1877

BOOK 2 IN THE BACK TO BILLY SAGA
2ND EDITION

A novel by:
Michael Anthony Giudicissi

Copyright © 2021 by Michael Anthony Giudicissi
2nd Edition

All Rights Reserved

No part of this book may be reproduced without written permission from the publisher or author, except for a reviewer who may quote brief passages in a review; nor may any part of this book be reproduced, stored in a retrieval system, or transmitted in any form or by any means electronic, mechanical, photocopying, recording or other, without written permission from the publisher or copyright holders.

This manuscript is a work of fiction. Any names, characters, businesses, places, events, locales, and incidents are either the products of the author's imagination or used in a fictitious manner. Any resemblance to actual persons, living or dead, or actual events is purely coincidental.

Mankind Productions, LLC

Albuquerque, NM

billythekidridesagain@gmail.com

Book Design & Layout: Mary Dolan

9 781088 087961

Retail: $18.00

"I seem to have loved you in numberless forms, numberless times, in life after life, in age after age, forever."

Rabindranath Tagore

I.

She heard the voices before she saw the "men" behind them, always. The catcalls, whistles, and comments about how she needed a "real man" followed Rosita Luna day in and day out in Lincoln, NM. As the great beauty proclaimed the "Belle of Lincoln" by many, she accepted that she simply had to live with the disrespect heaped upon her by the town's menfolk, at least for the moment. She wasn't at all happy about it, but live with it, she did. Her grand plan in life, her dream as it were, was greater than these small-minded men could ever fathom.

At 24 years old, Rosita was a younger and even prettier version of her mother Lourdes Luna. Lourdes and Sergio had married when they were only 19 years old. In his prime, Sergio ran the livery in Lincoln while Lourdes took in boarders. A handful of years after marriage, they were graced with a baby girl they named Grace. Grace was a precious, precocious little girl with wide, wondering eyes and a quick and easy laugh. As the apple of Sergio's eye, he couldn't imagine a more perfect little girl. Regrettably, in 1850, young Grace was stricken with pneumonia, and nothing Dr. Robash could do was able to save her. The image of Lourdes holding her little girl's body as she sobbed uncontrollably haunted Sergio for the rest of his life. Crushed by grief, Lourdes and Sergio buried her in a tiny pine coffin in Lincoln's only cemetery on the east edge of town. Sergio made Grace's grave a regular stop on his daily routine, picking wildflowers whenever they were in bloom to place on his baby girl's wooden marker. On the days when he had time, Sergio would sit by the grave and talk to Grace, sometimes for hours. His words would eventually turn to tears, and it was said that the level of the nearby Bonito Creek would rise from the runoff of his sadness.

Although Sergio stated he simply could not have another child for fear of losing it, and his mind along with it, in the fall of 1852, Lourdes became pregnant with a little girl who would be named Rosita. All jet black hair and piercing eyes, Rosita was fiery and feisty, as if demanding her father's attention. She was as quick as a whip and had a sharp tongue. While Sergio first attempted to mold her into another version of his beloved Grace, he soon saw the folly of his ways, allowing his young daughter the room to develop her own unique personality.

As she grew, it didn't go without notice just how stunning the young woman was. Young boys and older men secretly...and sometimes openly...pined for lovely Rosita.

Many a townsman sat at Sergio's eating table with their best of intentions and requested to court the young woman. If they thought Sergio was somehow in a position of authority on that measure, however, they were sadly mistaken. The fiercely independent Rosita took orders from no one and quickly set each potential paramour straight. She was waiting for the man that would match the yearning in her soul for love. A man that would bring both a sense of excitement and stability to her life. A man that could light a fire within her that the whole of the Gulf of Mexico could not extinguish. She searched and waited for a man that would come to her, and in his eyes, she could see an eternity…together. None of the men in Lincoln, NM, had shown her that potential. While still a young woman, Rosita was not getting any younger. She secretly agreed with herself that she would never settle. Never. If the man that strode through her dreams never appeared in Lincoln, then she would spend this life alone in hopes that he might appear in the next one.

On this windy and cold November day in 1877, Rosita hurried home only to have dinner with her mother. Sergio had passed away two years prior when a cancerous tumor took hold in his back. Again Dr. Robash tried every bit of modern medicine he had available to him, but to no avail. Sergio died on Christmas Eve, 1875, and was buried next to Grace, finally getting to spend eternity with the precious angel that had had an all-too-short time on this Earth.

Lourdes had taken her husband's death hard. Now 50 years old, she ran a laundry service that paid barely enough to survive. Luckily Rosita pitched in with her pay from serving as a cook at the Wortley Hotel, and the two ladies managed to eke out a subsistence in the far southwestern corner of the United States. Unable to bear living in the house where she had lost both daughter and husband, Lourdes moved into a room in the home of Monica Mills. The jovial woman made Lourdes feel welcome, and the house was just a few doors away from the tiny hut that Rosita now occupied as her home.

Her faith never shaken, Rosita felt sure that someday soon she would meet the man she would marry. Lincoln was growing and prosperity was settling in, at least for those that were aligned with the big House of L.G. Murphy and his partner, the pinched-face little Jimmy Dolan. Lately though, a gentle Englishman had also settled in Lincoln. John Henry Tunstall was a soft spoken, well dressed, genteel man. Rosita had made his acquaintance once or twice at the Wortley while he was in the company of Barrister Alexander McSween. If Tunstall had any interest in her, or any woman at all for that matter, he didn't betray it. That was all to the good for Rosita as she harbored no romantic notions for the man, even though they were the same age. It was simply nice to see a more refined crowd settling in than the scofflaws that hung around at Murphy's store in town.

Along with Tunstall, Rosita became aware of his ranch hands, who frequently made the trip from his ranch on the Rio Feliz to his recently opened store in Lincoln proper. With names like the big and strong Brewer, the impish Bowdre with the large ears, the serious Scurlock missing a front tooth, and the big dark-eyed French, they seemed at least a slightly better version of Murphy's and Dolan's henchmen. In any event, they were always polite to Rosita, and she returned the favor in kind.

On this day, while making her way home against the cutting breeze, she once again saw the man known as Doc Scurlock with his buddy Charlie Bowdre hanging around on the front porch of the Tunstall store. They politely doffed their hats to her, and just as she was about to walk out of eyeshot, a young, scrawny buck-toothed boy in a new jacket came bounding out of the store. He wore a large Mexican sombrero and seemed to have guns strapped to every appendage. His smile, crooked as it was, lit up his face, and Rosita could tell the boy was of a good nature. His friends clucked their tongues in approval at his new garb. Just as Rosita was about to turn towards her mother's house, the boy... a kid really...spotted her, and his eyes went wide. He immediately tipped his gigantic hat and bent into a deep bow, as one might while asking a lady for a dance. When he looked up at her, his smile seemed to engulf his entire face, his two front teeth leading the way over and through his lips. Rosita, hand on hip, smiled at the boy while tilting her head to the side. She had learned long ago that it's nice to be nice, but that being too nice invited unwanted advances from men she had no interest in having advance on her. While she was curious about who the boy was, she definitely wasn't curious about whether he was her soulmate. Within an instant of seeing him, she quickly ruled him out from the list of potential lifelong partners. He was a new face in town, but he wasn't *the* face she was looking for.

With a turn of her head and a snap of her skirt, Rosita flitted into her house to start dinner. Back on the Tunstall porch, the wide-eyed young man shook his head in disbelief at seeing such an incredible beauty and turned to his comrades to ask…

"Who in the hell is that?"

2.

Silence.

Martin Teebs had grown used to the silence of the past 18 months. His life before... well, before Billy the Kid...wasn't manic, but it was sane and predictable. His days used to meld into one another, with a rare treat of pot roast, ice cream, or his fantasy football draft providing the singular beacons of light in an otherwise mundane life.

Now, however, it was simply the silence.

Eighteen months earlier, in a scene that a screenwriter would have had a hard time imagining, Martin stood quivering with rage in his own guest bedroom. To his left stood the actual in-the-flesh outlaw Billy the Kid, who had come through time to warn him about a cowardly, atrocious act. To his right stood the man who had committed that act, Carl Farber. Farber apparently had decided that whatever belonged to Martin must also belong to him, and so he brutally raped Martin's century-ago girlfriend, Rosita Luna, while she was pregnant with Martin's son. So incensed was Teebs that he might have killed Farber with his bare hands, but Martin's present-day wife, Lilly Teebs, intervened. In the ensuing discussion and finger pointing, Lilly was forced to disclose her own secret: she was pregnant, and it was most certainly not by her husband. Upon the revelations that Martin had impregnated a 25-year-old Mexican beauty, who somewhere back in time was broken and desperate for her man, and that Lilly was with child by an actor turned bed & breakfast proprietor, both husband and wife trudged out of the room, totally dazed and definitely confused.

That was long ago and Martin had moved on in life. He had to. After a number of sessions of marriage counseling designed to save their union, they both decided that it must end. If Lilly was so willing to sleep with Dallas, whose only contribution to society was bad acting and 8-pack abs, she surely could not want a future with someone as substantial as her husband. Conversely, Martin had somehow (still unbeknownst to him) struck up a relationship with the great beauty of Lincoln, NM, and given her a son that would bear his name. He knew this to be true, both because he'd seen the historical photos of Rosita and little Martin Jr. and because he had made love to the woman on an open hillside under a white oak tree above San Patricio, just hours after Alexander McSween's brains had been splattered all over Martin's shirt. How any marriage could survive such betrayal and desire was beyond the Teebs, and ultimately their therapist agreed, even discounting their final session when the two jilted mates decided to call it quits after only five minutes. While Lilly didn't understand exactly what had happened in that guest room, she never believed or understood the possibility of Martin's time travel. She assumed he either had a girlfriend in the here and now or the entire episode was some bad ruse by Farber and whoever that buck-toothed boy in her house was. Martin had never reached out to any woman after that day, and she simply couldn't imagine him being so cold and callous that he would leave a woman all alone, pregnant with his child. She concluded that the whole story, at least on Martin's side, must not be true. At least, In her own confused and very pregnant state at the time, her mind couldn't seize on any other explanation.

And now Martin was met with only silence when he arrived home. Lilly and Austin (the name she had ironically given the baby boy) had at first lived in a garden apartment complex in Nutley, NJ; but then had moved to, of all places, Albuquerque, NM. Somewhere in the process of growing an entire human being in her womb, Lilly had discovered an artistic bent. She now spent her days in a bright art studio, creating abstract art that freed her mind from her past misdeeds and pointed to a brighter (she hoped) tomorrow. The money Martin had to pay in alimony, plus the half-of-everything divorce settlement, probably helped her pay the bills too, he imagined. More than once, Martin wondered aloud if Lilly and Dallas had yet another baby boy would they name him Fort Worth, or maybe even El Paso? He smiled each time at the thought...just before he felt that sinking feeling that this was all his fault. If he hadn't chowed down on a half gallon of ice cream, he wouldn't have been roiling in his bed in the early morning hours. If he hadn't stirred and watched *Young Guns*, he'd happily never have cared about Billy the Kid. And of course, if he had never cared about Billy the Kid, he would never have gone to Lincoln to do whatever it was he thought he would accomplish there. And he would never have spun the whirlwind that had created another complete life over 100 years before he was even born. In short, Martin had fucked up, royally. Now he was left here to pick up the pieces and live with the fallout.

Silence was all that greeted Martin Teebs upon his arrival home on this day, a day like all the rest. The house was cold and still, almost antiseptic. Not able to bear the silence he switched on SportsCenter immediately after entering the living room. The anchors would spar with each other over what seemed now to be insignificant topics, but at least they filled the air with noise.

Martin grabbed the mail from behind the front door and dropped it on the kitchen table as he went to grab himself a hard apple cider, having only recently found out that he was gluten intolerant…and therefore beer was no longer an option.

Teebs admired himself in the reflection of his stainless steel refrigerator. The lack of gluten in his diet had had the effect of putting him on a diet that neglected most of his favorite foods. He'd lost some 30 pounds in the past six months, and if he couldn't sport a Dallas-like 8-pack, he most definitely could usually break out a 2-pack on most days. If only, he lamented, he had someone to share it with.

Sipping on a cold one, he leafed his fingers through the mail, his eyes catching one letter in particular. The envelope was handwritten, and the return address caught him by surprise:

Highway 380
Lincoln, NM

Martin would soon find out that it was the letter of a heartbroken woman, pleading for understanding and commiseration as perhaps only he could share. Under any other of his former circumstances, Martin would most certainly have considered taking up with her, as warm, friendly, and sexually charged as she had seemed to be towards him. This letter, however, wasn't written to lure Martin into any sort of weird sexual tryst; it was written with the raw emotion of a woman whose life had been torn apart.

The letter was from Darlene Jones.

3.

Dear Martin,

Oh how I wished to never have to write this letter to you or anyone else. I'm so incredibly sad to note that Dallas and I have split up. He has moved to Albuquerque with Lilly and the baby. For months we have argued, cried, and tried to find a solution to this perfect mess we all made. Dallas and Lilly even introduced the idea of a polyamorous relationship...do you know what that is? I guess it's some way that Dallas would be married to both of us but we'd live separately. He did make some weird inference that maybe Lilly and I would grow to "like" each other...and I don't think he meant as shopping pals. In any event, I simply couldn't deal with the constant heartache anymore and we've called it quits.

I guess in a way I'm writing to apologize to you. Look, I know Dallas and I come on pretty strong. We're just highly sexual beings. We've always looked at our marriage as a safe space for us to explore each other and some of the people we come in contact with. When you and Lilly showed up, you looked like you could use a little fun. In my mind it wasn't going to go any farther than that...but I suppose Dallas and Lilly didn't see it my (or your) way.

I could probably have forgiven him for continuing the relationship when he went to New York, as well as the emotional bond they formed chatting on the internet, had it not been for Lilly getting pregnant. That's a deal breaker for me...and I see it was for you as well. I hope they are happy with each other, but having been married to Dallas for 10 years, I know his eyes will wander first, and then any body parts south of his belt will surely follow. I feel terrible for you, and for me, and I guess at some point for little Austin, who'll surely grow up without a dad.

Martin, I'm sorry that this all happened. You are such a decent guy. All you wanted to do was visit Lincoln, walk around the historical buildings a bit, and live out your dream of understanding Billy the Kid. Lilly has no idea of the good, solid, faithful man she let go. The Martin Teebs that I know would never touch another woman except his wife. I practically threw myself at you, and you were such a gentleman to not take advantage of that. Not only are you nearly a saint in my book, but I know you wouldn't hurt a fly. You are so gentle and calm I cannot ever imagine you lifting even a finger in anger. I guess if Lincoln had more men like you back in its heyday, there would never have been a Lincoln County War!

I'm going to stay here and run the B&B for as long as I can. It was our, or I guess, *my dream now. I love the peace and solitude of Lincoln and don't want to give up on it.*

I hope your sales job is still going well. In the middle of all this stuff that's going on, it's tough to focus on work, I guess, but I'll bet you are still setting records.

Martin…if you ever come through New Mexico again, please visit. The casita will be waiting for you, and the town of Lincoln will welcome you back just like your previous trips. I know maybe you know all about Billy the Kid now and don't need to visit here anymore, but there's always something new you can learn, no?!

Until then, take care of yourself and try not to hate that bitch of an ex-wife of yours too much. She got seduced by a man with the abs of a god but the IQ of a milk carton.

I hope to see you soon,
Darlene…
XOXO

Martin carefully folded the handwritten letter and placed it on the table. So Dallas and Lilly were together? Martin had thought of this, and wondered how much of Lilly's divorce settlement and the monthly alimony he was paying was going to support the man's non-existent acting career? He tried to tell himself he really didn't care. The Lilly he'd married and loved would never have had an affair, unprotected sex, and a baby long after she and Martin agreed they were too old. This had to be some new unimproved Lilly that had lost her mind. Despite Darlene's effusive praise in the letter, he knew she'd sing a different tune if she could somehow understand about Rosita, Martin Jr., Billy, and, of course, the spectacular death of Billy Mathews that Martin had perpetrated.

He let his brain play on Lilly's situation for a few moments, imagining Dallas sitting around the house while the baby cried incessantly. He could just see Lilly getting angrier by the moment as the smell of a full diaper permeated the air and Dallas willingly ignored it. Lilly would most certainly explode at some point, and Dallas would have to face the fact that the married woman he screwed was not the perfect little sex toy he imagined her to be, or at least that she was more complex than he imagined. A slight smile crossed Martin's face as he saw the scenario play out in his head. As quickly as he started smiling, he stopped. He didn't really want Dallas and Lilly to part. There was a baby involved, and if the last year and a half had taught him anything, it was that a baby needs its father…as long as its father has already been born.

"Martin Junior," said Teebs, mouthing the words carefully as if they were some sort of scripture. From his last meeting with Doc Scurlock in 1940, the same one where he rocked the elderly Billy the Kid into eternity, he knew that Junior had never been able to meet him. Martin certainly had no recollection of meeting the man who was his son. A tiny thought, like a ray of light, permeated Martin's brain. Is it possible that he, Martin, had been able to go see Junior, but that the boy was too young to remember? Even a few moments to hold his son and deeply kiss Rosita would surely serve him well for the rest of his days?

"My son," he said as he vividly remembered the picture of Rosita holding Junior, waiting...and waiting...for the man they say never arrived. "Hell, Billy changed the past, why can't I?" reasoned Martin to the empty kitchen. He only had to get back to New Mexico in order to try. He had to try. Lilly had a son and a new man, so why shouldn't he claim his son and the woman he apparently loved from the moment he was brought into the world, and for 140 years before that?

The COVID-19 pandemic had swept the globe the previous two years. Despite all the calls to "burn the mask" and "shun the vaccine" since the virus was merely "a hoax," over two million people had died around the world. It had turned Martin's life and job upside down. Only six months prior, he had been allowed back into the office, after having worked from his guest bedroom for almost a year. Zoom video conference meetings and hours of boring conference calls had become the norm, and no one was traveling once they found out how quickly the virus spread in airports and especially on coast-to-coast flights. Martin hadn't taken a sales trip in all of that time, yet somehow managed to virtually keep his sales growing. He also hadn't considered visiting New Mexico for any reason. Not Lilly nor Billy nor even Rosita could sway him from his firm decision to remain in the present. Yet, here he was, considering booking his first flight in forever and venturing back out into the world again.

His boss, Mr. Talbot, had been hinting strongly that Martin should get off his now-much-smaller ass and get back out on the road before his sales atrophied and his contacts found someone local to do business with.

The letter, the baby, the virus, and Junior all weighed heavily on Martin's mind that evening. At some point, he simply said "screw it" and popped open his laptop. He searched for his familiar route to LA and then back through Albuquerque. He was going back to Lincoln one more time. He might never travel far enough back in time to figure out how he met Billy and the Regulators, or how Rosita managed to fall in love with him, but he might just get back far enough to hold his own flesh and blood, Martin Teebs Junior, at least one time.

If the boy could talk, Martin wondered just what he might say to the father he most surely would love? What would that first meeting be like? Martin was sure it would be magical. For a boy meeting his father for the first time, it would have to be, right?

4.

Dick Brewer was a big, strong, twenty-eight-year-old rancher who had set down a set of shallow roots in Lincoln County after arriving from Missouri. Brewer owned his own ranch, but at the suggestion of Alexander McSween was also hired on as foreman of the new John Tunstall ranch on the Rio Feliz. Brewer had a keen eye for picking out hard-working men, men who also might be handy with pistol and rifle in the event such need arose. Most certainly, his boss Tunstall was pressuring the local monopoly of Murphy and Dolan to the point that everyone in town assumed the need would indeed arise at some point in the near future. Brewer hired on some boys he'd known from his time in town, including Josiah "Doc" Scurlock, Charlie Bowdre, "Big Jim" French, and Fred Waite, among others. When a scrawny but affable 17-year-old named William H. Bonney helped in the escape of outlaw Jesse Evans, but remained in Lincoln while the rest of the gang absconded, Brewer took notice.

Bonney fell in naturally with Bowdre and Scurlock and developed an even deeper friendship with Waite. Brewer noticed that the boy seemed to be missing something and seemed to be always searching for it. Other than his slight age, he seemed a lot like the rest of the vagabonds that made Lincoln their home. One day in early November 1877, as Brewer rode up to the nearly finished Tunstall mercantile, Bonney and Bowdre approached him.

"Howdy, Dick!" exclaimed the enthusiastic young man.

Brewer slid from his mount, looping the reins over the newly installed hitching post before he spoke. "Your name's Bonney, ain't it?"

"Indeed it is," said Billy, thrusting his hand out to the older man. "William H. Bonney. But you can feel free to call me Billy".

Brewer reached out his hand and shook Billy's vigorously, testing the boy for the strength it didn't appear he had. "Good to meet ya, Billy. Charlie here tells me you're lookin for a job?"

"Might," replied Billy. "Was thinking I might git my own ranch going but could use to make some money in the meantime".

"Mr Tunstall could use another ranch hand down on the Feliz. Things is getting hot up here and the more boys, the better." Dick looked down on Billy's hip to spot a .41 caliber Colt Thunderer and added, "You good with that thing?"

Billy removed the gun carefully and traced his finger along the barrel as if it were a woman. He cocked his head up slightly and smiled at Brewer before responding. "Better with this than I am with beef…and I'm pretty good with beef, Dick".

Brewer smiled, and the two men came to terms on Bonney joining the Tunstall company. If nothing else, reasoned Brewer, the kid could either sling lead or block it. Either way, he'd be an asset. Brewer excused himself and made a beeline for the store, eager to discuss with Tunstall some news he'd just heard.

"Congrats, kid!" said the always friendly Bowdre. "You got yourself a proper job now. Hell, coming here to Lincoln might jest make a man of you!" Bowdre laughed heartily at his own joke.

If Billy was offended, he didn't show it and simply replied, "Charlie, I been on my own since I was thirteen. If'n I ain't become a man by now, it prolly ain't gonna happen."

Just then Rosita Luna made the turn around the corner, walking quickly towards the two men. Billy, awestruck at the natural beauty of the woman, spit in his hand and slicked the sides of his hair back the best he could. Seeing the two men, and knowing they were at least aligned with Tunstall, Rosita gave them a quick but warm smile as she approached. Sensing his opportunity, Billy made his move.
"Miss Luna! Pleasure to meet you. My name is William H. Bonney," said Billy as he removed his sombrero and took a deep bow in front of the amused woman.

Rosita had been approached by all sorts of young and old bravos over the years and knew how to handle this one in the same way she had handled all of the others.

"Mr. Bonney. Likewise," she said with a slight nod of her head. "Now if you'll excuse me." Rosita began walking on, but Billy hop-skipped back a step to stay in her field of vision.

"Ma'am!" he said, fumbling for the words to connect with the most beautiful woman he'd ever seen. "I'm at your service. Day or night. If anyone, especially those bastards from Murphy's store, gives you any cause for alarm, well...I'm your man. I've signed on to work with the J.H. Tunstall company just now, so I'll be setting some roots here in Lincoln"

Rosita, amused, smiled at the charming young man. Knowing his true interests were less in chivalry and more in romance, she dismissed him gently, but quickly. "*Gracias*, Mr. Bonney. I'm quite sure you and the other...men," a word which she paused to emphasize, "in town have far more pressing matters to attend to." She looked up at the Tunstall store with a smile and a wave of her arm to reinforce what her meaning was.

"Good day, William, and congratulations on your new job," said Rosita as she whisked out of sight.

"Dang, Charlie, that's one tough nut to crack," sighed Billy, "but I might juss crack my nuts on her if she'll give me half a chance."

Bowdre shook his head in disagreement. "Billy, every man in Lincoln has tried to bark up that tree and ain't none even made it to the trunk. Kid like you damn sure ain't gonna be the first."

Billy looked at Rosita's hips swinging down the street and wondered how he might ever get on with a woman like that. As she grew smaller in his vision, he muttered, "I don't know Charlie. I just don't know."

"She done turned down every man in Lincoln once, and most of em twice. I don't think you got no chance," said Bowdre. "I don't know what the hell she's looking for. It's almost like she's waiting for some kind of man that don't even exist. You know what I mean?"

While Billy admitted that he didn't know what Charlie meant, he wondered what kind of man would finally win the heart of the Belle of Lincoln?

"The guy that gets her gotta be something special. Guy gets her, he probably just lives here and dies a happy man. Probably have to scrape the damn smile off his face when he dies," said Billy. "I hope I get to meet the lucky sonofabitch, whoever it is, so he can tell me what I'm missin."

"And so you kin smell his fingers too! Hahahaha!" roared Charlie, practically in fits at his own unique sense of frontier humor.

5.

Martin reached his fingers to his nose, sniffing them with interest. Somewhere in his travels from business class, through the jetway, and out of the plane, he had touched something damp, which left him wondering exactly what kind of bacterial swamp he was now carrying on his left hand.

The Albuquerque Sunport was busily humming along this Friday afternoon. Everything looked the same as the last time Martin had been here, many months ago. Martin guided his roller bag into the men's room and vigorously scrubbed the offending moisture from his hand. If COVID had taught him anything, it was the value of a good twenty-second hand wash.

Now free of the plague, he wound his way through the concourse, but not without some trepidation. While he felt that there would be no reason for Dallas or Lilly to be there, he most definitely did not want to run into them. What would he say? Martin had never been a fan of awkward situations and desperately wanted to get to his rental car and point it south in the fading November light. While he tried to fight it, his mind centered on Lilly. What part of town did she live in? Was she living in some luxurious artist's loft with an incredible view of the mountains or was it a regular run-of-the-mill house? What did Dallas do all day? Martin was sure that he hit the gym regularly, but lacking the income from his bed & breakfast, he must have needed some job? The thought that perhaps the only job Dallas could get was as an airport greeter or a rental car clerk momentarily chilled Martin. He doubted that Dallas would even have the sense to recognize that he should be ashamed of his actions. Teebs imagined that running into him would be a friendly "Hey, how ya doing?" moment that Dallas probably shared with everyone and anyone. In any event, Martin hurried down the escalator and to the rental car counter. Thankfully, the frumpy woman behind the counter bore no resemblance at all to Dallas Jones, and Martin was quickly on his way.

The ridiculously low angle of the setting sun blinded him as he exited the parking garage. It burned his retinas and had him bobbing his head from side to side in order to not run into anyone. No matter what he did, he could not escape the fiery glare. It was almost as if New Mexico, and Lincoln in particular, were trying to keep him away. Martin seriously started to consider whether this was a good idea. The last

18 months, while trying, had been at least peaceful. He never had to look over his shoulder to see if someone was coming for him, and he never had to make up any stories about where he'd been or whom he'd been with.

Martin edged his car towards the on-ramp of I-25 southbound and pressed firmly on the accelerator. Perhaps New Mexico and Lincoln didn't want him here, but he knew someone who would. His mind drifted to Rosita and Martin Jr. as the car built speed, every moment cutting the distance between him and the destiny he was sure to find in old Lincoln.

6.

Oncoming headlights, as rare as they might be, were blinding Martin on the otherwise dark and moonless night. As he made his way across the northern border of the White Sands Missile Range, he allowed his thoughts to drift off to the future...and to the past he hoped to find again on this trip. If he was even able to slip back in time, he had no idea where he'd wind up. The last time he saw Billy, at least the young outlaw version of him, he was standing at his front door in late 2020. Billy had come to rat out Carl Farber, but also to implore Martin to come and see his son. Would Martin Jr. be two years old now? Would Rosita have moved on and married someone else? Martin tried to make sense of the chronology of his previous time travels, but he couldn't latch onto a single thing that would help him determine what day it might be in old Lincoln if he were to make it back.

One thing was for certain: Martin still had no idea how he'd ever befriended Billy and had Rosita fall in love with him. That had obviously happened some time before he met both of them again during his first trip to Lincoln with Lilly. While his curiosity nagged at him, wondering what that first meeting was like, he was singularly focused on being a father to his one and only son. Hell, if Dallas could be a father, Martin figured he could be at least as good as some never-has-been actor who screwed all of the female guests at his B&B.

Martin guided the rental car carefully through the Valley of Fires, which was bathed in an inky blackness on this night. He had known he wouldn't arrive at the B&B until well after dark, but this was dark. Really dark. The kind of dark that New Jersey didn't traffic in.

As he approached Capitan, just 10 miles west of his destination, he stopped at the town's only gas station and convenience store. Knowing better than to roll into Lincoln with nothing to eat or drink at this time of night, he tanked up on water, snacks, and threw a couple cans of hard cider in for good measure. Maybe he and Darlene could commiserate over a drink before he headed off to bed? As Martin exited and approached his car, he was met by a giant of a man in a cowboy hat and with a six shooter on his hip. At first Martin wondered if this man was from the past, some spirit guide to take him back to old Lincoln and to his waiting family (or to prison), but his Wranglers, Apple watch, and giant belt buckle gave him away.

"Ain't from around here, are ya?" asked the big man, a smile spreading across his face.

"Well, no. I mean, yes. I mean…kind of." replied Martin, confused as to what this man wanted with him.

The big man threw his head back, taking in the night air before speaking. "Name's Steve. I used to be Mayor of this town. I expect I know just about everyone that comes through here on a Friday night. Saw your tags and just wanted to welcome you to Lincoln County."

While Martin was relieved that it was merely a welcome committee and not some time cop coming to bust him for killing Mathews, he was eager to get back on the road and get to Lincoln. "Thanks, Steve. I appreciate that. I'm just going to get on my way now," said Martin as he edged towards the driver's side door.

"Ain't too many people come visit Lincoln with winter coming. You must be some kind of diehard to be heading there, huh?" asked Steve, his eyes piercing Martin's gaze.

"Just curious. That's all," said Martin as he opened the door and quickly got in.

Steve took one of his big hands and rapped his big knuckles on the window, prompting Martin to reluctantly roll it down. "Listen, stranger, when you get tired of the sanitized version of history they teach down the road, come on back here and ask for me. I know things about the Kid that nobody else knows…or at least believes. There's a whole other history that those books and movies won't teach you. I'm telling you, you can't make this shit up," said Steve as Martin quickly nodded his head, started the car, and backed away. The big man continued to look at him smiling, almost as if he was implicating Martin in something. Teebs was creeped out. Did this guy know about his past? Did he have some revised history lesson that told about the great Martin Teebs, slayer of Billy Mathews, impregnator of Rosita Luna, and jackass who lost a book that allowed Billy the Kid to escape the grave?

Martin stepped on the gas a little too hard and threw up a shower of gravel as he sped towards Lincoln. In his rearview mirror, he saw the big man in the cowboy hat waving an eerie goodbye.

7.

Arriving in Lincoln in its stark blackness, Martin carefully drove the main street towards the east edge of town. Not a soul (of the living anyway) stirred in town, and there were but a few lights on. Although in modern day Martin had only been to Lincoln three times, he seemed to know every inch of the place. As he glided to a stop in the gravel driveway of the B&B, he remembered the first time he'd been there. His memory was vivid at the excitement of being in Billy the Kid country. His memory was just as vivid of Lilly's look of boredom and displeasure at his chosen vacation destination. Now Lilly was gone and Martin was here. The freedom of that thought intoxicated him as he stood breathing in the chilly mountain air.

"Martin!" cried Darlene, shocking him from his memories, "I was hoping you'd get here before too long."

Darlene Jones looked no worse the wear for losing her husband to Martin's wife. She was one of those women who needed no makeup and seemed to look better the less she tried to. She lunged down the porch steps and hugged Martin so tightly he thought she might break a rib. "Oh, Martin, are you a sight for sore eyes!" she gushed, squeezing tighter as if to force his very last breath from him.

"Hey, Darlene," said Martin seriously, "how are you doing?"

"Better," she replied slowly, then adding, "now that you're here."

Darlene led Martin up the stairs and into the main house. Leaving his suitcase near the door, he looked around the place, which seemed to be unchanged since his last visit. As Darlene walked into the kitchen to get something, Martin spied the now familiar picture of Rosita and Martin Jr. He bent in to see her face, looking more closely than before. Rosita had a vacant look in her eyes, as if somehow a little of the light was gone from them. It was a look he hadn't noticed the first time he'd seen the picture, but there it was, streaming across time, accusing him of abandoning everything he thought he ever had wanted. It crushed Martin to know what Farber had done to her, and that Martin had been powerless to stop. He stared deeply into her eyes, trying to see if there was even a small spark left in them. With the rape, the baby, and losing Martin, he could not blame Rosita a bit for believing all of the good in the world had deserted her. He only wished somehow to make this picture go away, to change it into a happy family photo of Martin and Rosita Teebs, and their bouncing baby boy Martin Jr. He resolved that if it were humanly possible to make that change, he would do it or die trying.

As Martin's thoughts wandered back in time, Darlene burst back into the room, holding two glasses with a very full pour of wine.

"Here, Martin," she said only slightly slurring her words, "let's relax and catch up."

It was then that Martin realized that Darlene had probably had a glass or six of wine before he even got there. He didn't remember her shirt being unbuttoned so much, or her breasts swaying so freely as they did now. Realizing that he had been brought to the main house to ease her pain of losing Dallas, Martin looked for a quick escape. Under any other circumstances, he would have gladly stayed and enjoyed the fruits of one Darlene Jones, but his heart belonged to a woman now long dead, who had given him a son, also now long gone. But if Martin could make magic happen one final time, he might be able to join them for a moment...or perhaps for an eternity?

With the picture of Rosita staring at them over his shoulder as if to dissuade him from doing anything stupid, Martin said, "Darlene, I'm sorry...I'm just so tired from the trip." Carefully helping to set the glasses down on the coffee table, he continued, "Listen, I need some sleep. Let's do this tomorrow night, huh? We can talk this whole thing out when you feel better and I'm not so tired, ok?"

Darlene smiled a drunken smile as she let out a big sigh. "You're one of the good ones, Martin Teebs," she slurred. "Any other guy would have come in here and taken advantage of me. I mean look, my boobs are practically falling out of my shirt!" Martin did indeed look and saw that she was right. Darlene laughed and pushed her tits together making her ample cleavage that much more impressive. If she got any more demonstrative, her breasts were absolutely going to make an unannounced appearance at the evening's festivities.

"Get some sleep, Darlene," said Teebs, "and I'll see you in the morning."

Martin grabbed his suitcase and made the short walk to the casita he had come to know so well. Dog-tired, he flung off his clothes and climbed the stairs to the loft. As he stripped back the blankets and slipped into bed, he wondered if Rosita had ever been here? Obviously the modern casita didn't exist in 1878, but had she ever stood on this very ground? Martin hoped so and tried to will the spirit of the woman he loved from wherever she was to lay with him in the cozy bed. His thoughts were in vain as he began to drift off to sleep, getting colder by the minute, and most definitely feeling as alone as he'd ever been.

8.

If John Henry Tunstall was worried about his life and livelihood in Lincoln, NM, he certainly didn't show it. 24-years-old in late 1877, Tunstall had come to Lincoln to carve out his share of the local economy. In direct competition with the House of Murphy, Tunstall seemed to believe that there was room enough in Lincoln County for two government beef outfits and two mercantiles. Murphy and Dolan thought otherwise and aimed to make the Englishman as uncomfortable as possible in his new environs. As the store that bore his name neared completion, Tunstall authorized his ranch foreman, Dick Brewer, to add some muscle to the payroll. One very small part of that "muscle" was a seventeen-year-old kid named Billy Bonney.

Tunstall had met Bonney at the ranch and in town several times. To him, Billy seemed much like the rest of the men Brewer brought on. Willing to do a fair day's work for a fair day's pay…and maybe willing to put a bullet in someone if the need arose. Billy was finally on a regular job with a regular pay envelope, and it felt good. He felt like… an adult. While running with the Jesse Evans gang had given him some momentary excitement, he clearly saw the long game, which was most likely the end of a short rope. This job seemed real to him, and he relished the opportunity. Besides, he fell in with a number of other young men of the west who shared similar aspirations and, presumably, futures.

Bonney quickly ingratiated himself to the good people of Lincoln, at least to those who were firmly in the camp of Tunstall and McSween. Monica Mills, the wife of former Sheriff Ham Mills, especially took a shine to the boy. She'd often flag Billy and friends down while they were in town with the promise of fresh baked biscuits or an apple pie. French especially like to rib Billy that Mrs. Mills was looking for more in return than a simple "Thank you, Ma'am." On this particular morning, Billy and crew were supposed to light out for Tunstall's ranch after breakfast. With Brewer already out of town, it fell to the men to govern themselves; and almost on cue, Monica Mills saw the boys and offered some eggs and fresh pork from a pig that Ham had slaughtered the day before. Seeing as they had no better breakfast prospects, the boys quickly thanked Monica and went inside, but not before French could grab his crotch in a mocking gesture to Billy about how they'd "pay" for the meal.

Lincoln was bustling with life on this chilly morning with a number of cooking and heating fires burning, turning the air into a mix of acrid smoke. The boys finished their meal with a genuine thanks to Mrs. Mills and were set to leave. Monica, however, could not let Billy go without a smothering bear hug. The rest of the boys snickered as Billy was lost somewhere in the woman's ample and sagging cleavage. When he came up for air, he offered his usual, "Thanks for breakfast, ma'am. We need ta be going now." Monica smiled deeply and pulled him in for one more hug, this time letting her hands fall down around the young man's buttocks, to which she gave a hard squeeze.

"Oww!" Billy yelled before backing a step away. He looked to see if he had hurt the older woman's feelings, but instead he noticed a devilish twinkle in her eyes. It was much the same as the look his mother had had when she had made an off-color joke or pulled some sort of prank on young Billy and his brother Joe. That Monica Mills reminded Billy of his mother made him sad for a second, and then revulsed that the woman seemed to want him to eat more than her breakfast. Before that thought set roots in his mind, he quickly tipped his hat and shuffled out the door to join the rest of his friends.

"You boys come back now anytime you want something to eat. You hear me, Billy?" offered Mrs. Mills, as the boys punched Billy on the shoulders and back, laughing their way to the Tunstall corral to get their horses.

Horses saddled, the boys made their way out of the corral just as the sun broke over the Capitan Mountains. Rosita Luna was making her way down the street, wrapped in a colorful woolen coat. Her hair was highlighted from behind by the rising sun, making it appear to glow to the hardened ranch hands. Her absolute beauty temporarily took their breath away.

"Holy hell!" exclaimed French before he could stop himself. The rest of the boys cast him a disapproving look as Rosita glared at him. While she was fond of most of Tunstall's men, she'd had enough unwanted advances on the streets of Lincoln to last her a lifetime, and then some. Always the life of the party, Billy spoke. "Hey, Rosita. If'n you could pick any one of these boys to *baile* with, who'd you take?" He cast his hand across the motley looking bunch.

In her most serious tone, designed to discourage anyone from thinking she had an interest in them, she responded, "Mr. Bonney, I don't simply *baile* with anyone off the street. So to answer your question, I send my regrets, but you chicos will just have to dance with each other, *si*?" The boys had a good laugh and expected Billy to be embarrassed, but his good nature took over.

"Well, ma'am, I been on some lonesome territory without much in the way of women around. I guess I danced with some real hags in my time, but none so ugly as this lot!" joked Billy, waving his hand at the crew. The joke stung the boys but made Rosita laugh, the first genuine emotion she'd shown young Billy. The discourse formed the first tenuous bonds of a friendship between the two, with Billy realizing he'd never be Rosita's lover but he surely could be her friend.

"Well done, Mr. Bonney," said the beautiful woman. "I must be on my way now. You and your 'lot' have yourselves a wonderful day."

Once again, Billy tipped his hat as the young woman walked on. Just as she was near to being out of range of their voices, Jose Chavez y Chavez bellowed in protest to his mates, "Who in the hell is she looking for anyway? Got her nose awfully high in the air for a poor girl from Lincoln!"

Perhaps a few steps further and Rosita wouldn't have heard the insult clearly enough to respond, but something in her snapped. She quickly turned and walked briskly back to the men. Seeing the glare in her eyes, they all made way so she could confront Chavez without interference.

"What I'm looking for, *Mr. Chavez*," she snapped, "is a REAL man. Someone of substance, means, and of the highest moral character! Someone who knows how to treat his lady like a wonder, not like a possession. In short, *Mr. Chavez*, I'm most certainly not looking for you!" For a moment her hand clenched, and it appeared she might hit the much bigger man.

Stung, Chavez looked sideways and then at the ground. Those among the boys who wanted to laugh smartly held it in for fear of being next in the line of fire. Only Billy was brave enough to speak up.

"I ain't seen that kind of man nowhere around Lincoln, Rosita. Where you think you're gonna find him?" he asked genuinely.

Rosita pondered the question for a moment before responding. "If he's not here, he'll get here. Somehow. Some way. Someday. And don't you worry, I'll know him the minute I see him!"

With that, Rosita Luna clicked her heels and spun quickly around to walk away, leaving Chavez brooding and Billy smiling. The rest of the boys were left wondering who the poor sucker was that would have to be on the receiving end of the barbed missives of Rosita Luna for the rest of his life?

9.

Martin woke early on Saturday and rolled his tired body out of bed. Lately he had noticed a lot more snapping and popping when he rose, and today wasn't any different. Here he was, suffering the common traits of aging, while hoping that today would be the day he met his young son. The dichotomy struck him as strange and a little sad. If he did meet little Martin, would he be too old and feeble to even keep up with him?

Tossing on a sweatshirt and pants, he slowly opened the front door of the casita to find a tray brimming with fruit, pastry, coffee, and assorted juices. Sitting on top was a handwritten note:

Good morning, Martin!
I hope you slept well. I'm soooooo sorry about last night. I was brooding all afternoon and clearly had too much to drink. I value you being here and being a friend and hope we can move past it. Come on by the house after you spend some time in town. I found a bunch of old Lincoln pictures and relics that were in the shed and you are welcome to them. Enjoy your breakfast.
Happy hunting!
Darlene
XOXO

So, perhaps Martin had dodged a bullet? Until he finally fell asleep last night, he had worried about how he'd stay at arm's length from Darlene. He wasn't in the right frame of mind to start a long distance relationship at the moment, despite the fact that he and Rosita did have a long time and distance relationship. Besides, he reasoned, he didn't want to take over the B&B and be forced to start having sex with every couple that bunked for the night. Martin considered himself a one-woman man…right up until the time he and Rosita slept together, and then just days later, was back in bed with Lilly in New Jersey.

Martin checked his luggage, but he knew what he sought wouldn't be found there. The original set of clothes that Sam Corbett had given him on a prior time travel had long since been thrown away. Teebs had considered donating them to Goodwill but feared that maybe the clothes contained some time-travel DNA, and he didn't want to encourage anyone else to follow his wayward path. In the end, he had pulled up behind a grocery store dumpster and pushed the clothes down deep into the piles of rotting bananas and lettuce.

Now he had nothing proper to wear for the year…..?

That was the rub, of course. Martin had no idea what year he'd wind up in…if he was able to make it back at all. He both hoped and assumed it would be after Rosita had given birth to Martin Jr. That would put the year at 1879 or perhaps even 1880. He reasoned that new fashion didn't come quickly to the southwestern frontier, and that what he wore in the past would suffice. Problem was, now he didn't have anything to wear from the past.

Another thought entered his mind. What if he came back at the very moment he last left? With Billy making his escape from The House and Farber glowering over him, what if Martin picked right up where he left off? For certain he would kill Farber. Happily, gleefully, to prevent him from the heinous act he would commit soon after. Could he then pick up and live his life with Rosita, being there for the birth of his son? The prospects were both intriguing and frustrating as Martin simply had no way of knowing where the pilot of his time machine would push him out of the door, leaving him to parachute down to old Lincoln at some point long before Martin had been born.

He picked his least conspicuous clothes from the remnants of his week of selling in LA and decided to get on with it. He didn't expect that The House or whatever was left of Tunstall's store would take a credit card or cash dated 2020, so he left his wallet behind. With a deep breath, Martin walked out the door and hopefully into his own history.

The morning was cold enough for him to see his breath, and he was glad for the heavy black sweatshirt he had put on. As he made his way towards the street, a car pulled up into the driveway.

"More guests today?" asked Martin of no one but himself. He wasn't even sure if Darlene was open for business for anyone other than him. The car rolled to a stop and out of the driver's side door bounded none other than Dallas Jones.

10.

"Fuck! No! You?!" exclaimed Martin before he could stop himself. "You've got to be kidding me!"

All smiles and good cheer, Dallas quickly stepped his way towards Martin. "Hey, buddy! How ya been?" chirped the man who had ruined at least part of Martin's life. Dallas actually leaned in for a bro hug before Martin backed away. How could this moron not understand the pain he'd caused? How could he actually think that he and Martin were "buddies" after the upheaval of all of their lives? In that moment, Martin understood what made Dallas Jones tick.

Nothing. Absolutely nothing.

The man was as vapid as a box of rocks. It's not that he didn't understand what he'd done. It's that he didn't even realize there were any rules to play by. Martin judged him to be so stupid that he wondered if he had to remember to breathe? Teebs' anger washed away like an ocean wave, and just as he was about to reply to Dallas, he got another surprise. Rising from the passenger door with a young smiling boy in her arms was none other than the former Mrs. Lilly Teebs.

Lilly glanced uncomfortably in Martin's direction before offering a simple "Martin" through her pursed lips.

Just as Martin's anger had receded, another bigger wave of it began to move towards shore. Here he was, seeing his former wife, her happy baby boy, and the dimwit she shacked up with, right in the middle of his own little personal paradise. "What could these two deviants want here in Lincoln?" he thought to himself. He couldn't bring himself to even mutter Lilly's name, so he just gave a disapproving nod of his head in her direction.

"So, what brings you here, big guy?" boomed Dallas, as if reciting a line in an audition.

"Never mind why I'm here, Dallas, what are all of you doing here?" Martin asked, waving his hand across the small family.

Lilly shifted uncomfortably as little Austin looked on with interest. The boy looked remarkably like the baby pictures he'd seen of Lilly when they first met. "Poor kid," thought Martin, "doesn't even know what a bad hand he drew in the father department." While Martin heretofore couldn't present himself as any better of a father than Dallas, that was an issue he was at least intending to change, starting today.

"We're just here to pick up some of my stuff," said Dallas. "Darlene said she found a box of old Lincoln stuff in the shed. Lilly is going to paint pictures of it. She's good, man, have you seen her work?"

Before Martin could answer, Darlene came out from the main house. She seemed as shocked and angered by the sight of Dallas as Martin was at seeing Lilly.

"What are YOU doing here, Dallas?" she asked accusingly. "Remember, you don't LIVE here anymore?" Darlene emphasized the words to make sure that he understood just how unhappy she was to see him. Darlene allowed her scornful gaze to rest on Lilly and Austin for a moment, until Lilly shuffled away towards the street, wanting no part in the coming fight.

"Babe, I just came for that box of stuff you said you found. The old Lincoln stuff, remember?" Dallas replied as smooth as silk.

"Babe this, asshole!" said Darlene, making an obscene gesture with her crotch more often seen among professional baseball players. "I'm giving that stuff to Martin. He's come all the way here to pick it up, and I'm NOT going back on my word now!"

Amidst the rising protests of Dallas about making a three-hour drive with an 18-month-old toddler, Martin excused himself to let the formerly happy couple fight out the rightful owner of what was surely a bunch of junk. His date with destiny waiting, he walked to the road as Lilly gazed wistfully to the east. Hearing him coming, she turned to catch his gaze. No one spoke for a moment as Martin tried to remember the wife and the life he'd grown to like just a short year and a half ago. It seemed so far away that chasing the memory was hardly worth the effort.

"Martin?" said Lilly softly, about to ask something that would either anger him or force him to doubt his cause. Having none of it, Martin simply waved her off with his hand and walked towards town. If he heard her softly sob "I'm sorry" as he left, he gave no indication of it.

II.

Martin crunched along the dry grass on the edge of the road. While he knew exactly where he wanted to be, he had no idea where he was going. The mess that had been left in his wake at the B&B fresh in his mind, he pushed his thoughts to old Lincoln, to Rosita, and to his son. The current look of the town began to annoy him. The electric lights, modern signs, and cars parked here and there revolted Teebs, and he longed for the good old days of Billy, the Regulators, and hell, even the War.

The cold air began to cut through his sweatshirt and reminded Martin that most of his other time travels had come when some cold fog blew in. In the crystal clear mountain air that was already cold, his old method of conveyance into the past seemed a lost cause. He shuffled to the west, passing the Tunstall store, Dolan's old house (which gave him cause to retch just thinking of the sniveling little douche), and finally came to a stop when he ran out of town at the old Murphy-Dolan store. The store, which had once held the Kid before Martin aided him in blasting his way out, had been converted to a museum that was not set to open for a few hours.

Martin sat sullenly on the steps, wondering what his next move should be. He wondered at what point Dallas and Lilly would come driving by with a trunk full of the crap that Darlene had promised him. He almost decided to hide around the corner near where the old outhouse had been so that he wouldn't have to see them, but his last experience on that piece of real estate and down in the hole was fresh enough in his mind to avoid it. Lost in his self pitying thoughts, he hardly noticed the sound of an approaching vehicle. When Martin looked up he saw a pickup truck slowing down as the passenger window opened. The giant cowboy hat and bigger smile were a dead giveaway: this was Steve, his welcoming committee at the Capitan convenience store of the past night.

"Hey! Thought I might find ya here," boomed the voice from behind the wheel.

Unsure of what this guy wanted with him, Martin gave a slight smile and said, "Steve, right? From last night?"

Steve dropped the gear selector into park and slid across the seat towards the passenger window. "You're on the trail of the Kid, ain't ya?" he said with enough self assuredness that Martin felt exposed.

Who was this guy? What did he want? And why on earth did he pick Martin to buddy up to? Even if he couldn't get back in time, Teebs wanted this man to leave. He simply wanted to sit on the steps of The House until he went back in time or dropped dead trying. He never asked for any help and damn sure didn't want any from a former Mayor of Capitan, NM.

"Yeah, kind of," Martin finally replied, "but no, not just Billy…I mean," Martin couldn't finish the thought and didn't feel obligated to divulge his sordid past to Steve, so he just shook his head.

Steve smiled right through him and slipped the truck into drive. Just as he was about to pull off, he leaned back in and said in a low and serious voice, "I hope you find what you're looking for." With that, he swung the truck into a U-turn and gave Martin a last glance with what appeared to be a laugh as he drove out of sight.

As the sound of the truck's engine faded farther and farther away, the silence that Martin craved had returned. Closing his eyes and taking a deep breath, he was surprised to hear someone come up behind him and ask in a perfect Hackney accent, "Why are you shopping here, mate? My prices are better just a bit down the road."

Martin turned quickly around and was surprised to be looking directly into the eyes of one John Henry Tunstall.

12.

Stunned as Martin was to be in the company of Tunstall, he had to glance around to understand what year he was in. The quick turn to acknowledge the Englishman had taken Teebs out of 2020, but where did it put him? Historically, Tunstall had been killed in February, 1878, just weeks before Martin first arrived back in time. This time, he reasoned, must be earlier since the soft-spoken young man was very clearly alive.

"Come on, then," said Tunstall, looking over Martin's odd clothing, "you look like a man that could use a new kit. We'll get you fixed up right as rain."

Teebs could barely protest and rose from the steps to walk with Lincoln's newest merchant. "Ummm, I'm Martin. Martin Teebs," said Martin as he thrust his hand towards Tunstall.

"Jolly good to meet you, Martin. My name's John. John Tunstall," said the young man, while vigorously shaking Martin's hand in return.

Martin slowly walked down the cold main street. Lincoln was already buzzing with fires lit and smells of all types (good and bad) emanating from the various homes and businesses. He assumed that if it was still 1877, the bad blood between Murphy and Tunstall hadn't yet boiled over. While he was still on guard against an ambush from Dolan's bullies, Tunstall's devil-may-care attitude put Martin at ease that a fight wasn't about to break out imminently.

Making progress towards what he knew was the Tunstall store, the two men passed by an impressive U-shaped adobe house that Martin knew all too well. It was the McSween house that he had barely escaped from with his life. Thinking of two tiny plots and crosses behind the store in the year 2020, Martin shuddered, knowing the refined gentleman he was having a casual stroll with would very soon be a corpse. As they neared the McSween house, out from the front door came the man himself, very much alive, and in good spirits, Alexander McSween. The last time Martin had seen him, it was while using the man's dying body as a human shield to escape the rain of hell and bullets from Dolan's and Dudley's attack. In the very brief time they'd had to get to know each other before the escape, Martin felt a bond with Alex, and seeing him brought joy in that the man was still alive. Before he could think any further, Martin walked up and embraced the lawyer like a long-lost brother.

"Alex! Oh man, you're alive! So good to see you!" gushed Martin with genuine happiness.

The look on both Tunstall's and McSween's faces couldn't be any more telling as they both looked at each other in curiosity and concern. McSween drew back, smoothed his topcoat, and hitched his pants up before replying, "I'm sorry, do I know you? Sir?"

In an instant, Martin realized his faux pas. Of course he had met McSween before, but that was in July of 1878, while ushering Alex to his untimely death. This trip back had placed him earlier on everyone's timeline except his own, and McSween had definitely never met this big man from the future before today. Tunstall stared back and forth at the disconcerting quiet between the two men, unsure as to what to make of the exchange.

"Oh, Mr. McSween. My apologies. I mistook you for someone else," said Martin, with as much conciliation as he could manage.

McSween, still on guard, relaxed a bit and began chatting with Tunstall about some legal matter involving an insurance policy. Martin wandered to the front of the store and wondered if Billy and the boys were around. His goal was to get back in time to see his son and Rosita, but he had clearly overshot the mark. He'd gone back too far to meet Junior, and now he had to find out if he even knew Billy yet.

After the men chatted a few minutes, Martin noticed Tunstall pointing towards him. "Probably telling McSween not to bother counting on me to save his ass in a gunfight," muttered Martin to himself with some surprising bitterness. Tunstall walked over to Teebs, saying, "Come now, Martin, let's get you equipped."

Martin couldn't resist one last look at the troubled McSween, and as he turned away, he missed seeing a pile of horse shit that caused him to slip. While overcorrecting, he wound up diving forward into Tunstall, taking the younger and much smaller man to the ground. In seconds, Martin heard the cocking of a number of guns that were very near his head, just inches away. Trembling, he slowly put his hands up to show he wasn't a threat and rolled over to wind up face-to-face with a very young-looking William H. Bonney and his Regulator pals.

13.

"Billy! Don't shoot. It's me," stammered Teebs.

With French and Bowdre helping Tunstall up and Billy holding the stranger to the ground, the rest of the boys relaxed and holstered their weapons. The Kid pressed the barrel of his Colt to the big man's temple. Martin felt the cold of the steel and wondered if this might be his final moment on earth?

"Who's me, fat boy?" Billy growled as Chavez broke out into laughter, "and how do you know my name?"

Martin swallowed hard, realizing this was it, this was his first meeting with Billy the Kid. Although in Martin's mind they were close friends, Billy had yet to meet this weirdly dressed man who walked around unheeled. Just as he began to speak, Tunstall jumped in, "Easy, William. This is Martin Teebs. He wasn't attacking me. I believe he just slipped on some manure."

Billy kept his gun firmly to Martin's temple but looked up at Tunstall. The Englishman seemed no worse for the wear and wasn't alarmed at being taken down in the middle of the street. With a snort, Billy released the hammer on his gun and shoved it back in his holster. Martin, still wary of being shot, slowly rose with his hands up to show the men he meant no harm.

"I'm sorry, John," said Teebs, "somebody didn't clean up after their dog, or horse, or something."

The Regulators all looked confused as they tried to understand what the hell this stranger was implying. Even Tunstall was caught off guard momentarily before giving a half smile at Teebs' obvious joke. "Right then, Martin, let's get you a proper kit," declared Tunstall, as he and the big man marched up the step into the store.

Summoned from the corral by the commotion, Dick Brewer made his way into the street to see why his men were standing around and not getting any work done.

"What's this?" exclaimed Brewer to the still confused men. "Why are we not on our way to the Feliz?"

"Wasn't nothing, Dick," replied Doc. "Just some new friend John made that kicked up some dust is all."

"Well, then, all's clear, let's git!" yelled Brewer to his men.

Billy stood in the street for a beat longer than Dick expected, still staring after the man whom he almost killed a few moments ago. "Bonney, what's the problem?" questioned Brewer of his new ranch hand.

"Something…something weird about that new guy. Can't put my finger on it, but I will," replied Bonney, more to himself than to Dick.
Brewer swung a leg over his mount and replied firmly, "Let's go," before spurring his horse up the road.

Billy walked towards Tunstall's corral, past one of the new windows in the store. He paused just long enough to see the big, weird man staring back out of the window at him.

14.

Dallas carefully moved to the right lane as his car approached The Big I, which in Albuquerque meant the intersection of I-40 and I-25. Swinging off on I-40 east, he piloted a few more exits until he, Lilly, and Austin could be home.

"Well, that was nice seeing Martin, huh?" asked Dallas innocently. Lilly looked at him like he was crazy. How could anyone, Dallas included, think that visit was nice? She looked over at the pearly teeth and great head of hair and wondered how long that would keep her from killing him?

"Nice?" she replied tersely, "no, it wasn't nice. It was uncomfortable. Geez, you even tried to hug him. What's wrong with you, Dallas?"

Ever the optimist, even Dallas was wounded by Lilly's dissection of him. "Nothing's wrong with me, Lil," he said. "I just like being friendly. That's who I am."

"Don't call me Lil, ok? That's what Martin used to call me, and now it just sounds weird coming from you," said Lilly as matter of factly as she could.

With the thickening mood inside the car, Dallas chose not to reply and swung off the highway at their exit on the east side of the city. Austin was amusing himself by seeing how much drool he could pool up between his legs for when one of his parents came to unbuckle him from his baby seat. Sensing that she might have gone too far, Lilly changed the subject.

"So what are you going to do for work, Dallas?" she asked, "being that the B&B isn't really making any money, and you're not working there."

Lilly was worried about spending her less-than-a-fortune divorce settlement and having to support the struggling actor-turned-hotelier-turned back to actor. Martin may not have been the most exciting husband, but he was always a good, solid provider. Lilly fondly remembered the days of paying their monthly bills without having to check an account balance each time. That luxury was now well in the rearview mirror of her life. While she loved little Austin and she could tolerate Dallas on most days (especially the days when they had sex), her life had spun off in a direction that she never planned nor imagined. From the manicured fescue grass of her front lawn in New Jersey to the weed-infested bland gray gravel in her New Mexico front yard, this life was as different from the old one as it could get. She often gave herself a mental game: would she go back to her old life if she could snap her fingers and make everything right? She tended to play that game most days, and as of this moment, the results were running in a virtual dead heat.

Dallas finally perked up as they made the turn onto their street. "Well, there are a LOT of movies being made here now. I'm going to get me an agent and start auditioning."

This was not the news Lilly wanted to hear. She'd heard about the booming New Mexico movie industry, but she'd also heard from some of her new friends that all of the big roles went to actors out of LA. The locals might snag a small speaking part here or there, but it was hardly enough to support a family on. Sounding worried, she asked, "Is that it? I mean, is that the only plan? What if there's not enough work to support us?"

Dallas looked over at Lilly with a bit of a frown, not used to being doubted by any woman. "Listen, Lil, acting is going to work out. Just you wait and see. And besides if it doesn't, I've got a plan with the B&B. In fact, it's already in the works."

Now it was Lilly's turn to frown. She could only imagine being sent to clean up the casitas by her "boss" Darlene while Dallas and little Austin played toy soldiers in the main house. If he again had some weird idea that there was going to be a three-way marriage or relationship, she'd set him straight in an instant. Tired of arguing and tired of thinking, she simply shot back, "I told you not to call me Lil."

15.

"Sign right here, Martin," said Tunstall, pointing to the line of credit he extended to his visitor, who had somehow misplaced his money.

Martin signed his name and was now in debt to J.H. Tunstall and Company for a total of $6.25 for an entire "kit," as Tunstall liked to call it. Rather than the fighting man's clothes that Billy had secured for him in the past/future, these were more gentlemanly. Martin felt like he'd fit right into a Luden's cough drop commercial with his west end's finest on.

"Thanks, John, I appreciate this," replied Martin. "I'll get this paid back just as soon as I get my finances in order." Martin felt a little bad about the lie. He knew that he'd probably never earn a dime's worth of 1877 money. In fact Martin could be sent back to the future at any moment, leaving Tunstall holding the note that would never be collected. Martin also knew that unless history was somehow about to be dramatically changed, Tunstall wouldn't live long enough to call the note, and neither would McSween, who would be entrusted to keep the enterprise running after the Englishman's death.

Tunstall carefully inspected Martin's original outfit with some interest. He felt the fabrics and looked closely at the workmanship. He couldn't imagine a place on earth that would consider these clothes a acceptable look. He reasoned that Martin must have come across a tailor with too much time on his hands, and an idea to build the world's most repulsive clothing. Tunstall judged that whoever the man was, he had succeeded admirably. No matter, once Martin was properly outfitted, he commanded store clerk Sam Corbett to burn the offending garments so no one else in Lincoln would have to suffer the misery of seeing them.

While Martin had attempted to sneak his modern-day boxer briefs under his new wool suit, Corbett's insistence that he take the whole mess to the fire pit left Martin with a scratchy pair of part-cotton, part-steel-wool underwear that constantly itched everything they touched.

Noticing his guest's discomfort, Tunstall chimed in, "Ah, the drawers have got ya, have they, mate?" Martin smiled a rueful smile as he again grabbed his junk and repositioned it. "They'll break in after a good sollywagging or two, you know, Martin?" said the cheery Tunstall.

Martin felt as out of place as if he'd been transported to Mars. His privates itched like he had poison oak, and all he had to do to cure it was to have a good "sollywagging," whatever the hell that was? Rather than ask, he decided to try to walk the underwear into submission and headed to the door.

"I think I'll take a walk, John. Just to get some fresh air," said Martin.

"Cheers then, mate, have yourself a dozzel," replied the young man, as Martin strode out the front door and out of sight.

Martin scanned the street to the east and west. From past experience, he knew he'd be here again on March 31, 1878, just four months in the future. Everything looked the same as he remembered it, yet there seemed to be a great number of people that he'd never seen. He surmised that some of them would leave town once the War started, wanting to protect their families as the Regulators and Dolan boys were shooting up each other like the Bloods and Crips. Martin's feeling of being out of place didn't subside while walking the town. All of his other trips here had been with Billy and the Regulators as his friends, while this morning they had nearly killed him. He also had gotten used to Rosita pining for him. Knowing a beautiful woman would be throwing herself at him the moment he arrived in town made the trip back in time easier too. Now he was totally alone…a stranger in a strange land…and he did not like the feeling.

Rosita.

Martin now had the clarity of mind to wonder where she was? Clearly in just a few months, she'd be desperately in love with him. How did it happen? Where did it start? What did he do to convince her that HE was the man that she had spent her entire life waiting for? Martin had many questions, but no answers. He set off to see if he could at least find her and gaze at her from afar. One crystal clear concern burned in his mind, however: if he didn't befriend Billy, and never approached Rosita (however that happened), would history go back to the way it was written? If he and Billy didn't become friends now or in the near future, would the other version of Martin still have a front seat to Brady's murder? Would he kill Mathews and lose that damn book?

These were not the kinds of questions with answers one would find on Google anyway, even if Martin did have his mobile phone. He tried to reason with himself that he might have been put back here by the mysterious Steve in order to fix all of the things he had screwed up. If he avoided the two people who had come to mean the most in his life, maybe, just maybe, he would go back to his old life with Lilly. He could escape this past and wind up back in the casita with her, furiously packing his bags and heading back to New Jersey, never to return to New Mexico. No Billy, no Rosita, no Farber, no Dallas, and definitely no baby Austin.

It felt like Martin had his finger on the trigger of life and the hammer was pulled. Pull the trigger, and the past and future are changed forever. Release the hammer and go back to whence you came. For Teebs, it was an unfathomable choice. His life in the future had been ruined, and based on what he saw of Lilly that morning, hers had been too. In fact Darlene and Dallas had their lives thrown into turmoil as well. With one swift, sure decision, Martin felt he could make everything as it had been.

Then his mind went to the photograph of Rosita and Martin Jr. Without their love, Junior would cease to exist. Martin shook his head sadly at the thought, and then more sadly, remembering the strain on Rosita as he came and went from Lincoln (and from her existence) at the drop of a hat. Would he sacrifice his own happiness to make sure she didn't live a life of longing and loneliness, always waiting for him to reappear?

Martin felt like his world was spinning out of his control. "Make a decision!" he thought to himself. The cold wind cut through the topcoat that Tunstall had picked out for him, and he found himself cursing Corbett for burning his other clothes. The stiff leather shoes hurt his feet as he shuffled along Lincoln's only street. His crotch was on fire from the cat-scratch underwear that he'd been given, and the strain of 140 years worth of decisions stung his brain like a migraine tsunami.

With rapid, shallow breaths and his heart racing, Martin feared he was having a heart attack. His mind played a timpani drum roll, with an audience of millions awaiting his decision. He began to sweat in the cold November air, which only made his fiery crotch even more uncomfortable. Finally Martin simply snapped.

"Fuck it! I'm going home!" he yelled in the middle of the street. His decision made, he turned to the west, to the place he had met Tunstall, and to the place he hoped would return him to present day. He'd get in his rental car and head right back to Albuquerque. He'd stop in Capitan along the way and let Steve know he left his precious history of Billy and Lincoln just as it was supposed to be. All the books would be right. Nothing would be changed. He'd get home to Lilly, and pot roast, and ice cream, and the life he'd grown completely comfortable with. He was done with Billy the Kid and done with Lincoln. Martin was going home….

In a huff, he spun around quickly and took one giant stride towards The House without looking. In doing so, he slammed into and knocked to the ground the beautiful Belle of Lincoln, Rosita Luna.

16.

"Oh, my God! Rosita, I'm sorry!" exclaimed Teebs, reaching for her hand to help her up. If he expected a warm welcome from the woman who did not yet know him, Martin was gravely mistaken.

"Maniaco! Estas loco!" she yelled to the big, awkward stranger. Martin grabbed Rosita's hand to help her, which only served to stoke her ire further. "Let me go! Haven't you done enough?" said the clearly agitated woman, as she slapped his big mitt away.

Martin backed off as if bitten by a snake. He wasn't used to this treatment from Rosita. In his rose-colored time-travel glasses, he had assumed that when they met, it would be love at first sight. This was anything but.

Rosita made her way to her feet, dusting off her skirt and adjusting her coat. She glared at Martin with the look a person gives to something they need to scrape off his shoe. Martin put his hands up in front of him, trying to diffuse the situation. "Listen, I'm sorry. Ok?" pleaded the big man. "It's my fault. I wasn't looking. Are you ok?"

"I am fine, thank you," she snapped back at him. "Now I must be on my way."

Rosita walked firmly past Martin towards the Wortley. His plan of returning to his safe and comfy future abandoned, he took one more shot. "Rosita," he said softly and in the way a lover might. Disarmed by the clumsy man's tone, she turned once more.

"Who are you? Why do you know my name?" she demanded, without an inkling of love for him in her eyes or tone.

If Martin had a lifetime to prepare to answer this question, it still wouldn't be enough. What should he say? Was it the right time to tell her that he'd come from the future to meet his soulmate, to have a baby with her, and to try to live his life making her the happiest woman in Lincoln County? Even with his limited experience wooing any woman other than Lilly, that seemed like a farfetched plan to him. What then? Should he make up a story about being a friend of Tunstall's? Would she be impressed that he knew (or at least would know) Billy the Kid, the greatest outlaw in New Mexico history? Clearly Martin knew he must say something, but that something must be enough to start him on the love affair with Rosita that his history (and future) demanded. In the end, all Martin could present was the truth.

"My name is Martin Teebs," he offered with a weak smile.

Rosita didn't much care for more of an explanation, being that she was late for work. She delivered her parting shot before turning to walk away "Well, *Martin Teebs*, next time *abre tus ojos, si?* Open your eyes!"

"Nice job, Martin," said Teebs to himself, as Rosita walked quickly away. Standing there in the middle of the street, he replayed the scene in his head and wondered if he had just ruined any chance he had of happiness with her? Aside from everything else that had gone wrong, his groin was crying out for attention from his ticklish underwear, so Martin reached down for a quick scratch and adjustment. He stood there, absentmindedly watching Rosita fade into the distance while cupping his itchy balls. Just then, somehow caught by the mystery of the big oaf, Rosita stopped to turn around. Glancing back, she saw him staring at her with his hand on his crotch. Her eyes narrowed and her face hardened. Just another loser who thought the way to her heart was through her legs. She hissed and spat on the ground in his direction, turning away for a final time.

Martin released his manhood and stared at the offending hand as if it had a mind of its own. He was tempted to scold it, but the damage had already been done. He looked helplessly up and down the main street, unsure of what to do next. He was a man out of both time and place, and seemingly without a friend in this strange old world.

17.

With no place to stay, and with no certainty he could return to present day, Martin made his way back to the Tunstall store. Happily, Tunstall had taken a liking to him and extended his line of credit to include a room and dinner at the Wortley Hotel. Sending Martin along with a letter of credit on his behalf, Tunstall returned to the duties of his new store's grand opening.

Martin checked into the Wortley that afternoon. Having walked the town vainly in search of Billy or Rosita…or anyone that remotely knew him…he decided to warm up in front of the small fireplace in his room. With the flames defrosting the day's effort, Martin began to feel sleepy. He couldn't actually remember a time when he had stayed overnight in the Lincoln of old. Even the night he and Rosita first made love had ended with him waking up alone in the hills above San Patricio and clearly back in the present. Fighting it no longer, he undid his pants and laid on the bed, quickly drifting off into a fitful sleep.

When Martin awoke, it was pitch black outside his window. He wondered how long he'd slept for? Tunstall hadn't seen fit to include in his kit the Benedict & Burnham pocket watch that Martin had been eyeing, so he had to guess that it was either at or past dinner time. Zipping his pants and putting on his coat, he made his way to the dining hall.

"Just you, Sir?" asked Sam Wortley as Martin walked into the room.

"Yes, table for one, please," replied Martin, glancing around the half-empty room. Once Martin was seated, Wortley pulled out a small pad and looked inquisitively at him, waiting for his order. "Umm, is there a menu or something?" Martin asked.

Wortley cocked his head and smiled at the stranger. He figured the man must be from the east coast, since asking for a menu was a big-city kind of thing. Rather than explain that the Wortley hadn't had a menu since the doors opened in 1870, he simply replied, "What would you like, Sir?"

Martin looked around to see what the other guests were eating, but in the dimly lit room he couldn't make out even one dish. He decided, when in Rome…

"What do you recommend?" asked Martin, assuming he wasn't going to get bat wings or fried rattlesnake in such an establishment.

"For a cold night like this?" said Wortley. "How about a nice bowl of *posole*, Sir?"

Fearful of looking even more out of place than he felt at the moment by asking what *posole* was, Martin simply replied, "Excellent, thank you!" as Wortley scurried away.

A hunger rumbled in Martin's belly as he realized he hadn't eaten since breakfast back in his casita. That morning seemed like a lifetime away, yet here Martin was... sitting less than one mile from the spot he woke up in, but 140 plus years distant in time. While earlier his plan had been to abandon the past and assume his old boring life, he now wasn't so sure. The intrigue of how his relationships with Billy and Rosita would play out commanded Martin's attention. Would it happen tomorrow? A week from now? Or had his appearance in Lincoln somehow upset the space-time continuum and changed the course of future history yet again?

As he pondered such unfathomable mysteries, Wortley arrived with a bowl of a rich, aromatic red soup. The sharp aroma stung at Martin's nose, hinting at the spiciness of the dish. Always searching for the mild jars of salsa on his trips to Shoopman's Grocery, Martin worried that this *posole* might do him in, but he was too hungry to care. Just as the first spoonful of the dish coursed through his body, warming him like a giant bear hug, Wortley returned with a small dish containing two small berry-topped pastries.

"*Pastelitos*, Sir, for your dessert," said Wortley, motioning at the dish. With the posole taking effect, Martin's head began to perspire, so he choked out a simple "Thank you!" as Wortley retreated again into the kitchen. Caught between the genuine deliciousness of the *posole* and the heat that was currently kicking his ass, Martin allowed himself only a few more spoonfuls before deciding that he could not go on. With the fire raging on his taste buds, he inspected the small pastries carefully. Delicately picking one up, he popped it whole into his mouth. The combination of the sweetness of the berries and the firmness of the pastry momentarily tamped down the burning in his gut. Judging it to be delicious under any circumstance, he quickly ate the second one too.

Wortley approached Martin, looking disapprovingly into his bowl. "Is it not to your liking, Sir?" he asked the big stranger.

"Oh, no! It's delicious, it's just a bit spicy for me is all," said Martin, not wanting to insult Wortley or the chef. Wortley smiled a knowing smile. He'd seen a number of easterners come through Lincoln and suffer the same fate as the man seated in front of him. Even the Englishman Tunstall had suffered a bout of explosive diarrhea after eating his green chile stew, or so Wortley had heard.

"More *pastelitos*, then?" said Wortley, motioning to the now empty plate. Taking Martin's nod as a yes, he grabbed the plate and quickly returned with two more of the tiny pastries. Almost before Wortley had left the table, Martin scarfed one down and waited just a beat before eating the second.

After serving a table just across the room from Martin, Wortley looked in his direction, and Martin raised his hand slightly to flag him down. "Could I get a few more of these, *pastel*....what do you call them?" he asked.

"*Pastelitos*, Sir, small pastries," said Wortley, looking down at the vacant plate. "I will bring you four this time."

He turned to walk away just as Martin asked, "And a glass of milk too?" Wortley looked strangely at the man before giving him a quick nod of his head, and then disappeared into the kitchen.

As Martin sat and contemplated another spoon of posole, he heard footsteps behind him, and a familiar voice say, "Who is this man who loves my *pastelitos* so much he might eat the entire tray?" Martin's head snapped around to see Rosita with a tray of pastries and her apron on. The food he'd been enjoying had all been made by her.

Seeing the man who knocked her to the ground earlier startled Rosita. "You!" she cried. For the third time that day, Martin found himself with his hands up to show he meant no harm.

"Rosi....I mean, Miss Luna, please accept my apologies for earlier today," he stammered, hoping she wouldn't throw the plate of pastries in his face.

Rosita's face softened a bit and she breathed deeply. How much trouble could a man cause that was stuffing his face with her pastries? She decided to give the stranger a break. "It's fine. No damage done," she said more gently. "So, you like my cooking?"

Martin smiled broadly at the minor breakthrough, realizing that this might be his only chance to spark a flame with the beauty. "I do indeed," he said happily, "although I'm not sure I should be eating so much gluten, you know?"

Indeed Rosita had no idea what gluten was or what the man was talking about, and her expression showed it. Martin quickly realized that gluten free was a trend that wouldn't be popular for another 140 years or so, give or take.

"The food is delicious, thank you. Again, my name is Martin Teebs," said Martin, realizing he should stand in the presence of a lady. Rising, he offered his hand, which she could not take due to the pastry tray and glass of milk he had requested. Rosita put the food and drink on his table and slowly reached out her hand. Shaking hands with a man was one of the strangest things she'd been offered to do, but this Martin Teebs seemed nice enough. He felt the warm embrace of her palm touch his, and it was like a jolt of electricity had gone through his veins. He stared into her eyes to see if she felt it too. If she did, it didn't register.

"I'm glad you like it, *Martin Teebs*," she said sincerely. "My name is *Rosita Luna*."

For a moment Martin just took her in. She had a smudge of flour on her forehead, and her long hair was tied back. Judging by the look of her apron, she had been working a long day and was not done yet. More than anything else in the dimly lit room, her eyes shone like the sun and took Martin's breath away. He now understood, maybe more than ever, that this was the place he was destined to be, and this was the woman he was destined to be with. His decision to stay had been the right one. He was sure of it.

"It's my pleasure, Rosita," he said, trying to catch his breath. "Thank you for allowing me to explain about earlier."

"*Si, Martin Teebs*, all is forgotten," she said through a broad smile. "Enjoy your *pastelitos* and milk, and I shall get back to the kitchen."

With that Rosita turned and walked away, leaving Martin gasping for air, staring at her wake, and longing for a lot more than milk and cookies.

18.

Martin was practically dancing on air as he exited the dining hall. So abuzz was his mind at the breakthrough with Rosita that he decided to step outside and get a brace of cold mountain air in his lungs. He inhaled deeply and exhaled a stream of foggy breath into the night sky. At minimum, he felt he was on the right track with her. She had been friendly with him, which was more than he could say for their first meeting of the day. "Friendly" was a start, he reasoned. Standing in the blackness, he wondered if he should wait for Rosita to be done for the evening and walk her home? She hadn't shown anything that let on any romantic feelings, so it might be considered premature. "Better not to rush it, Martin," he said to himself, "no sense rushing forever." Forever. Could it really be? He and Lilly were most definitely over, no one but his coworker Colin would miss him, and it might even take Mr. Talbot a week or so to realize Martin was gone. "Why not?" he said aloud. What would be the point of heading back to his modern-day life when he had no one to share it with?

Then there was Billy. Certainly he and the young man hadn't forged the kind of friendship that Martin had seen in the coming months. He wondered if he could still win Rosita's heart, yet keep far enough away from Billy so as not to change his future? But hadn't the future already happened? Martin asked himself. Hadn't he already lost his book, killed Matthews, slept with Rosita? The backwards and forwards calculations began to hurt his head, and he felt a tension headache coming on. Martin decided to head to his room, hoping that a solid night of sleep would give him the clarity he desperately sought. As he turned, he caught his foot on a loose board on the porch and fell forward. His hands instinctively went out in front of him, and just before he hit the door sash, he caught himself with a loud thud. Scared that his clumsiness might have knocked him forward into present day, he peered through the window to satisfyingly see Wortley serving up another tray full of the devilishly hot soup.

"Slip in any horseshit lately?" came a soft voice from the shadows behind him. Surprised, Martin whirled around and instinctively went for his gun, realizing in the last second that he didn't have one.

"What you gonna shoot me with, your finger?" cackled the voice again as Billy stepped forward out of the shadows. Half relieved and half scared that this Billy might indeed kill him, Martin took a deep breath before talking.

"Hi, Billy, my name is…"

"How do you know my name?" asked Billy with a stern enough tone for Martin to know he wanted an answer, and quick.

Martin grasped at his flagging thoughts. He only knew that he and the Kid were already good friends when he first went back to Lincoln. He had no idea how they got that way. Should he tell him he was from the future? No, that would make him seem insane. Maybe he could come up with some well crafted lie about knowing his mother? Martin silently voted no to that idea as well, not knowing how sensitive of a subject that was for the young man. Finally Martin decided to just tell as much of the truth as he could without alarming Billy.

"I've just heard a lot about you, Billy. That's all," said Martin plainly.

Not about to let the moment go, Billy dug in, "From who?"

"From Mr. Tunstall and Mr. McSween," Martin replied. "They both think a lot of you."

This seemed to surprise Billy. He quickly raised his head and squinted his eyes, something out of the one known picture of him in front of Beaver Smith's saloon. "They do?" he asked. "Of me?"

"Well, yeah, Billy, everyone was, I mean, is impressed by you," said Teebs, quickly catching his mistake.

Billy pondered that thought for a moment before shaking his head with a smile, "Awww, you're full a horsefeathers, man. Ain't nobody around here even cares who I am. Just some damn orphan trying to make my place in the world."

The weight of Billy's easy dismissal of how much he would mean to people around the world nearly crushed Martin. He felt a fatherly affection towards the boy and seriously considered going to put his arm around him. The Colt hanging from his belt and the Winchester he was using to prop himself up with made Martin think the better of that plan.

"Well, if I look into my crystal ball, I can tell you that the name William H. Bonney will be known by people all over. No one's ever going to forget you," said Teebs, wondering if perhaps he was giving away too much.

"If anyone remembers me, it sure as hell can't be for nothing good," stated Billy as he pondered the thought. Deciding that pondering his past wasn't the best idea, he shifted moods in an instant. "Hey, what did you say your name was again?"

"It's Martin. Martin Teebs"

"Where ya from, Teebs?" asked the now jovial young man.

Again Martin paused. New Jersey was a state already in 1877, so he could easily tell Billy the truth. He'd sure like to avoid a lengthy discussion of how he got to Lincoln though. He decided to slow play it.

"Well, New Jersey originally, but I've been making my way out west for some time now," said Martin and hoped that would be the end of that.

"Figured you for a Yankee! Damn, I told the boys you had too many manners to be from round here," laughed Billy into the night. "No wonder you get on so well with John. Both of ya are cultured, ain' ya? Probably went to a university and all too!"

Martin smiled an embarrassed smile, happy that they were getting on so well.

"I'm from New York, at least that's where I was born," offered Billy. Until that moment Martin hadn't been sure of the fact, being that a birth certificate for the Kid had never been found. "But I've been making my way out west for some time too, Teebs."

Feeling more assured, Martin stepped down onto the street and offered his hand. "Nice to meet you, Billy." The young man grabbed Martin's much bigger hand in his rather small one. Billy's grip was solid and his hands rough in a way that Martin's would never be from his ad sales job.

"Same here, *hombre*," replied Billy. "Well, I gotta get this brood mare in the corral.

Tunstall wanted her here where he could keep his eyes on her, you know?"

Martin had little idea what a brood mare was but nodded knowingly anyway.

"Night, Teebs," said Billy as he turned away, not giving Martin a chance to respond. As the outlaw disappeared into the darkness, Martin stood in wonderment. He'd done it. He'd met Billy the Kid. While every book he'd read and movie he'd watched portrayed the Kid differently, none of them captured the real living, breathing man that had been in front of him. The Billy that Martin was getting to know was a complicated man in a complicated time. His morals were questionable, but driven by need and, sometimes, reckless desire. This Billy seemed to range from class clown to dark, brooding, goth punk...and everything in between. He was a hard young man, living in a hard land and trying each day to stay alive. Martin could only observe the real Kid but never truly understand him. Teebs had grown up with an intact family, good food and education, and in a city where he didn't have to carry a gun to stay alive. He'd never faced the kind of long odds that Billy had, so he never had to make some of the choices the young man made either. The more Martin thought about it, the more he admired that Billy could ever be lighthearted and fun. With the shadow of potential death around each corner each day, one could be excused for being a little moody.

About to turn in for the night, he saw the boy emerge from the shadows, leading a pretty chestnut mare. "Hey, Teebsie, you any good with the iron?" asked Billy in a voice loud enough for half of Lincoln to hear. The vision of Mathews' brains flying out of the crater in his head popped into Martin's mind as he replied, "I'm pretty good. Can hold my own. Why?"

"Might could use a few more boys down on the ranch. I hear you owe John some money. If you're staying in town, I'll talk to Dick for ya," came the reply as the boy again sauntered out of sight.

"Hmmmph," said Teebs to himself. A job? While chasing cattle around the plains wasn't his idea of fun, it would at least allow him to pay back his debt to Tunstall and, just maybe, to learn a trade that would allow him to provide for Rosita. While Martin had no idea how long he'd be able to stay in this early version of Lincoln, he did know that, as in present times, he wanted to be a good provider for his family. Lacking any other frontier-worthy skills, a job with Tunstall might be just what the doctor ordered.

With Billy now gone, Martin thought about the possibility of an extended stay in the past. The money would come in handy so he didn't need to rely on the kindness of strangers.

From his history books, Martin remembered Tunstall buying Jesse Evans a suit while he was in "the pit," which was Lincoln's hole-in-the-ground jail. Apparently, Tunstall was trying to woo Evans to his side of the coming fight and thought a suit and a bottle of whiskey would win the day. Martin wondered if Tunstall was trying to woo him too? Maybe he never expected to be paid back for the suit or his stay at the Wortley? Maybe Tunstall would call in his favor when bullets started to fly? Maybe, just maybe, the Englishman hadn't been acting nice to Martin, maybe he'd been calculating...looking to expand his army with men that were in his debt and would feel obligated to fight, kill, or die for him? The thought chilled Martin. Had he been played that easily by the affable Englishman? For the price of a suit and a few plates of pastry?

Now feeling more cold than he had since stepping outside, Martin turned to return to his room. As he grabbed the door handle, however, he knew things were all wrong. There were no lights on and no one inside the hotel, which appeared to have aged 100 years in the past five minutes. He didn't have to look back to see if Billy was still there, for he knew he was not. Martin could only manage to mutter "shit" as he turned and walked to the road and back to his very modern-day casita. His heart sank. He had just made major progress with Billy and Rosita, and now they were just dust in the ground. He wanted to find a portal back to 1877, but there was none apparent.

Maybe Darlene was awake and they could split those two ciders he bought the previous night? After what Martin had just been through, he wished he'd bought an entire case.

19.

The next morning dawned clear and cold as Martin made deal after deal with himself to exit the warm bed. Finally rising, he shook off the night and stretched mightily. The main house had been dark when he got back the night before, so he'd gone straight to bed. Now he wanted to see if there was a delicious breakfast waiting for him. He trudged down the stairs in the B&B branded robe and happily found a tray loaded with goodies and granola for breakfast. Martin placed the tray lightly on the table and directed his attention to the coffee maker where he would concoct a pot of dark-as-night roast of New Mexico pinon coffee.

As Martin sat munching on a banana while waiting for the coffee to percolate, he reflected on the previous day. It seemed like his relationships with Billy and Rosita were headed exactly where they had to go in order to meet up with his other visits in a few months. (Which of course had already taken place. Which of course was a maddening jigsaw puzzle to Martin.) He wondered how hard he should push to move them forward? He was scheduled to fly out tomorrow, so he had the entire day to see if he could rebound back to 1877. Then he wondered how he could even be sure that's the time he'd go back to? What if he went back to 1879 and was finally able to meet Junior? How could he make sense of his relationships with these people if there was no consistency?

Hearing the chirp of the coffee maker, he poured himself a big, steaming mug and sat down with the Sunday newspaper Darlene had left for him. Splashed across the front page the headline blared:

COVID-19 MUTATES, U.S. INFECTIONS SOAR

Well, good morning to you, too, thought Martin. He had assumed the country would be done with COVID two years after it had hit America's shores, but the virus had stubbornly hung around and mutated from time to time. Those mutations made the vaccines that were quickly pressed into service worthless within months. While the paranoia about COVID was at an all time high, Martin had somehow been able to avoid being infected, or, if not, he never developed any symptoms that he even noticed. Suddenly a chill shot through him. What if he was an asymptomatic carrier of the virus. Could he bring it back in time? Would he wipe out his entire group of friends and family that were left to call on doctors who had no idea what the plague was? Would Billy the Kid simply cease to exist, the victim of a virus that half the world claimed was a hoax?

Martin wasn't sure how all of this could work. When he traveled back and forth, some things came with him and some didn't. Most times his guns remained in the past while his vintage clothing stayed on his body. The lack of consistency was maddening. Martin's revolver did finally make it back to present day with him, but that was only after he had shot Farber with it. Was that the key? Did he need some interaction with someone from his own time? And what of this virus? If he had it, would he bring it right to Rosita's front door, or would it be trapped in some vacuum in time, waiting for him to return? If Martin was going to figure it out, it would have to be another time, as a sharp rap on the screen door jarred him from his fog.

"Hey, Martin! Is it ok to come in?" asked Darlene cautiously. She was wrapped in a fleece jacket and her usual tighter-than-skin yoga pants, but this time she had on a pair of giant woven boots with what looked like a lion's mane coming out of the tops of them.

Still in his robe, Martin made a mental check if he'd put underwear on. Thankfully he had. He rose and opened the door for her, saying, "Sure, Darlene, come on in."

Martin noticed a giant mug in her hand that was only half full of coffee so he brought the pot over and freshened it up.

"Oh, thank you, Martin. That's so sweet," she said. "I didn't see you last night. You were gone all day, and I was starting to worry!"

"I'm fine. No worries," he said, unsure of how to continue. "I was doing a lot of exploring and wound up meeting a guy from Capitan. We talked for quite awhile and had a couple of beers over there. I guess I lost track of time."

"Martin, I'm sorry about all that mess with Dallas yesterday. I had no idea they were coming. I would have warned you if I did," said Darlene with genuine concern and, it seemed, sadness.

Martin studied the woman. In any other lifetime, he would have gone gaga over her. She was pretty, kind, had a killer body, and seemed to have the sex drive to use it. Unfortunately, it was not any other lifetime for Martin, it was this one, and he only had eyes for Rosita. "Hey, it was tough for everyone. You didn't do anything you need to apologize for. If anyone should apologize, it should be them for showing up unannounced."

Darlene took her hand, still warm from holding the coffee mug, and placed it on Martin's. For a split second, he thought she might be trying to go down a path he wasn't willing to, but he quickly saw it as a gesture of friendship and camaraderie. He smiled gently back at her and lifted his mug to toast. "Hear, hear. Here's to new beginnings for everyone, and fondly remembering the good times in the past!" Darlene clinked her mug to his, and they both downed a shot of the hot, black liquid.

"Oh, the other thing was this," she said, while reaching into the pocket of her fluffy jacket. "Dallas took everything in that box that I wanted you to have, but this was left behind. It's some kind of really old book." Darlene pulled out a tiny book, no more than 20 pages and maybe four or five inches high by three inches wide. It almost looked like a bunch of notes that someone wrote, but it had a real cover and binding. He looked carefully at the worn title and was able to make out:

LINCOLN COUNTY DAYS
BY
JUAN PANCHITO BACA

Martin flipped through a page or two. The book was written in some of the worst handwriting he'd ever seen, so he wasn't sure he'd even be able to read it. Nevertheless, he thanked Darlene for the gift and put it on the side table to decode later.

Rising to leave and get her Sunday chores done, Darlene gave Martin a gentle hug on her way out the door. Being a man and susceptible to the physical responses of contact with the opposite sex, he stepped back and leaned his torso into the hug, lest he send Darlene a pointed seven-inch message that they should be more than friends.

After watching her bound down the steps and out of sight, he climbed the stairway to the loft to fetch his "kit" and see if he might be able to arrange another day in the past... the splendid, glorious past that Martin sought so eagerly.

Now, if he could only figure out how to stay there?

20.

Being as he'd stayed in bed longer than planned, by the time Martin made his way out onto the main street of Lincoln, things were jumping. A number of tourists were out and about as the sun peeked over the Capitans and began to warm the valley. Martin always felt a little self-conscious wearing his throwback gear among these modern-day tourists, but rather than scorn, the men at least frequently looked at him with that appeared to be admiration. So, decked out in his new kit from the store of J.H. Tunstall and Co., Martin walked towards the west.

"He must be impersonating Pat Garret," whispered a midwestern man to his corn-fed wife. The wife looked Martin up and down as they walked by and gave him a little wink. Martin obliged her with a slight nod and tip of the cap.

"Pat Garrett," he said to himself, "as if...." While he now knew that Billy had escaped Garrett's bullet in Fort Sumner, he had no idea how. The Kid had lived to be an old man in Magdalena. He had either made a deal with Garrett or decided to just head somewhere else on July 14, 1881. In any event, it was clear that Billy the Kid got the better of his former friend on that night. The thought of Garrett plagued Martin's thoughts. Even now in his history books, Garrett was the hero that killed the Kid. How could this be so? Martin himself had held the Kid as he died in 1940. Without a Billy to kill, what act had Garrett completed to make him famous? Even though every single thing in Martin's life pointed to the fact that history was irrevocably changed due to his actions, the only ones that seemed to know it were Martin and perhaps Farber. Why hadn't the books changed? Why hadn't history been revised to show all of the changes that one Martin Teebs had caused? It was then, for the first real time, that Martin considered that he might be clinically insane. Was it possible that he had lost his mind two years ago? Was he living in some bubble of his own creation that only he could see? He even went so far as to wonder if he was caught in some drug-induced coma that had lasted for years, and that all of this might be a multicolor trip of his mind's design?

If he had been in a coma, it would have to be from that first time he fell in a ditch in Lincoln during his and Lilly's first visit. While Martin arose and met Billy, Rosita, and the Regulators, perhaps in the real world an ambulance had taken him to the hospital and they drilled a few holes in his head to relieve the pressure. He wondered, was Lilly sitting by his side all this time? Was she crying herself to sleep while gently holding

Martin's hand, begging him to come back to her? What of his job? Did Colin take over his sales position? Martin wondered where he even was if he was in a coma? Were they still in New Mexico or had Lilly arranged some expensive medical flight to bring him back to New Jersey? Then a thought struck Martin heavily…how much was all this costing them? If he'd lost his job, surely his insurance was cancelled. Now thoughts of dread filled his mind. Had Lilly sold the house? Was she stripping in one of the sleazy bars in Passaic County to make money so Martin could have his oxygen? Maybe times were so bad she had to start hooking? "Geez," he said to himself, "you really screwed the pooch on this one, Martin."

As Martin delved deeply into the coma possibility, he couldn't shake the notion that all of this had felt incredibly real. Meeting Billy, making love to Rosita, the pain when Lilly announced she was pregnant with Dallas' baby, and much more. He knew he must be alive. There was no way this could be a dream unless he was in a matrix-like simulation. Wanting to feel something, anything, Martin pinched himself hard. "OUCH" he cried. Unconvinced, he slapped himself across the face even harder. "Ah-hhh!" he grunted through the sting. He had hit himself so hard a few tears welled up in his eyes. As he stood there blinking them away and contemplating what more painful act he could commit, two mountain bikers sped towards him from the east. Just as Martin regained his composure, he heard one of them yell, "Jackie, watch out!" and a diminutive girl, covered in tattoos, slammed right into him hard enough to knock him all the way back to 1877.

21.

Martin came to next to Reverend Ealy's hut. He writhed against the pain in his hip where the crazy cyclist had hit him. It was one of those pains where the sufferer knows it will pass, but it's taking its sweet time to do it. As he grimaced and gritted his teeth, the pain swelled and eventually did subside to a level that allowed him to get to his knees. Never taking his time-travel arrival for granted, Martin looked for signs that he had arrived in 1877 and not some other year where he'd make a fool of himself… again.

One thing he knew for sure was that if he'd arrived on the heels of his last departure, the Tunstall store would still be open. Martin peered around the corner of the hut and looked towards the store. People seemed to be coming and going, just like the last time he'd been here. While he didn't spot Tunstall or the boys, Martin had a reasonable assurance that he was in the right time. Making one last check, he peered further and saw the still-standing adobe of Alexander McSween. The last time Martin had been in that house, it was very much on fire and McSween was very much on his way towards being dead.

Rising and dusting off his pants, Martin scanned the street before stepping out. Just as he did, he heard a familiar voice in distress just down the street.

"No!" cried the woman. "Leave me alone, you pigs!"

Martin jogged a few steps to get a better look and saw Rosita, half in fear and the balance in anger, lecturing her attackers. As soon as Martin saw who the perpetrators were, he grew nauseous. Billy Mathews and Jimmy Dolan stood laughing and pointing at the beautiful woman. They seemed to have no fear and no respect for her wish to be left alone.

"Come on, Rosie," growled Mathews in an exaggerated deep voice, "let me show you how a man treats you!" Dolan smiled a pinched smile on his narrow face. Martin couldn't tell if he was going along because he wanted to or because Mathews wanted him to. Dolan swayed back and forth with what Martin determined to be nervousness.

Rosita's face grew hard at her tormentors as she hissed, "That will *never* happen, *maricon, nunca!"*

Just as Martin was about to walk over and step in, the real Jimmy Dolan stepped out of his shell.

"You'll do what I say," he said smoothly, "everyone here will. Murphy's on his last leg with that cancer. You know who's going to take over this town when he's gone?"

Rosita stared in disgust at the tiny man. She simply sneered at him, not giving him the satisfaction of an answer.

"Time's up. The answer is that I will," said the sniveling little bully, "and when I do, you'll do what you're told, Rosita Luna, IF you know what's good for you, that is. Lincoln is *my* town, and you're all just living in it."

Mathews got way too excited, clapping the small man on the shoulders. Dolan swatted his hand away and glared at him. Rosita couldn't resist taking a parting shot at the two men.

"*Cuidado*, you might break the little man!" she said with a hearty laugh. Always having been teased for his diminutive height (among other things), Dolan growled and stepped towards her, "Hey!"

Martin walked up quickly and stood in front of Rosita, shielding her with his body. "Leave her alone, man," he said in a vernacular that was way too modern for the situation.

"Who the hell are you, *man*?" said Dolan, his voice dripping with sarcasm.

Martin glanced over his shoulder to see if Rosita was ok. Her surprised face at the intervention of Teebs was apparent. She didn't seem disappointed, which gave Martin some confidence.

"Never mind who I am, just leave her alone," said Martin with what little authority he could command. Mathews stepped up close enough that Martin could smell what he had for breakfast on his breath. Martin could only picture what would take place just a few months from now, as a 44-40 Winchester slug that Martin fired would permanently drain the brains of Billy Mathews on a spot very close to here.

"You have no idea who you're talking to, stranger," threatened Mathews. "You picked the wrong damn side in this fight." Mathews' eyes bulged out of his stupid bully head, looking as if they might pop out onto Martin's coat. Martin thought about punching Mathews square in the nose, but the sight of a gun on both his and Dolan's hips made him think the better of it. Mathews craned his head even closer, causing Martin to lean back as the man's breath created a noxious fog that spread quickly to Martin's nose.

"Well, do something, dummy. Make us leave her alone," he said.

Lacking a gun, Martin couldn't really make a fight. He looked at the pitifully small Dolan and figured that in a wrestling match, the small man would be easily beaten. Mathews on the other hand didn't look like a pushover. Martin tried to remember his last fistfight. He remembered back to the seventh grade when he fought under the bridge against Glenn Gowan. Gowan was a punk who regularly got beat by his alcoholic father. Martin just happened to be the piece of fresh meat that the kid liked to take his retribution on. On that day, Gowan got Martin in a headlock and repeatedly punched him in the face until Martin wrestled free, screaming his lungs out in frustration. While he couldn't be sure, Martin didn't think he got even one punch off. Now here he was, face-to-face with yet another bully looking to take his failures in life out on Martin, and this time there were guns involved.

"*Senor Teebs*, come!" said Rosita, sensing that a real fight was about to break out. Martin held his hand out firmly to his side to signal that he had things in order.

"You two are going to leave Rosita alone. Not just now either," said Martin in his best *Dirty Harry* voice. "She doesn't want anything to do with the likes of you two. Is that clear?"

Even Martin surprised himself with how strong he'd come off. He was even more amazed when both men took a step back. He considered pressing his defense, but both men continued to edge away. He'd done it. Martin had saved the damsel in distress. *THIS* must be the reason Rosita fell in love with him. He felt heady, giddy. The power of backing down two armed men with only his voice inspired Martin to speak. "And don't come back!" he said enthusiastically. Dolan and Mathews had what appeared to be fear in their eyes as they backed away, never letting their gaze wander from Martin. Just then, he heard the unmistakable "click" of the hammer being lowered on a Colt. With a shiver, Martin assumed another one of Dolan's boys had gotten the drop on him. Turning around, he was met with the barrel of a Thunderer .41 and the smiling face of William H. Bonney behind it.

"Billy!" Martin cried in relief. "How long have you been there?"

Billy smiled the crooked little smile that Martin would come to know so well and simply replied, "Whole time, Teebsie."

Martin got a sinking feeling as Mathews and Dolan walked away. They didn't turn yellow because of him, they'd been looking down the barrel of Billy's gun the entire time. He felt the life go out of him as he looked at Rosita. To his surprise, she beamed at him with a look of genuine appreciation. She had seen that Martin had no idea the Kid was there. She was intrigued by the big stranger who carried no gun and seemingly had no fear of those who did. Reaching up to touch his shoulder, she said, "*Martin Teebs*, you are a brave man. Thank you for standing for my honor." Behind her Billy started smiling and winking the way a high school boy might, urging Martin to make his move and get laid.

"It was nothing, Rosita. No one should treat a lady that way. Especially a lady like you," Martin replied respectfully.

Billy rolled his eyes and tossed back his head at Martin's missive. As a young boy driven by hormones, his first goal with any attractive woman he met was procreation, and he couldn't understand why this strange man didn't feel the same way.

"You got everything under control here, Teebsie? If so, I'll juss be on my way," said Billy.

Martin, sensing a few moments alone with Rosita, quickly replied, "Yeah. Thanks, Billy. I appreciate the backup."

Billy lifted his chin with a smile and walked off towards Tunstall's corral. Martin was free to turn his gaze back to Rosita, who still smiled warmly at him.

"No one has ever stood for me like that since my papa died, *Martin Teebs*. You are a good man," gushed Rosita. Martin was rendered speechless by the woman, and all he could return was a smile. "Tonight," she said, "I will prepare dinner for you as my thank you. *Si?*"

Martin wrongly assumed that Rosita meant at the Wortley, and in her capacity as cook. "Um, I'm not staying at the Wortley. I mean, I don't have a room there…or anywhere tonight, I guess," he stammered out.

"*Tu no entiendes, Martin!*" said Rosita to a man who understood tacos and cerveza as his only Spanish words. "Not at the Wortley, at my home," she said, pointing to two little shacks on the north side of the street. "Mine is the one with the blue door."

Martin was stunned. Things were moving faster than he imagined they would. Here he was, getting a dinner date with the love of his time-traveling life after only meeting her for the third time. Not wanting to tempt fate, he quickly agreed, "Yes, thank you, Rosita. That sounds wonderful. What time should I be there?"

"At sunset, *Martin Teebs*," said Rosita through her big, bright smile, "and bring your appetite!" With that, Rosita twirled away and walked down the street towards church. After a few steps, she stopped to look back, wondering if this man was still gazing at her. He seemed frozen to the spot, his eyes in a state of disbelief. She could only laugh at him and snap her flowing hair around as she walked out of sight.

Martin breathed heavily, taking the last few minutes in. He had a date! His good fortune had put him back at precisely the right time to make an impression on Rosita. Five minutes sooner or later and he wouldn't be in this position. He wondered if there was some divine intervention pulling the strings on his experience? He always seemed to wind up where he was supposed to. Of course, he reasoned, he just might be showing up wherever he landed and only in looking back could he see how the pieces fit. In any event Martin was thrilled at the prospect of some alone time with Rosita. Now all he had to do was stay here throughout the day and find some way to make himself useful.

22.

Lilly glanced at the blinking cursor on her computer screen. It was silently pointing to her shrinking bank account balance. She hadn't sold many paintings at the weekly flea market at the fairgrounds, and that was before COVID hit. Now that the flea market was closed down, she had few options to sell her amateur-but-getting-better artwork. She mused that she might be able to build a website and sell her paintings online, or maybe find a small gallery that would hang them? Her other last resort was to put her artwork in one of Albuquerque's two thousand eight hundred and seventy-six brewpubs. She wasn't sure if that number was right, but it sure seemed like it, with a new one opening up every few days.

That Dallas hadn't gotten any acting jobs...nor had he sought any other semblance of work...annoyed her. Whatever money he was worth was tied up in the B&B, and that didn't seem to be going anywhere soon. So here she was. A woman with a toddler, a partner that acted like a toddler, and a shrinking supply of money. For a brief instant, Lilly wondered if she could get Martin back? He would be a far better father to little Austin than Dallas would. Martin was kind, sensible, and reliable. Hardly the stuff of a torrid romance novel, but Lilly had had that…and didn't like where it had gotten her. She had a vision of groveling on the front steps of their New Jersey home while little Austin toddled around the extra-green front lawn. She reasoned she could throw herself on the mercy of the court and plead temporary sex-induced insanity. Martin must be able to understand that. Surely at some point in their marriage, he must have had eyes for someone else? Lilly remembered back to that day in the spare room with Farber, Martin, and that strange kid. Martin was accused of having a girlfriend and a child, but Lilly had seen none of it. Martin never mentioned it while they tried marriage counseling. She was certain he wasn't sending money to anyone, and he didn't disappear for days or even hours without explanation. Could it be that he was a deadbeat dad? Lilly couldn't believe that. The whole thing must have been some giant misunderstanding.

So here she sat, planning the rest of her life out while wishing the plan included going back to her previous life. The thought of it made her sad and melancholy. Just as she thought she might cry, Dallas popped up behind her, grabbing her breasts and squeezing them hard.

"Come on, Austin is asleep. We've got time for a little trip around the world!" he whispered in his cheesiest sexy voice. Dallas rolled his tongue around her ear in a move that used to take her breath away, but now just made her want him to stop breathing.

"Ok," she sighed and rose from the chair. If her lack of enthusiasm somehow slowed his roll, it was only by a second or two.

What the hell, she figured. At least she could take her mind off of her troubles for awhile. Lilly followed her biggest trouble into the bedroom as he let his pants slip to the ground, and she gently closed the door behind them so as not to wake the baby.

23.

With time on his hands, Martin headed to the Tunstall store. He knew he'd need to settle up with Tunstall at some point, and he had no idea how he'd get any period money to do so. He imagined some little time-travel airport with a currency exchange in it. He'd bring in his circa 2020 fifty-dollar bills and pocket some of 1875's finest cash in return. If only there were a bigger time-travel trade, he thought. Climbing onto the porch, Martin strode through the front door to be greeted by the store's clerk Corbett. Nodding his head at the man, he walked on by to gaze at the pocket watches.

"Martin! Splendid to see you, old chap," said the overly enthusiastic Tunstall. "Treating you right as rain at the Wortley, are they?"

"Oh, yes, ummm…right as rain, John," came Martin's hesitant reply.

"Right, right. It's brass monkeys out there today, no?" queried Tunstall.

Martin had no idea what "brass monkeys" meant and was too embarrassed to ask, so he simply gave Tunstall a knowing nod.

"Excellent, so what can we do for you, Mr. Teebs?" inquired the Brit.

Martin realized now was as good a time as ever to talk money.

"Well, John, you've been so generous to help me out in getting started here. I don't want my tab getting out of control, so I would like to find a way to start paying you back. Do you perhaps need some help around the store?" offered Teebs.

"S'not where we need it, mate," said Tunstall quickly. "We need more men on the ranch. Trying to fatten the herd in anticipation of winning one of the Fort's beef contracts. You any good with beef, Martin?"

Martin had to ask himself, was he any good with beef? He certainly had a lot of experience eating it. His grilling skills were better than mediocre too. Martin wondered if his experience in eating steaks and hamburgers gave him any sort of insight into the way the animals act? With no better prospects for work, he decided to gild the lily just a bit.

"Yeah, I've had a lot of time around beef in the past, John," answered the big man.

Tunstall looked him up and down before responding. "Splendid, chap, how's about you ride for me? Pay is forty dollars per month for a start. What say you, Martin?"

Before Martin could balk that he would make almost forty dollars per hour in his own time at his sales job, he stopped himself and was reminded this was a perfect way to pay off his debt.

"Thank you, John, that sounds great. I accept," said Martin.

"Jolly good man! The boys will be back in town later this afternoon. I'll get you a mount ready, and you can head back to the ranch with them this evening."

This evening? Martin had a date with Rosita. Tunstall must have seen the look of panic on his face. "What's the issue, mate?" he asked.

"It's just that I had plans here in town tonight. Ummm, Rosita Luna invited me for dinner," said Martin sheepishly.

"Top job, Martin!" gushed Tunstall. "Rosita Luna. Blimey, she's aces, mate. Just go on with yourself, and you can ride out to the ranch with me tomorrow."

"Thanks, John. I appreciate it," said Martin genuinely.

Now with a job, a date, and some clothes that didn't have cats and fireworks on them, Martin was feeling more at home in New Mexico than he ever had. Martin strode out to the main street and took in a deep lungful of clean mountain air. He had arrived. He was here. If the time-travel airport ever broke down and he found himself stuck, Martin imagined he'd get on just fine.

24.

"Something different bout you, Teebsie," said the boy who would grow to become a legend. "I know you ain't from around here, but you don't even seem like you're from around anywhere. Can't put my finger on it, but I will."

As promised, seven of Tunstall's men came to town that afternoon with a buckboard to carry provisions back to the ranch and to deliver to the corral two more horses that Tunstall intended to sell. Billy always seemed like the eager younger brother to these men and always seemed to be in good spirits.

"Don't look so hard, Billy. I haven't had much of a life until I got here," warned Martin.

Billy looked in interest at his new friend. A man who would stand down Dolan with no gun but was afraid to ask a woman to dance or take supper with him. The question of who this man really was gnawed at Billy. "You got kids, Teebsie?" asked Billy.

Ugh, thought Martin, how do I answer this one?

"Umm, yeah. Kind of. But not yet, kind of," stuttered Martin as his mouth emptied out the jumbled thoughts in his head.

"Clear as mud," said Billy. "Now you feel like givin me one answer stead of three?"

Martin tried to focus on what to say. A simple no would be a lie, or would it? In this land, in this time, Martin clearly did not get Rosita pregnant yet. Of course in the world he recently stepped out of, he did have a son he'd never met who was long since dead. He figured it was useless to try to explain any of this to the young man, so he simply replied, "I don't have kids yet, but I plan to soon."

"Ahhh, I get it. That's why you're all steamed up about Rosita!" laughed Billy.

Martin must have turned a shade of red Billy had not seen before because the young man quickly added, "Hey, I'd be steamed up too if Rosita was takin a shine to me, Teebsie. I'm happy for ya!"

Martin muttered a quick "thanks" and looked for a way to change the subject.

"So I'm going to be working for Mr. Tunstall. I guess I'll see you out at the ranch tomorrow?" asked Martin.

"Sure nuff, Teebsie. It's gittin cold in the mornings so wear your heavy knickers. Don't want to freeze your stones off before Rosita's got a chance to see em!" laughed the boy.

Martin rolled his eyes at the comment but smiled, knowing he was enjoying Billy's company.

"Hey, Teebsie?" asked Billy.

"Yeah?" came the cautious reply.

"I asked you if you was good with the iron. Was you telling me the truth?"

Martin thought carefully back over his firearm experience. In his entire life, he'd only pulled the trigger twice. The first time, with Mathews, it was one shot, one kill. The second time, with Farber, he had at least hit his target in the arm. He considered two-for-two a pretty good average. "Yes, I usually hit what I'm aiming for. Why do you ask?" inquired Martin.

Billy leaned in, looking serious. "There's gonna be blood. I can feel it. Them Dolan boys is just looking for a way to get rid of John and Alex. Might be tomorrow, might be a year from tomorrow, but it's gonna come down to who shoots first and who shoots best."

Martin stared at the boy's blue eyes and saw none of the good cheer that was there a minute ago. How he switched so rapidly from friend to fighter alarmed Martin. Knowing the history of what would happen, Martin could only nod his head in assent.

"So, if you're gonna ride with this outfit, you'd best be ready to shoot first. And Teebsie…don't miss," said the boy seriously.

Martin wondered what his immediate future would hold. Was he just here for a dinner with Rosita, or would he be taking a role in the bloody troubles to come? In his first trip back in time, it was March 31 of 1878, the day before Brady was murdered. There was almost four months of time between now and then, and in that time, John Tunstall would be brutally murdered. The thought of his new employer shot through the head gave Martin more of a chill than the late November air. He took a deep breath before answering, "I won't miss. You can count on it."

"That's my boy, Teebsie!" said Billy through a big grin. He slapped the big man on the shoulder and began to adjust his pants. "I gotta git. Help them boys load the wagon. See ya out there tomorrow," said Billy as he sauntered away. Just before he reached the wagon, he called back to his new friend, "Oh yeah, have a nice dinner. And keep them stones warm!"

Martin gave a rueful smile as he watched the Kid walk away.

25.

Just as the sun was peeking over the western rim of the Capitan mountains, Martin stood at the blue door of the house of Rosita Luna. He'd walked circles around Lincoln all day, taking mental pictures he hoped he'd remember when he inevitably went back to his own time. Constantly gazing at the sun, Martin almost willed it to go down as the temperature began to plummet. With his knuckles freezing, he gave the door three solid raps. He heard footsteps on the floorboards inside and the door latch being lifted.

"*Martin*," said Rosita warmly, "welcome to my home." Rosita swept Martin inside with a wave of her hand. He walked into the cozy house, warm from the cooking fire. While the home certainly wasn't luxurious, it was as neat as a pin and looked welcoming.

"Please, sit," she said, smiling all the time at her dinner guest, "and let me take your coat?"

Martin shrugged off his jacket, thankful for the gluten-induced weight loss he'd managed early in the year. Hanging the jacket on a nail near the door, Rosita sat at the table across from Martin.

"So you see my home?" she said with a wry smile. "Not many people have been invited here, Martin, so you are special, *si'*?"

Martin glanced around the room and answered, "I feel special, Rosita. This was a wonderful surprise to be invited here."

Rosita straightened up and said, "Of course I would invite you. You defended my honor. Most in Lincoln just look the other way."

The fact that Rosita was in distress and people looked the other way infuriated Martin. What happened to that old-fashioned chivalry that he saw in all of those old cowboy movies? Was it just the overactive imagination of screenwriters in the fifties? Did these men treat women as badly as some of the men Martin knew in his own time? He shook the thought from his mind and replied, "I think you were holding your own, but I was glad to step in just in case. I really figured I'd have to save those two from you!"

Rosita laughed at the joke and leaned in closer. "So, *Martin Teebs*, tell me of yourself. Where do you come from?" she asked.

Martin had already decided he was going to be honest in every way with Rosita...well, except for the whole time-travel thing. That might be a bit much to lay out there on a first date. He knew that they would be together in the future so nothing he said now would change that...or so he hoped.

"I'm originally from New Jersey. I've been out west for a couple of years now," said Martin, without a hint of regret.

"New Jersey!" exclaimed Rosita at the thought of a cross-country journey, "*Dios mio, Martin*. So much of the country you have seen."

Before Martin could stop himself, he blurted out, "None so beautiful as this." He looked directly into Rosita's dark eyes as he said it, so as to leave no doubt he wasn't talking about the mountains. Rosita actually blushed a bit as she tilted her head and gave Martin a big smile.

"And you had no *esposa*? No *ninos*?" she asked, almost afraid of the answer. Martin remembered the first time he screwed up and mentioned his wife, so the Spanish term for it was clear in his mind. Using deductive reasoning, he assumed that *ninos* meant kids. He was relieved that he could easily and honestly answer this question.

"No. No wife, no children," he said plainly, and then added, "At least not yet."

While she attempted to hide it, Rosita exhaled and her entire body seemed to relax. She had no intention of even having dinner with a married man. She understood this easterner didn't understand Mexican culture, so he might not know how big of a deal being invited to a single woman's home was.

"Well then, *Martin*," smiled Rosita, "let me serve dinner. I hope you are hungry?"

As Rosita served dinner, Martin continually rose to attempt to help her. Each time she playfully shooed him away from her kitchen, not knowing what the big stranger was trying to accomplish. Dinner went swimmingly, and Martin enjoyed her cooking even more the second time than the first. Rosita had made a small tray of *pastelitos*, based on how much Martin had liked them the first time, but this time he deferred after eating only two. Post dinner, Martin had to be shooed from the table yet again after trying to help Rosita clear the plates. Although she'd never been to New Jersey, she assumed it couldn't be that much different from New Mexico and men should wait to be served by their woman.

As she thought about Martin's home, she reflected on her own life. She'd been born in Lincoln. The farthest she'd ever gone was on a trip to Roswell, 70 miles to the east, with her father when she was much younger. She barely remembered going to a general store; and with two pennies her father had given her, she bought two chocolate hearts from a pale man whose name was Ash, if she remembered correctly. To travel all the way to New Jersey was as unfathomable as she could imagine. She'd seen pictures of New York City in the occasional newspaper that she read. The buildings looked like brick and metal mountains, and it appeared as if every person in the world was crowding the streets. She tried to imagine this gentle man in her home shoulder-to-shoulder on those streets, pushing people to and fro to get where he was going, and she simply couldn't resolve it. Although he seemed out of place in Lincoln, in her mind's eye, he seemed much more out of place anywhere else. As they sat looking into the fire, she spoke. "I'm glad you are here in Lincoln, *Martin*. This is a place for a man like you."

Martin had to restrain himself from reaching to grab her hand, not knowing what the proper courting etiquette was in 1877. He turned to her with a smile and replied, "I am too, Rosita. Honestly, there's no place I'd rather be right now."

If Martin was too shy to make a move, Rosita certainly was not. She had waited her entire life for the man that would treat her like the queen her father had always told her she was. Her blood was literally boiling with desire, and she quickly rose from her chair and stepped towards Martin. Facing him, she hiked up her skirt enough to straddle his legs and sat down heavily on them. Martin's heart began to beat more quickly and he breathed rapid, shallow breaths, trying to keep up with his oxygen needs but clearly losing. He didn't dare speak for fear of passing out, so he stared directly into Rosita's eyes.

"I've waited for you so long, *Martin Teebs*," she said in a breathy whisper, "and I don't want to wait anymore." She grabbed the hair on each side of his head and pulled him to her as her tongue parted her moist lips. Instantly they were locked in a deep, soulful kiss as her tongue probed his. Martin wrapped his hands behind her waist and pulled her closer to him, not knowing at what point he should stop. Rosita's body language gave him no inkling that he was approaching any point of no return. They kissed even more deeply, and Rosita twined her hands through his thick mane of hair. Martin's hunger for her knew no bounds. While he had no idea if they were going to make love, he was certain that if the possibility presented itself, he would not pass it up.

They kissed and groped for what seemed like hours before Rosita slowly pulled her head back and smoothed out his hair. She breathed in deeply and smiled as she exhaled. Continuing to arrange his hair, she looked at him with satisfaction. "*Martin*, my body wants to go further, but my mind says we have many days to get to know each other, *si'*?"

Nearly out of breath, he recovered enough to agree with her. "Yes, Rosita. I loved that…*really* loved that… but let's not rush things."

Grabbing his cheeks and pulling him in for a last hard kiss on the lips, she gently lifted herself off of the big man. Remembering Billy's last instructions, he took note that he'd have no problem at all keeping his "stones" warm on this cold evening. Martin rose from the chair and felt a bit woozy upon standing, needing to brace himself on the chair back to avoid a dive into the fire. Rosita stood admiring him the way someone might look at a beautiful landscape.

"*Martin*, I must get some sleep. I will work early tomorrow, you understand?"

Martin was amazed the night had gone so well. This was more, way more, than he imagined their first "date" would be like. He could see himself sitting in the Wortley, replaying the night over and over. Although tempted to ask Rosita for her phone number so he could text her, he didn't want to spoil the evening with a joke she couldn't possibly understand.

"I do, Rosita. Thank you for dinner and, well, everything," he finally answered. Rosita helped him slip his coat on, brushing off the shoulders and running her hands down his back. As he turned to say goodnight, she stretched to give him a quick peck on the cheek. Never the smoothest with words, Martin decided to throw caution to the wind. "I hope I can see you again, Rosita?"

Her smile positively beaming, she cocked her head and answered, "*Si, Martin*, of course. This is Lincoln. Such a small town. All you must do to see me is to open your eyes, and I will be there."

Martin gave her one last hug, trying to press himself into her so the feeling would last until tomorrow. They exchanged goodnights, and Martin stepped out of the front door. He heard the latch behind him and Rosita giggling giddily. Her words rang in his head…"just open your eyes, and I will be there."

Just then, a heavy fist crossed Martin's jaw as Billy Mathews, hiding in the shadows, paid him back in spades for the earlier embarrassment. Martin fell like a sack of heavy rocks. A time later when he came to, he did pry open his eyes, but all he saw was the dark streets of modern-day Lincoln and not even a remnant of where Rosita's house had been over 140 years ago.

26.

Martin rose wearily just as the sun was coming up. Having had only a few hours sleep after he arrived back in the present just down the road, he dreaded the rest of today. He had to quickly pack, drive to Albuquerque, and catch a plane to Newark, NJ. For a guy that just spent two days in the divine past of 1877 Lincoln, NM, all these modern plans were almost too much to bear.

With the taste of Rosita's lips still on one side of his mouth and the blow of Billy Matthews' fist on the other, Martin flicked on the coffee maker while he began to pack. He really hoped to avoid Darlene this morning as he was in a hurry and wasn't in the mood to listen to her tales of woe. He had planned to go straight to the car and perhaps wave at her, if necessary, as he jumped in and drove out of town.

He grabbed his last clean outfit from his suitcase and began jamming clothes, old and new, in their place. The coffee maker chirped that it was finished, and he poured a long, hot cup to steel him for the day ahead. Through the pain in his jaw, Martin could only remember his last moments with Rosita. She wanted him. She really wanted him and that fact amazed him. That a woman as impeccable as Rosita Luna could see something in Martin Teebs that made her lusty was almost unfathomable to Martin. He walked over to the mirror so perhaps he could see in him what she did, but all he saw was an ugly red welt where he'd taken a sucker punch. For the first time, Martin began to feel ok about his upcoming killing of Mathews. Once again he'd be hiding in the shadows behind a wall, but this time, it would be Martin Teebs who'd deliver the knockout blow…permanently.

Slugging down the coffee, he showered and dressed as his departure time drew near. Martin made the final once around he always did when leaving a hotel. It only took leaving his phone charger behind in LA eight times for him to adopt his new modus operandi. He switched off the coffee pot and headed for the door. At the last moment, he swept the room with his eyes one more time. From the corner of his eye, he spotted *Lincoln County Days*, the tiny book that Darlene had left for him. He figured maybe it would be something he could try to decipher on the plane flight to NJ, so he picked it up and dropped it into a pocket on his luggage.

He quickly rumbled down the walkway past the main house and popped the trunk on the car. Just as he was about to get away cleanly, Darlene came calling from the porch.

"Martin! Hey, you leaving now?"

Sighing that he didn't make a clean getaway, he walked slowly towards the house. Darlene looked unkempt, like either she hadn't slept or she had slept restlessly in the clothes she was wearing. Her usually smoothly braided hair was frizzy and sticking up in every direction of the compass. She looked a bit sad that her guest was about to leave.

"Time to go, huh?" she asked in an innocent tone.

"Yeah, my flight's at noon so I need to get on the road," replied Martin. "Hey, are you ok, Darlene?"

With a look that usually preceded tears, Darlene pursed her lips and nodded her head, but in an unconvincing fashion. "It'll be alright, Martin. Just something with Dallas. I'll figure it out…don't worry," she said, her bloodshot eyes looking to Martin for a ray of hope.

"I'm sure it will. Listen, give me a call if you need anything, ok? Really," said Martin sincerely. "I'm here to help. I need to go now."

Darlene looked up at him with such hope and gratitude that Martin was almost embarrassed. He imagined if he asked Darlene to head to the bedroom with him at this moment, she'd about do anything he wanted. She was frail and on the razor's edge, and he didn't like being in the position of power with her or any woman. His life was lived on equal footing with either gender or any sexual orientations. More often than not, he was the one in the subservient position, and it suited him. He had never wanted to be a hero, and he had never really wanted anyone counting on him that much. That revelation as they stood in the morning chill did nothing to cut the insidious breeze that was making him shake. Seeing his discomfort, Darlene finally released him, "Go, Martin. Have a great trip and let me know when you're coming back. I'm always open for you."

The phrasing of Darlene's last line caught him off guard, but he gave her a quick hug and a smile and trotted down the stairs to his waiting rental car. Firing up the tiny four-cylinder engine, he eased the car onto Lincoln's only street and drove to the west. As he spotted building after historical building, he realized he was driving through 145 years worth of history that he himself had lived in only the past two days. Passing the Tunstall store, Martin's guilt got the better of him. In 1877, he was supposed to be riding to Tunstall's ranch this morning to begin his work as a ranch hand. He owed the Englishman a solid ten dollars, and he could only wonder what Tunstall and the boys thought of him for running out. Martin made a mental note to find some way to acquire the appropriate funds to pay Tunstall, if he even made it back to Lincoln before the young man's soon-to-be demise.

Martin cleared the courthouse and pressed firmly on the gas pedal. His feelings ranged from sad to be leaving Rosita and Billy, to happy to be leaving the modern version of Lincoln, which only seemed to contain despair to him. Where he once thought living in the historically preserved town would be a dream come true, he now viewed it as a place of sadness and loss. It wasn't the bustling vibrant town he knew in the past. It was a ghost, a still standing martyr of what was, and what never would be again.

Martin saw the last vestiges of Lincoln fade in his rearview mirror, and for once he was happy to be heading to New Jersey.

27.

As Martin's car faded out of sight, Darlene walked to the mailbox. It had been at least three days before she thought to collect whatever had been jettisoned there. Crunching along the gravel drive, she heard the inescapable sounds of silence that permeated Lincoln in winter. She had no upcoming guests and wasn't at all sure how she'd afford to make it financially through the season. She had come here with Dallas, full of love and hope, and now she was stuck here, hopeless and full of hate.

After retrieving a stack of envelopes, she carefully shut the mailbox door and retreated to the main house. Mail, she thought, who sends mail anymore? There was essentially zero need to be sending paper from one human to another with the wonders of the internet available to everyone. Bills, ads, money…all could be transmitted digitally online and save the need for killing yet more trees that the forests didn't have.

She entered the house, shutting the door solidly behind her. Dropping the letters on the coffee table, she went to pour herself a steaming mug of coffee and then settled on the couch.

"Ok," she said to the stack of envelopes, "let's see what's so important you had to travel all the way to my mailbox to get here." Filtering a few obvious "you need this credit card!" mailers, Darlene grabbed a thick envelope addressed to her name. She cautiously observed it was from the law firm of Chacon, McLaughlin & Chacon. Darlene steeled herself for whatever sure-to-be-bad news was coming next as she tore open the letter. She grabbed a deep sip of coffee before she unfolded the contents. About ten seconds in, her coffee cup crashed to the floor, spewing its red-hot contents over the couch and sofa. The letter, and its suddenness in arriving, felt like a hard, cold slap in the face on this cold and lonely morning.

Darlene seemed not to register that her leg was burning from the hot liquid and simply stared at the letter for what seemed like hours.

28.

With the coronavirus pandemic raging again, Martin was relegated to his home office for the rest of the winter. While he didn't really mind working alone, he did miss the occasional interaction with his office mates, especially Colin. A year ago, Colin had proposed to, and almost walked down the aisle with, Desiree. His stripper-turned-girlfriend thought that maybe marriage was just what she needed as she approached thirty years old, but after having sex with four male strippers (and a female one) at her bachelorette party, both she and Colin thought the better of it.

Winter had arrived in northern New Jersey, and the gray gloom associated with it staked its claim on this day. Martin pecked through a few emails and answered a call or two before the midmorning slump arrived. Because his clients were on the west coast, there was usually some business that would come in after hours. Martin would spend the first couple hours of the next morning wading through the backed up correspondence, and then...usually by midmorning...the deafening silence of nothing to do would set in.

As Martin waited for the west coast to wake up and get down to business, he drifted to his bedroom and eyed his overstuffed suitcase. He'd gotten in later than he expected due to the ever present traffic on the New Jersey Turnpike and had left the bag to be unpacked another time. He grabbed an empty laundry basket from his closet, tossed the bag on the bed, and unzipped it. He quickly filled the basket with an assortment of dirty-from-the-trip clothes and only slowed when he arrived at his kit that he still owed Tunstall for. He lifted the kit's shirt to his nose and deeply inhaled, hoping to catch the scent of Rosita between the smell of stale airplane air and the miasma of a week's worth of dirty clothes. He was delighted that the shirt seemed to have the tiniest of his woman's aroma on it, and he was instantly transformed to her sitting on his lap in front of the fire. Rosita's hunger for him seemed to know no bounds that night, and only her (and Martin's) common sense prevented them from full consummation of their new relationship.

Having just returned from New Mexico, Martin wasn't in the headspace to plan any returns just yet. If time-travel experiences had taught him anything, it was that that past was written (or rewritten by a large middle-class schlub from New Jersey), and it would take place for him whenever he got there.

For a brief instant, a thought flashed across his brain. What if his untimely exit at the fist of Billy Mathews was the last time Martin was in Lincoln until his arrival on the eve of Brady's death? He sat and thought seriously through the timeline from his first trip to Lincoln with Lilly over two years ago. He remembered arriving in old Lincoln that first time and wandering up to the Tunstall store. The boys, including Doc and Chavez, had seemed way too friendly to him for never having spent any real time with him. Billy had been delighted to see him, but that could definitely have been on the heels of their last interactions. But Rosita?

Rosita came around the corner on that day like a heat-seeking missile, launching herself into his arms. Could she be that in love with him after only one evening together? It didn't seem logical that she or the boys could be that familiar with him after his last trip to Lincoln. He reasoned that he must have had some additional history before the Lincoln County War turned deadly and he'd carelessly thrown Bachaca's book away, thereby changing history. Martin decided that, yes, he must have at least one more trip to old(er) Lincoln to deepen his relationships before his ill-fated visit in March 1878 would happen.

Dumping the remainder of his dirty laundry into the basket, Martin zipped up the suitcase and carried it to the closet. As he stretched to put it on the high shelf it would reside on until his next trip, he remembered the little book Darlene had given him. Bringing the case back down, he unzipped the small top pocket and retrieved the worn little treasure. In all of his time studying Billy the Kid, Martin had never heard of this book. Surely his endless searches on Ebay or Amazon would have come up with a rare copy of something so important to his fellow historians and fellow Billy worshippers? The book looked more like a journal, but the cover had certainly been printed on an ancient printing press. Small tatters of the cover and pages hung off the book, and as Martin inspected it further, he realized that the binding was torn. It was as if half of the book had been cleaved from the spine. Whatever Martin now held in his hand was most definitely incomplete.

The author escaped Martin's knowledge of history. Juan Panchito Baca didn't seem to exist in any history book Martin had ever read about the War. Sure there were plenty of Bacas in New Mexico, but this particular name seemed to elude Martin's research. In his experience, books like this were often poorly written but contained some first-hand recollection (usually many years later) of some ridiculously brief encounter with the Kid. Martin had seen 87-page books that tortuously described a three-minute meeting with Billy on some remote plain that could never be verified anyway. While the books were most often historically worthless, they often fetched high prices on auction sites due to their rarity. He wondered if he had such a book in his hand.

Martin walked the book into his office to fetch his reading glasses. Based upon what he'd seen, the book was handwritten in English but seemed to be mostly illegible. He didn't figure to learn anything new about the Kid. Certainly he couldn't learn more than the rich history he was cultivating personally with Billy and the rest of Lincoln County's finest. Martin plopped heavily down onto his expensive office chair and looked up at his bookshelf. Row after row of Billy the Kid books adorned the shelves. At one point after he and Lilly had split up, he had boxed them all and threatened to donate them to anywhere that would have them. The boxes sat in the hallway for months before Martin's stance on anything to do with the past softened and he allowed them to inhabit the shelves once again.

As he scanned the titles, he found himself thinking through all of the days and nights he had obsessed over silly, arcane facts of Billy and the Regulators. What kind of gun they had in a particular circumstance, whether Billy wore that silly crushed cap from his famous photo while riding on the plains, and how many rounds Colonel Dudley brought for his Gatling gun during the five-day Battle of Lincoln?

What of that really mattered to the story? he wondered. Had the Regulators time traveled to 2021, what would they think of the obsession with minutiae over every aspect of their lives? These were real men, fighting and dying for a cause they believed in (or were paid to believe in), and they most likely couldn't have cared less what kind of gun fired the bullet that ended their lives. They rode every single day of their mostly short lives knowing someone could be drawing a bead on them, yet they persevered to create the history that so many followed today like a religion. Martin decided that none of the men he met would give a damn about these books. They would probably laugh at the losers who spent so much time studying the Regulators' lives that they failed to live their own. The thought pinched Martin as he realized that he too was among those "losers."

Book after book, row after row, dollar after dollar, Martin added it all up in his mind.

He'd spent a lot more money on these books than he cared to admit. He had pored over them time and again, hoping somehow to know more, feel more about the men and women they were written about. As he thought about it, he realized that no matter how many books he read or how many lectures he attended, he never really "knew" Billy or the Regulators. He was still an outsider to them. Had these books been his only exposure to the past, he would only have been a wealth of knowledge on a subject that would bore most people at parties to tears. No, only through his fortuitous travels back in time did he really get to know those who would fight, kill, and die in Lincoln County. The books meant nothing and his experiences meant everything. Martin's experiences (and blunders) had reshaped at least part of history. While he couldn't be sure, Billy's deathbed confession told Martin that the only thing the young outlaw used Bachaca's book for was to save himself. Was that true? Martin couldn't tell anymore. After all, not one of the many books that lined his shelves had changed to reflect the "new" version of history that Martin had helped create. Billy might have changed a lot more and in his final moments decided not to cop to it. The thought of it strained Martin's ability to reason, and so he left that riddle for another day.

Picking up the ancient book, Martin pried open the cover. Just inside was a handwritten cover page with the title, author, and a date he assumed to be the publication date:

July 15, 1881

That's weird, thought Martin. Was it just coincidence that this book was published the day after history tells that Sheriff Pat Garrett had shot and killed Billy in Fort Sumner? Was the author in Fort Sumner that day and helped put Billy (or whatever was in the coffin) in the ground? Perhaps the author was a friend of the Kid and had stopped writing once Billy was gone? Martin assumed that any answers to his mounting questions must lie within, so he turned the cover page and began the arduous task of trying to read the almost illegible cursive. As he decoded the first two lines of the tiny book, his blood froze in his veins and his heart stopped:

In the year of our Lord 1877, a stranger from a strange land arrived in Lincoln and would change the course of many lives. Liked by some, hated by others, Martin Teebs blew into town like the distant winds from the four corners of the Earth.

29.

Martin Teebs…

Seeing his own name in print in anything other than an email shocked Martin, especially in this ancient book that he would have otherwise ignored. While this obviously was no mass-printed historical tome, it was a first-person account of the Lincoln County War, and Martin Teebs was in it! It had nagged at Martin over the past two years why there was no record of him anywhere in Lincoln during those times. It wasn't like he wanted to be known for his indiscretions, but it amazed him that somehow he wasn't. Surely Doc or Chavez would have mentioned his name. Charlie, French, some of Dolan's boys?

Immediately Martin wondered who else might have seen this book? It identified him in the first two lines, so Martin assumed that wouldn't be the end of his appearance in it. A million times (or so it seemed), Martin had Googled his own name in conjunction with Billy the Kid and had always come up empty. Usually he did it as a precautionary measure to make sure some time cops weren't chasing him through the centuries, ready to hand out his punishment for killing Mathews. Not once was there an inkling of any book written about his time in the late 1800s in New Mexico.

But now there was.

As difficult as it was to decipher what was written, Martin wanted to know more. He struggled with the rest of the first page, which made some allusions to Tunstall and McSween. Suddenly curious about how far the book went, he turned to the final page. From the little bit he could make out, it talked about Billy's escape and murder of Olinger. A few lines later, he saw his name again and was doubly shocked to see the name Carl Farber. While he couldn't make out the passage, he assumed it was the report of their final showdown in Lincoln. The last couple of lines talked about a bucket and dust in the wind…and ended up with the name Rosita Luna. It mentioned *llorando* which Martin had to look up to understand it meant "crying." This book, or at least the part that Martin held in his hand, ended at the very time his last visit to Lincoln ended. He assumed if he were able to pick through the pages, he'd find many of his other escapades as well.

Who was this Juan Panchito Baca anyway, and why the hell was he so interested in Martin Teebs? If he had indeed taken the time to document that a Martin Teebs and a Carl Farber had existed in Lincoln in 1878, then why didn't that news make it into the local newspapers, oral history, or books about the Kid? This made so little sense to Martin that he suspected maybe someone was putting him on...but who? The only person that knew everything that Martin was guilty of was Farber. Was Juan Panchito Baca really Carl Farber? Did Farber write a running history of his rival while they were backwards in time, and then leave it to be found by someone 140 years later? As Martin examined the torn spine of the book, he could clearly see that the author, whoever he was, had more to say. It was hard to tell, but it looked like an appreciable chunk of pages was missing. Martin's finger drifted along the spine. What story did those pages hold? Was it more of Martin's future-in-the-past or something else? Did they even exist anymore? If so, where were they and who tore them out? It all seemed just a bit too convenient to Martin that the pages were torn out at exactly his last moment in Lincoln.

His eyes hurt from trying to read the book and his mind hurt from trying to understand it. He silently realized that this portion of the book ended before that scumbag Farber had raped his beautiful Rosita. Just the thought of it made Martin gag. He only wished for the ability to insert himself at just the right time to ward off that monster...and maybe kill him. Martin understood that if he were ever to find the missing pages, he'd likely have to read through that painful chapter. The very thought of it made him start to tear up. Here, only two days ago he had the love of his life sitting on his lap, kissing him as if she could never let him go, and now his mind went to the unthinkable horror that Farber had perpetrated on her. Before he went too far down that rabbit hole, Martin laid the book on his desk and dusted his hands off. He wiped a tear from the corner of his eye as the silence of his home permeated his being. He couldn't remember a time in his life when he'd felt as alone and helpless as he did in this moment. While Lincoln was 2000 miles away, Martin felt like his life in Lincoln was in another galaxy. He wished he could open his front door and walk out onto the main street. He'd tip his hat to a few ladies, laugh at one of Billy's jokes, and walk to Rosita's house to sweep her off of her feet. Of course, Martin's front door only led to his once green front yard and not to Lincoln.

He looked sadly out of his office window and noticed a few snow flurries swirling in the easy breeze. He thought that maybe one of those flurries had once been a drop of water in the Bonito Creek running near Rosita's home. Maybe she had even tasted its sweetness as she pumped water for her household. It might have even been the bucketful that Martin was carrying just before his last showdown with Farber. He remembered that matter cannot be created nor destroyed and water is eternal...or at least Martin hoped it was. Grasping for any connection to the past, he lost himself in the circular logic and was only shocked back to reality when his phone rang. Picking it up, he was greeted by a very hysterical Darlene Jones.

30.

Try as he might, Martin could not make a good case to his boss for traveling cross country in December. Business was always slow at this time of year, and Mr. Talbot was on guard for anyone intentionally looking to escape a cold northeast winter on the company's dime. While he knew that there must be another trip to old Lincoln in his future, he had no choice but to wait it out.

Over the past few weeks, Martin had struggled to read the tiny book by Juan Baca and had managed to roughly follow the events he had already taken part in. There was some dire warning about Tunstall's death, which Martin already knew would happen, but he hadn't been able to decipher anything else of value from the book thus far. He had scoured every single book on his shelves for mention of Juan Baca but had come up empty. Endless internet searches yielded the same result.

As the year closed out and faded into January, Martin, along with just about everyone else on the planet, hoped for a true renewal. The world had been living with this COVID pandemic for almost two years now. Every time he had to go out, he got halfway from the car to his destination before cursing himself for leaving his mask in the car yet again. He'd been out to have a beer with Colin exactly two times in the past two years, both at intervals when there had been a temporary lift of lockdown restrictions by the Governor. While never a social butterfly, Martin still struggled with the isolation of quarantine. Just the freedom that he could go somewhere if he chose to was enough for him, but winter was the worst season for a pandemic, so locked away in his house he stayed.

Lilly had sent him a Christmas card, which remained unopened until he finally threw it away, and she'd texted him on two occasions, asking how he was. Both messages went unanswered. In his imagination, Lilly had just finished shagging Dallas; and as her beau went to do one thousand or so sit ups, she laid there in bed, still reeking of sex, and wondered, "How is that guy I used to be married to?"

Martin wanted no part of a dialogue with her, Dallas, or Darlene. He longed for his life in old Lincoln. Back when he and Rosita first made love, she'd asked him if he would stay with her forever. While he had said yes, he knew that it was most likely a lie. He was still (at the time) mostly happily married to Lilly. He had a life, a wife, a mortgage, and more. To simply disappear into time sounded like the ultimate escape but wasn't really practical. Now things were different. If asked to stay in old Lincoln (and if he had any idea how to accomplish it), he could vanish and few people would miss him. Martin could live out the rest of his natural life in the past, and no one would be the wiser.

The problem with all of this was that he still had no real control over his travels. Something as simple yet painful as a Billy Mathews punch could knock Martin out of time. It was maddening to him that he couldn't stick in one time for more than a few days. He wondered if he would improve his travels with more experience? Was it like playing the piano? Would more practice yield better results? Martin hoped so. He hadn't as much as cast an eye at a modern-day woman in over a year. Rosita Luna occupied his waking (and often his sleeping) thoughts and desires. Sometimes he could almost see her sitting there with him in his living room.

Martin once entertained the thought of trying to bring Rosita to his own time. He imagined the idyllic life they'd live, with Rosita discovering the modern conveniences of a microwave oven and the internet, while he got to know and raise Martin Jr. and live happily ever after with his dream girl. When he got too far down that line of thinking, Martin castigated himself for his silliness. How could he possibly bring Rosita forward in time? What would be the vehicle? Sure, Billy had briefly visited Martin in modern day, but look at how that had ended! Even if he could bring Rosita forward, would he want to? While 1877 wasn't an easy time to live in, it had a simplicity that allowed people to focus on each other. Martin furrowed his brow at the vision of Rosita updating her Facebook profile on her iPhone, watching the latest installment of The Bachelorette, and distractedly trying to listen to him tell her about the road construction on the Garden State Parkway.

No, he vowed. He'd have Rosita in the past. This future he lived in contaminated people. It spoiled them. Just look at Colin's fiancée. Just look at Lilly and Dallas. This future had too many options and too many trap doors that you could fall from grace through. He would somehow, some way establish himself in the past, and he would right the wrongs of his life. He'd be a better husband. He'd be a good father. He would become a provider for his family no matter how hard he had to work. Martin Teebs would live and die in the past he had created for himself (along with his friends and enemies), and he'd never look back.

Late in January, Martin got word that the very large client he'd been pursuing in Las Vegas was ready to sign on. When the email arrived, it made his head swoon. The commission on this sale would provide him with the type of disposable income he hadn't had since Lilly cleaved their net worth in half and moved to New Mexico. He had money. He had options.

That day Martin sat down to book himself a weeklong trip to New Mexico that wouldn't be shortened by work or family obligations. He was prepared to stay as long as it took to connect with Rosita and pay his debt back to Tunstall. If he found a way to close the door to the future behind him, he didn't plan to shed a tear. Martin was going to New Mexico on the next available flight. He was going to Lincoln. Martin was going home.

31.

Dallas held the phone far from his ear. Due to the volume that Darlene was screaming at, there was little need for him to get close. Almost everyone in the neighborhood could probably hear her. He hadn't expected her to receive the news well, but this was beyond the pale. After all, the B&B belonged to both of them. Darlene could not have expected that he would simply walk away from his investment forever. When he moved to Albuquerque with Lilly and little Austin, he simply left Darlene in charge, knowing she'd run a tight ship and have the chance to make a little money. Never did he have an inkling that she would get the entirety of the Jones estate.

"You did this! And now I have to suffer, you jerk!" screamed Darlene into the phone. Dallas winced at the name calling. The one major blind spot in his life had always been the lack of awareness of other people's feelings. Somehow, whatever he did seemed to have an impact on others, yet he always seemed surprised when they didn't agree with him. He simply assumed that everyone agreed with him since he had a great smile and such winning ways. The irate voice on the other end of his phone told him that once again he had missed the mark.

"Listen. Listen, Darlene!" he said, trying to get her attention. "This is good for you too. We'll sell the place, split the money, and then you can go live anywhere you want to. I don't see what you're so upset about?"

Dallas' plan was to put the B&B up for sale. He and Darlene would split whatever profit they made, and it would be a clean break. Buying property in Lincoln wasn't an inexpensive affair, and he was sure that they would have a handsome sum left over after paying off the mortgage. With half of whatever they made, he was certain that Darlene could establish herself somewhere. She'd buy a little house, meet some nice guy, and settle down. Darlene was hot, thought Dallas. There's no way she wouldn't score some rich dude who'd give her the life he was sure she deserved.

Hot. The word settled in his mind. Hot. Would he like to have sex with Darlene again? Sure he would. It was never a question of Lilly being better looking or even better in bed. Somehow Dallas liked the fact that Lilly seemed to look down on him. He'd always been idolized for his smile, his abs, and his chiseled features. Most women dropped their underwear before he could undo his belt. He'd been fed a diet of willing partners since he was 14 years old, and there was no one woman who could satisfy all of his needs. That's why his and Darlene's relationship had worked so well.

Darlene was no slouch herself in the looks department or in bed. She and Dallas had had an agreement that playing around with others (even if the others were their guests) was fine as long as they were safe. They began to look at it as a challenge each time a new couple checked into their B&B. It was all working fine until the Teebs wound up at their front door some two years ago. While Martin wasn't much to look at, he was a nice man with a solid head of hair. Darlene figured at least he'd be fun with the lights out. Rarely had either of them been refused by a guest. Dallas took an immediate shine to Lilly and knew that before their trip was over, he would be getting to know her in the biblical sense. When Martin showed no interest in Darlene after that first day (and not much more in his wife either), it seemed like the game was off, but Dallas didn't see it that way. He and Lilly had a tryst or two while Darlene put buns in the oven. At some point, Dallas wound up putting a bun in Lilly's oven, and the game was changed forever.

With Darlene screaming in his ear, he looked around the cramped house he and Lilly lived in. It was the best they could afford under the circumstances, but Dallas had big plans. Once the B&B was sold, he'd take his half of the cash and move his little family to Los Angeles. He'd played around being an actor long enough, and the bit parts he was being offered in New Mexico had bit paychecks to match. Finally, he figured, he'd be seen for what he was worth if he just got a fancy LA agent and manager. He envisioned movie premieres, red carpets, and Hollywood parties that he and Lilly would attend. Of course, his plan was to make a similar deal with Lilly once they were settled: play with whomever you want, just keep it clean and safe. This time, he promised, he'd actually live up to his end of the bargain.

The giant blind spot that he was born with, and that followed Dallas around, never allowed him to see that perhaps Lilly wasn't interested in an open relationship. She might just want to be a wife and mother and live some normal, peaceful life. She'd made her mistakes in her marriage to Martin and had learned that sometimes the grass is not only not greener, but sometimes it's actually dead on the other side of the fence. Dallas saw her eye rolling and condescending looks at him, however, and figured that she'd eventually be looking for some escape.

"And don't bother showing up here ever again with your whore!" Darlene continued. "I'll take care of selling this myself. The less you're around, the better the price I'll get. Asshole!" And with that, Darlene hung up, leaving Dallas to wonder just what he'd done that was so wrong that she'd resort to name calling?

Placing the phone on the table, he walked towards Lilly's studio and called out before he got there, "Hey, Lil, have you ever been to LA?"

32.

Usually in a hurry on these trips, Martin took his time driving down I-25 south on this sunny Thursday afternoon. While the sun warmed the interior of the car, the temperature outside stood at 39 degrees. New Mexico was a high desert climate; while it avoided the cascading snows of Colorado, it could still deliver up the cold weather when it wanted to. Martin eased off the interstate at San Antonio and stopped for a burger (minus the bun) before continuing on. At this pace, he would arrive in Lincoln well after dark, but he was familiar enough with the route that he didn't mind driving after sunset.

Martin created a mental checklist of what he wanted to accomplish on his trip. First and foremost, he must find Rosita. It had been two months since he'd seen her. There would be a lot of explaining to do, but he had cooked up a story about his mother dying in New Jersey and he had had to take the first train out of Santa Fe to attend her funeral. He had rehearsed it a number of times, and while he wasn't an actor like Dallas, he was impressed enough with his performance to rate it award worthy.

His second task was to connect with Billy, the boys, and Tunstall. It bothered him that he bailed out on them when they needed him. The fact that he still owed Tunstall money also gnawed at Martin. If only he could bring some of his commission from the Las Vegas deal, he could almost buy the entire town, or so he convinced himself. He was intent on getting to work and paying the debt while getting to know Billy better. When they had last talked, the Kid had seemed somewhat fragile, which surprised Teebs. He knew the boy had had a tough life and had been abandoned by his stepfather, but he assumed it had calloused the young man to be immune from vulnerability. The Billy he met was at times unsure of himself. He vacillated from cocky to frail and happy to morose, sometimes at the drop of a hat. The history books had missed a major portion of what made him Billy the Kid. Martin had had aspirations of writing the seminal Billy the Kid book and correcting that impression, but he figured he'd changed enough history for one lifetime.

Third and finally, Martin was on the hunt for the last handful of pages from Juan Baca's book. He thought they might still be at the B&B. Perhaps if Dallas had somehow dropped the book while taking the other items to his car, the missing pages could be in the Jones/Teebs household in Albuquerque? If so, Martin would count them as lost forever as he couldn't fathom talking to either Dallas or Lilly to ask them to locate a few ancient pages of a book. Whatever was in those final pages spelled out what happened to Rosita, and if Martin had a future in the past. Just the thought of having "a future in the past" made Martin's head spin. There were times when all of this made him feel as if he were insane. He was edging dangerously close to that right now, so he forced his thoughts aside to focus on the last bit of his drive.

Arriving in Capitan, he gassed up his rental rig and entered the convenience store to score some bottled water and beef jerky. Standing patiently at the counter, he sensed an imposing presence over his shoulder. The giant shadow cast by the harsh fluorescent lights helped amplify the feeling. As he reached for his debit card to pay, he felt a strong hand on his shoulder.

"Hey, Martin. Good to see ya around here again," boomed the voice of Steve. "How ya been, cowboy?"

Martin had managed to forget about his weird interactions with this man, and it annoyed him that he couldn't simply buy a bag of jerky and a tankful of gas without Steve somehow finding out about it. Martin looked over his shoulder dismissively and replied, "Hey. I'm good, thanks." Steve kept his hand firmly on Martin's shoulder and let out a big smile.

"Good to hear, Martin. You headed back to Lincoln, huh?" the big man asked.

Martin slipped his shoulder from Steve's massive grip and made his way to the door. Realizing he was being followed, he spun around quickly. "Hey, what do you want with me? How did you know I'd be here? In fact, how do you even know my name? I never gave it to you?" demanded Martin.

"Martin Teebs," replied Steve, "people talk. You're in small-town America, son. This ain't no big city living out here."

"Steve, no offense, but I'm not looking for any new friends. Ok?" said Martin with surprising courage. "I'm just going to get on my way if you don't mind?"

Steve smiled an easy smile again as he adjusted his cowboy hat. "Sure, sure, Martin.

No problem, *amigo*."

Satisfied, Martin slipped into his rental car and fired up the engine. He turned the heat up to deal with the sudden chill he felt as Steve about-faced to walk back into the store. After a few giant steps, however, he turned around and waved a hand in Martin's direction, prompting him to roll down the window.

"Yes?" asked Martin, clearly wanting to get out of the parking lot.

"Martin, I was just wondering," said Steve as his lips turned into a knowing smirk, "have you read any good history books lately?"

The blood drained from Martin's face faster than a chipmunk runs through a cheese factory. He knew! Steve knew about the book! "People talk," my ass, thought Martin. Steve knew his name because Steve knew about *Lincoln County Days*. That damn book that he could barely decipher had ratted him out. Although Martin wondered if Steve had a complete copy of the book, including the pages that would describe Martin's future in Lincoln, he dared not ask. He now knew that Steve wasn't some friendly ex-mayor and cowboy. He was on the inside. Inside of what, Martin had no idea, but this man knew things that no one in modern times should know. Martin was so stunned in the moment, he couldn't respond.

"Cat got your tongue, huh, Martin?" came the friendly voice. "No problem. If you ever want to talk about it, I'll be here."

Martin stared at the man while he backed the car up. He was so flummoxed that he forgot to roll the window up. As he drove away, he clearly heard Steve offer a parting shot: "Watch yourself out on that road, Martin. If you get sideways, you never know where you'll wind up!"

33.

Martin walked up the driveway towards the main house. Even if he wanted to avoid a long, drawn out conversation with Darlene, he had to check in so there was no way out. The last time he had talked to her, she was hysterical after receiving a demand letter from Dallas' attorneys. In it they asked for half of the equity in the B&B, as well as the value of half of the remaining possessions. Darlene protested that, aside from the house, she owned only some ordinary things that wouldn't be worth much. Still, the dollar figure loomed on the letter from Dallas' lawyers, and she certainly didn't have that kind of cash lying around. Darlene knew the only way she would was to sell the business. Martin was still unsure of why she had called him with the news. Perhaps as her most regular guest, she thought he might have some wisdom, but all Martin did on the phone call was continually tell her how sorry he was.

He reached the front door and gave a steady knock. Seeing a figure approaching, he stepped back into the porchlight.

"Martin! You're back. So good to see you," she said, pulling him again into her ample breasts. If Martin feared a dramatic replay of the phone call, it appeared that none was coming.

"Hey, Darlene, thanks for keeping the lights on for me. It's good to be back," he said with a warm smile. As he looked around the living room, it appeared as if Darlene had packed away a number of items. It wasn't vacant, but it definitely felt less homey than he was used to.

She noticed his gaze and cut in, "I've been downsizing. Getting rid of lots of stuff. I don't really have a choice but to sell the place, Martin. In fact, the real estate agent will be here tomorrow to get the listing started." Darlene seemed a little quiet, a little sad, but not out of her mind like the last time they had spoken.

"I'm sorry, Darlene," said Martin sincerely. "Who do you think will buy it?"

"Don't know. Hopefully someone that'll love it like we did. As much as you come here, you should buy it, Martin!" she said, with her spirits brightening a bit.

That thought had definitely *never* crossed Martin's mind. While he did love Lincoln and hoped to find a way to stay (at least in the 1877 version), he didn't relish the idea of a bunch of Billy the Kid afficionados coming through his house everyday, spilling mistruths and repeating tales that had been proven untrue 50 years ago. He imagined himself forever explaining that Billy was actually not left handed and getting into the intricacies of tintype photography.

"Oh, Darlene," Martin apologized, "I'm not cut out for being a host. You and…well you have that rare gift of making people feel like they've known you forever the first time they meet you. That's why you're so great at this. That's just not me."

Darlene smiled at him as her eyes began to well up. The raw emotion of her divorce, Lilly's baby, and now selling the place she'd called home for a decade was almost too much for even her to bear.

"Where are you going to go after you sell it?" Martin asked. He was curious about the next steps after divorce as he too had contemplated his future if he didn't wind up living in the 19th century.

"I'm not sure. We came from LA, but I don't think I want to go back there. Maybe Colorado, maybe Oregon? Someplace clean and fresh where I can start over again. Someplace I won't make the same mistakes I made here," said Darlene.

Martin saw the slightest suggestion of strength in her answer. It wasn't much, but it was enough that he surmised the woman would be ok. She'd taken some bruises, but she was a fighter and would go on to live a good, happy life. At least that's what he was hoping for.

"I hear you. I know exactly what you mean, Darlene," said Martin. "Hey, I think I'm going to get some sleep. It's been a pretty long day."

Darlene smiled and handed him the familiar key to the casita. "Sleep tight, Martin," she said, "and, hey, one of these days, would you take me on a proper tour of Lincoln? Believe it or not, I don't know all that much about this Billy the Kid stuff. You seem to know everything. If I'm not going to be here much longer, I'd like to see it all before I go."

Martin was surprised. Not so much that she'd asked him to lead the tour, but that she cared at all about the history of Lincoln. Lilly couldn't seem to wait to roll her eyes every time Martin mentioned the Kid. This was nice. This was refreshing. Martin assumed he wouldn't be spending the entire week back in time (if he could get back there at all), so he happily agreed. "Sure! That'd be fun. Count me in."

Darlene gave him a slight wave as he made his way across the darkened yard to the casita where the blankets would be warm and, in the morning, the coffee would be piping hot.

34.

Wandering down Lincoln's main street the next morning, Martin began to question the logic in coming here in January. It was bitter cold and a hard easterly wind pushed through the canyon, creating a venturi effect that chilled him to the bone. If he had wanted to be alone in Lincoln, past or present, there was no better time to do it than today. The vacant road was only upset by the occasional gust of leaves blowing to and fro.

It occurred to him that there wasn't much left for him to see in modern-day Lincoln. He'd been through the town so many times that he'd worn out any newness that remained. Martin felt like he'd inspected every inch of the place. There simply wasn't the draw for him like the past contained. In present day, he was a divorcee with his only friend being the woman whose husband impregnated Martin's wife. Even she would be gone soon, once the B&B was sold. Teebs wondered what it would be like coming to Lincoln when the only person he knew was the one staring back at him in the mirror. It might be freeing, he thought. Not having to befriend anyone could allow him to easily punch out of the present and into the past more quickly. Maybe, he thought, without any draw to bring him back to present day, he could simply live out the rest of his natural life in the late 1800s? Maybe it was the Darlenes, Dallases, and Lillys of the world that kept pulling him back to a time he no longer wanted to exist in?

With that thought in mind, Martin briskly walked across town towards the House. His last venture back in time started with Tunstall inviting him to shop at his store versus the monopoly of Murphy's place. He thought his best chance to skip backwards in time was to begin at the same place. Pacing back and forth on the portal didn't produce the desired result, so Martin walked around the corner to the death marker for Bob Olinger. He stood next to the white stone and looked up towards the second story window where Billy appeared and shredded Bob with his own shotgun. While Martin had no desire to face down a double barreled load of buckshot, he looked hopefully at the window, thinking his friend might appear there. With no such luck, he simply continued to the east, passing the site that marked where the McSween house used to be and then onto the wooden walkway of the Tunstall store. Try as he might, Martin could not find the portal back to 1878 anywhere in Lincoln. After a couple of bone-chilling hours, he decided to pack it in and head back to his casita.

"Well, maybe tomorrow?" Martin said to himself as he warmed up a last cup of coffee in the microwave. Spying Darlene coming and going with boxes from the front door of the main house to the shed, he remembered one of his missions. Find the final pages of Baca's book. Grabbing the steaming mug of coffee, he walked outside just as she made her way back to the house.

"Back so soon? You always seem to stay in town for hours when you come here, Martin," said Darlene with a warm smile.

"Yeah. It's pretty cold and I figured I have a whole week, so what's the sense of losing a few toes to frostbite?" he replied. Darlene had a shocked look until she realized that Martin must be attempting to make a joke. She gave a wink and nod of her head to let him know that she finally caught on.

"Hey, Darlene," Martin continued. "Remember that little old book you gave me?"

"Sure do. Was it any good?" she asked.

"Well, it has some interesting information. That's for sure," he said in what amounted to the understatement of the year. "But the last handful of pages is missing. Have you seen those pages anywhere?"

Darlene cocked her head in thought, giving Martin hope that she was about to divulge where the mystery pages were hidden. "You know, Martin, I haven't. The weird thing about that book is I never remember packing it. After Dallas left, it was just kind of there on the floor. I'd never seen it before, and it for sure wasn't in that box that he stole from me."

Martin's confusion was apparent. How could Darlene give him a gift of something she had never owned? Where did she think it came from?

Another thought quickly entered Martin's brain. Had Darlene looked in the book? If so, she surely would be able to make out the name Teebs in it. Was his secret already out? He decided the casual approach was best. "So did you get a chance to read the book before you gave it to me? It was pretty interesting."

"I didn't, Martin," she replied. "I was so flustered that day, I just picked it up and put it aside for you."

Problem averted, Martin wondered what his next move would be to locate the missing pages. If they were here at the house, Darlene would surely have found them in her packing and purging. They must be in someone else's possession or, more likely, long gone like so many documents relating to old Lincoln and the War.

"Hey, how about that tour tomorrow, Martin?" asked Darlene as she blew a wisp of hair out of her eyes. "I'd love to take a break from all of this." Martin didn't need an explanation to understand that "this" referred to Darlene's life at the moment.

"Umm, sure. That sounds good," he said, secretly afraid that Darlene was cutting into his available opportunities to see his friends. "But don't you have the real estate agent coming?"

"She called and said it would be late in the day. She's selling some ranch on the Rio Feliz and is going to be there most of the afternoon," said Darlene as if she didn't care if the agent ever showed up.

Martin wondered, was it the old Tunstall ranch that was being sold? He'd never seen it in person since it was privately owned and not open to the public. While he didn't think he'd get any keen insight into Tunstall by seeing his ranch so many years later, it would be something he could scratch off of his bucket list. "Darlene, I think that might be John Tunstall's old ranch. How about we start your tour there? It's about 30 or 40 miles from here, but I've never seen it. What do you think?"

Darlene shrugged her shoulders and replied, "Sure, why not? I'll call my agent and make sure that's it. Maybe we can just see her there to sign the paperwork on this place, and then we can check out the ranch."

Martin had long ago stopped being fascinated by every old Billy the Kid site, but even he had to admit that the ranch held special meaning. If not for Tunstall buying the ranch and running cattle, the Lincoln County War would probably have never taken place. That piece of ground led to one of the greatest grudge matches of the Old West and introduced the world to his new friend William H. Bonney. If the ranch was being sold, this would probably be his only chance to see it, to walk in the footsteps of Tunstall and his Regulators as they set off on that fateful day, running nine horses back to Lincoln and into a date with death from Dolan's posse. Martin's excitement was starting to build. If not for the Mathews' hook to his jaw sending Martin forward in time, he would surely have seen the ranch already, being as he had been summoned by his new employer to do some actual work for actual money.

"Cool!" he replied. "Let me know for sure, and we can get out of here about what, 9 am?"

Darlene brightened at having an actual thing to do that didn't involve divorce or selling her home. Even a day away from the mental drain would be refreshing, she thought. "Sounds good, Martin. Thanks!" she replied happily. "I'm looking forward to it. Let me get back to work, and I'll see you around 6 pm for dinner?"

Martin gave her the thumbs up that he was sure had won him the sales job from Mr. Talbot as he shuffled back to the casita. His coffee had gone lukewarm, and he wanted it piping hot to stave off the chill. Depositing the mug back in the microwave, he thought about the trip tomorrow. Darlene was a real decent person. It'd probably be fun to spend a little time with her. If he never wound up finding a way to stay in the past, it would be nice to have a friend that he shared something with in the present…even if that something was the illegitimate love child of their former spouses.

"Yeah," he said out loud, "this should be fun. She seems like she actually wants to learn…not like Lilly." Just the thought of Lilly invited the dark clouds into Martin's thoughts, so he quickly pushed them aside lest a raging storm of anger sweep through.

He reached into the microwave, burning the tips of his finger on the molten-lava mug handle. Cursing as he ran his fingers under cold water, he decided a nap was in order. Tomorrow was going to be a big day.

35.

Leaving Martin's tiny econo rental behind in favor of Darlene's pickup truck that morning, the two adventurers bounced along a dirt road, approaching a gate. The "For Sale" sign indicated they were at the correct place. Having graciously allowed Martin to drive, Darlene put her co-pilot skills to good use calling out every giant rut in the dusty road. Looking ahead, she saw her real estate agent outside of a seemingly old but well preserved house.

"There she is," pointed Darlene, as if Martin could aim anywhere else except the lone figure standing 50 yards in front of them. He was a slight bit fascinated on the drive here, imagining how many times Tunstall had made the trip on horseback or wagon from Lincoln to his home and back again. The ground those men covered in the saddle amazed Martin, and he wondered if he too would ever make the same trip during one of his time spasms?

As they approached the woman, Darlene leaned out the window to say hello, just missing the opportunity to let Martin know he was about to drive into a wheel-swallowing rut that ran along whatever semblance of driveway there was. As the truck pitched wildly to the left, Martin's head whipped hard against the door frame, and Darlene was thrown up against him. His head sounding a muted but sickening thud, Martin's vision went black and he slipped from consciousness. As he started to come to, he could hear Darlene gently slapping his face and calling his name. The slapping picked up in frequency and intensity, and he rolled his head to avoid it. When, he wondered, did Darlene acquire a British accent? Furthermore, when did her voice get so low and husky? As he tried to answer his own questions, he pried open his eyes to see a wide-eyed John Tunstall imploring him to get up.

"Up and at em, mate!" said Tunstall, staring directly into Martin's eyes. As the big man came around, Tunstall gave him another perfunctory slap or two, just because he could. "Come now, Martin, who's done this to you?" the Englishman asked.

Martin blinked away the pain in his head and checked to make sure he wasn't dead by pinching himself before speaking. "John? Hi there."

"Do you know where you are, Martin?" asked Tunstall. "Someone's dumped you here at the ranch. Was it Dolan?"

"Darlene," mumbled Martin, still woozy from that blow to the head.

"Well, I must admit I don't find him so much of a man either, Martin. From henceforth, sure, let's call him Darlene!" laughed Tunstall at the insult to his rival.

Tunstall reached out a hand and helped Martin struggle to his feet. Martin looked around to see the ranch had taken on a decidedly less modern feel than it had when he and Darlene drove up just a few seconds ago. Looking down, he noticed he was wearing clothes that were far too modern for the time and place. As he did, he felt Tunstall's eyes on him as well. "Where on Earth did you get that kit, Martin? I've not seen anything like it in Victoria even."

Unable to come up with a lie that would be better than the truth, Martin simply answered, "New Jersey."

"Right then. So that's where you disappeared to? A man has a tab and a job to pay it off, and he just ups and leaves? That's not the sort of cloth I sensed you were cut from, Martin," said Tunstall. The young man's dissertation made Martin feel guilty and childish. He was saving the big lie for Rosita but figured it could be of use here too.

"My apologies, John. My mother was sick, and I was sent for to reach home before her passing. I caught the first train out of Santa Fe," sulked Martin. He peered up to see if his sob story was working.

"Bad news. I see, Martin. So did you arrive in time?" asked Tunstall, as if he suspected the story was a lie.

"I didn't actually, John. They don't make trains fast enough to beat the grim reaper, I guess." Martin was pleased at his turn of a phrase and hoped that it at least threw Tunstall off the trail for awhile.

"Well, top job for trying, Martin. Family is the only thing. Glad to see you back. Are you ready to go to work?" said Tunstall, so casually that Martin was almost angry that the young man wasn't more sad about his fake dead mother. Martin nodded his assent, and Tunstall began walking him towards the main "house," which was not much more than a hut at that time. Tunstall turned around once more to look at Martin's kit before announcing, "Well, then, those clothes from Jersey won't do now, will they? You and Frenchie are about the same size blokes. Let's see if he's got some proper gear for a working hand, eh?"

As Tunstall guided him towards the bunkhouse, Martin felt it was time to catch up and find out exactly *when* he was.

"So what have I missed, John? What's going on here?" he asked.

"Nothing more than Dolan's…I mean Darlene's pissing and moaning about the Stanton beef contracts," laughed Tunstall at his own joke. "There's some business about an insurance policy from Emil Fritz that Alex is mixed up in. Dolan is up in arms that Alex stole ten thousand dollars from him. I'm sure he'll get it sorted before long. In any event, it doesn't involve me, so I don't involve myself in it," proclaimed Tunstall with an air of aristocracy.

Oh, how wrong the Englishman was, thought Martin. That policy would be the kindling upon which the fires of the Lincoln County War would be lit. Had Tunstall known what the coming weeks would hold, there is no way he'd be casually dismissing it as someone else's problem. Had he known what would transpire in the next few days, he would advise Alexander McSween to immediately turn the money over to the Fritz estate and divorce himself from any further proceedings. Had Tunstall known what an insurance policy that had nothing to do with him would cost him, he might have up and left Lincoln behind forever.

If he had known

One man knew what the outcome would be, and his name was Martin Teebs. Martin was at a crossroads. He couldn't bear the thought of changing history. He also couldn't bear the thought of Tunstall losing his life over something he had nothing to do with. Martin wondered: If he told Tunstall the coming truth, would the young man believe him? Would Martin even be able to change the history he was fighting so hard to protect? What was the sense of protecting history anyway, he thought? He'd already lost his book (although it wouldn't happen for another two months) and given Billy the ammunition he needed to change almost anything he wanted. He remembered Billy's deathbed confession that he had only used the book to save himself. If true, Billy must either have been the most stand-up guy Martin had ever met for refusing to change the course of history, or he was the biggest bastard Martin had ever met for refusing to change the course of history. Standing here with Tunstall, Martin now understood the duality of those choices, and he wasn't having any easier time than he imagined Billy did. Finally Martin decided he'd screwed enough things up in his own past and Billy's future, and he didn't want one more thing weighing on his conscience.

His decision made, he simply nodded at Tunstall and said, "Right, no sense getting involved in another's business, John."

Tunstall waved him into the bunkhouse and retrieved some of Big Jim French's clothing. Leaving it lying on a straw mattress, Tunstall departed for Martin to dress and get ready for work. Exiting the bunkhouse, wearing a checked shirt, tan vest, and dark pants, Martin looked the part of a working cowboy.

"Splendid, Martin," chirped Tunstall. "Let's get you mounted and out with the boys calling up the herd." Tunstall called for old Godfrey Gauss to saddle up a pony for their new hand and turned to Martin to speak. "So you think you'll be staying put here for a time now?"

Martin looked at the young, twenty-four-year-old man and thought to himself, "Yeah, I'll be here a lot longer than you will." But luckily the words stayed trapped in his head and didn't portray the pity that Martin looked at him with. Instead Martin simply nodded in the true hope that he would be and set off to mount the pony that Gauss was patiently holding for him.

36.

Martin looked at the slight figure of Charlie Bowdre as he bobbed slightly in the saddle. Having been ordered to ride along with Martin to join the boys, Bowdre's horse now walked a step or two ahead of Martin's. While Martin had indeed ridden horses (and ridden them well, he thought) in his previous time travels, this felt like the first time he'd ever been upon such an animal. He rocked and swayed in the saddle and got his undercarriage pummeled every time his horse moved at anything faster than a walk. He studied the tiny Bowdre and saw how he lifted himself just a bit in the stirrups to take some of the strain off of his groin every time they picked up speed. It reminded Martin of the time Lilly bought him a bike for Christmas. Once the New Jersey winter weather cleared (maybe five months later), he ventured out on a local bike path. Within two miles, his ass was screaming and his junk had gone numb. The numbness so worried him that he manipulated his manhood several times to see if he could feel anything, the last time coming when an obviously disgusted female cyclist rode up on him and yelled "Creep!" as she raced by. With the current pain invading his backside and rattling his molars, he knew he'd have to learn on the job quickly or risk having to muscle out Gauss for the job of camp cook. He wondered with amusement how the boys would respond to his now-famous, gluten-free red rice pasta as their dinner after a hard day in the saddle?

"John says you come from New Jersey?" asked the easy going Bowdre.

"Ummm, yeah. Up in the northern part," replied Martin.

"Ain't never been that far east. Must be sumthin to see, those big cities and all," speculated Bowdre.

Martin couldn't tell if Charlie was just making conversation or really was interested. While trying to figure it out, he let his guard down. "Yeah, New York is cool. The property taxes will kill you, though."

Charlie cocked his head to the side and stared at Martin. "You mean it's always cool? It don't never get hot in New York? I never heard that before. Why's that?"

Martin's vernacular didn't exactly fit in a conversation with an 1878 cowboy. He realized the error of his ways and was about to answer when Charlie cut back in. "How much you pay for them taxes? I got me a little piece of ground in Mississippi, and I gotta pay twelve dollars a year on it."

Twelve dollars, thought Martin. How much time would twelve dollars pay on his middle class home in Waldwick? He did a little mental calculation and decided that his tax bill of roughly a thousand dollars per month meant he was paying thirty-three dollars per day. Charlie's twelve dollars would cover enough of Martin's tax bill to let him eat breakfast and perhaps think about lunch before he'd be evicted. Even if he wanted the shock value of telling Bowdre that Teebs' property taxes were a thousand times more expensive than his, he knew the diminutive man wouldn't, or couldn't, believe him.

"Twelve dollars, huh?" asked Martin. "That's not too bad. I pay a little more, but I guess you always do back east."

Martin watched how easily Bowdre commanded his mount as if he'd done it a thousand times, which of course he had. Charlie wasn't long for this world either, thought Martin. While under indictment for the killing of Buckshot Roberts, he continued to ride with Billy. Although he wanted to go straight and settle down to ranching or farming with his wife Manuela, the lure of Billy the Kid was just too much for him. He would even meet with Pat Garrett at some point just outside of Roswell, asking for help to put his past behind him. Garrett would promise to do all he could for Charlie but demanded that he end his association with the Kid. Easy to say, yet hard to do. Charlie had the best of intentions, right up until Garrett mistakenly put a bullet in his gut, thinking he was Billy exiting a rock house at Stinking Springs. Sad, thought Martin. This man seemed like a genuinely good guy. He'd probably have lived a productive, nondescript life, had a few kids, and be buried on some private land where Billyphiles would flock each year to oooh and ahhh over the man that had once ridden with Billy the Kid.

"Sure enough," said Bowdre, as he nudged his horse over the brow of a hill. Arriving a step behind him, Martin peered down into the valley and saw some of Tunstall's ranch hands bringing up a few dozen cows. Among them, he spied Dick Brewer and Billy, who drifted off the back and seemed to be singing a song of some sort. As they approached the men, Brewer rode up to meet them.

"You're back, huh?" Brewer asked Martin matter of factly.

"Yes. I was back east for awhile. John knows about it," replied Martin.

"Whatever, Teebs," said Brewer. "Just don't go running off without telling someone next time. Ok?"

Too intimidated to speak to his foreman, Martin just nodded a serious assent.

"Charlie, ride point on these. I'll sweep. Teebs, head back with Billy and get them strays," directed Brewer. With that, the two men simply rode away and left Martin to follow his orders. Seeing Billy fifty yards away, he gently raked his mount with his spurs and made his way to his young friend. As he approached, he could hear Billy singing a not-very-good song in a slightly off-key voice:

"In the moonlight
In the canyons
Cross the prairies
Cross the field

Oh I'm bound for
Oklahoma
Dirt beneath this
Wagon wheel"

"Teebsie! You old son of a bitch. Where ya been?" greeted Billy through his perennial smile.

"Hi, Billy. Good to see you. Nice song," said Martin as tactfully as he could.

"Ya think? It's one I made up. I call it 'Wagon Wheel.' Wonder if a song like that'll ever catch on?" Billy asked enthusiastically.

Remembering the 30 or so people that karaoked to the oft-played hit "Wagon Wheel" at his company's Christmas party, Martin drolly replied, "Probably so, but you might have to change the words a bit."

Unaffected by Martin's critique, Billy continued to ride on, searching for strays. "So where ya been for two months, Teebsie? We missed you," asked the boy.

Getting better at the lie, Martin decided to embellish a bit. "I had to head back to New Jersey. My mother got sick and passed away. I barely made it in time to see her off."

"Oh, damn. Sorry about that, Teebsie. I know what it's like to lose your mother. I lost mine just a few years back in Silver City," replied Billy earnestly.

Martin knew the story well. Billy's mother had been stricken with tuberculosis or "consumption," as it was called in the day. She had sought drier and higher altitudes, as was the recommendation of her doctors, finally settling in Silver City, New Mexico. The dry air didn't provide her much respite, however, and she died when Billy was a teenager. Legend had it that he was forced to help dig her grave due to the almost constant absence of his stepfather William Antrim. If Martin wanted to verify that particular fact, he decided now wasn't the time. Consumption was an ugly death in most cases, and Martin had no desire to ask the young man to relive that period of his life.

"Thanks, Billy," Martin said simply, "I'm sorry to hear about your Mom, too."

With a somber, thoughtful look, Billy turned away, and Martin thought the boy might be crying. Billy scratched at his eyes and proclaimed, "C'mon Teebsie. These cows ain't gonna round theyselves up."

37.

Martin's posterior was getting the mother of all workouts. His cheeks stung like fire every time he bounced in the saddle. He wondered why they didn't make those soft gel butt pads for saddles like they did for bike seats? When he thought about making a living if he somehow was permitted to stay in the past, he figured he could open a saddle butt pad company and make a fortune. Of course, the raw materials wouldn't be invented for another sixty or seventy years, so he might need to find another job in the meantime.

"Go on and bring her back, Teebsie," said Billy, motioning to a fat heifer that had wandered up a hill. For some reason...perhaps because he looked like the most inept horseman in Lincoln County...Gauss had given him a solid cow pony. The horse seemed to know what to do even when Martin did not, which was basically all the time. He'd simply aim the horse's head towards the wayward cow and let nature take his course. Trying to deflect the pain in his rump from his mind, he chatted casually with the young man.

"So what's next for you, Billy? You going to stay on with Tunstall?" asked Martin, as they pushed a small group of cows forward.

"Might. Could," said Billy in return. "Course, I'd love to have my own ranch one of these days. Been planning with Waite to do that if I could raise the money."

Martin knew all too well the future of all of these men, and very soon some of them would be in the ground. There would be no ranch for Billy or Fred Waite, and certainly no long-term retirement plan for the men either. Life in the 1870s in Lincoln County was...well, fragile. Many of these hard cases didn't worry about tomorrow because, with the funnel cloud of war looming on the horizon, many suspected that their tomorrows were going to be severely limited.

"So what are you doing all the way out here, Teebsie? You damn sure ain't come here to work beef," stated Billy emphatically.

Martin looked at him and wondered how much he knew or suspected about how and why Martin had come to Lincoln. "I don't know, Billy," joked Martin in return. "If I could only get this horse every day, I'll bet I could do a respectable job. Maybe I'll be foreman!"

"Oh, that ain't never gonna happen," replied Billy just as jovially. "That horse is gonna have a sore back for a month just from having a big boy like you riding him today!"

Martin smiled and laughed easily with the boy. As they picked their way along the rocky trail, Billy popped his head at attention as if something important had just come to mind. "Hey, Teebsie, what's going on with Rosita?" he asked. "You just up and leave a girl like that without saying goodbye? She ain't good enough for you or something?"

"Good enough? Oh, man, that's not it at all," stammered Teebs. "I think I'm probably not good enough for her."

"You could be right on that one," said Billy without a hint of sarcasm. "Every man in town has taken a shot at Rosita Luna, and you's the only one who finally hit the mark."

Martin wondered if the "hit the mark" term meant more than Billy was letting on, but he didn't pursue it. If nothing else, Martin aspired to be a gentleman around women, and bragging about his moments of intimacy with Rosita hardly qualified as gentlemanly.

With their horses bobbing along, Martin asked, "Have you seen her? I'm sure she's mad, huh? I wish I'd had time to explain."

"She ain't mad, Teebsie. She's sad more than anything, I think. Seems like that woman really likes you, but for the life of me, I can't figure the hell why!" joked Billy. "If you ain't seen her since you got back, you best get up to Lincoln quick before some other *gringo* from New Jersey shows up and steals her away from you!"

Martin was taken aback. Another *gringo* from New Jersey? What was Billy talking about? Was it Farber? Could he somehow have gotten back here too? His blood boiling, Martin decided to innocently prod Billy to see what he knew. "Is there someone else here from back east? Anyone I should know?"

"Naw, Teebsie. Ain't no other tenderfoot here. I's just saying that if Rosita could fall for a soft hand like you, then you best get her back cause she might fall for just bout anyone!" Billy cackled at his joke, leaned over in the saddle, and gave Martin a friendly punch on his arm to reinforce how funny he found himself.

Temporarily relieved that his dream girl wasn't running around town with another man, Martin set his mind to more serious matters. "So things are bad with Dolan? John doesn't seem too concerned," said Martin, hoping he didn't betray that he already knew the Englishman wasn't going to live much longer.

"For sure they are," answered Billy, "and getting worse every damn day. I say John got in over his head on this deal. We'll fight to the last man for him, and hell, we might just have to." For once, Billy's face clouded over, and Martin could tell the young man was troubled. From his history books, he knew that Billy had joined Tunstall's outfit with the hope of going straight and giving up his outlaw ways. In Tunstall, and more specifically in Tunstall's men, he saw the kind of "mostly" law-abiding citizens that lived, worked, drank, gambled, and chased ladies together. The Kid having been on the run since he was a young teen, Martin assumed that this life would have appealed to Billy. If he expected to punch cows for a living until he and Fred Waite had raised enough money to buy a ranch, the likes of Dolan, Murphy, and the Santa Fe Ring had other more urgent ideas.

While Martin had certainly already done enough damage to history, this one moment in time would be his best opportunity to change the course of the life of William H. Bonney. If he could somehow convince Billy to quit Tunstall's employ and leave Lincoln, the boy might live to be a happy old man somewhere in Texas with a passel of kids and a loving wife. However, as tempting as it was to steer the Old West's most famous outlaw into a life of law abidingness, Martin knew too much had gone on already and attempting to derail Billy's future would be fruitless.

"Let's hope not, huh?" said Martin, "even though I am pretty handy with a gun."

"Says you," replied Billy drolly. "You ain't ever but talked about how good you was. Nobody here has seen it."

"Alright, alright. Let's get back to the ranch. You loan me that Winchester, and I'll put 10 of 10 shells wherever you tell me to," replied a surprisingly confident Martin Teebs.

Billy smirked a little in surprise at his friend's boast but agreed to the deal on one condition. "Them shells ain't cheap. If I do, you're gonna have to break out some of that old New Jersey money and buy me a box, ok?"

"Billy, I don't have a dime to my name right now. That's why I'm working here. I promise, once I get paid, I'll replace the shells. You've got my word," replied Martin.

"I know you's good for it, Teebsie. Long as you don't up and disappear like a feather in the wind again, that is," said Billy with as much friendliness as he could muster.

The two men rode on, spying the ranch in the distance. The few cattle they drove walked listlessly forward as if in protest against rejoining the herd.

"You think you'll ever take Rosita to New Jersey, Teebsie?" asked Billy.

The thought had never occurred to Martin, at least not in 1878 terms. He wondered if he'd fit in any better in 19th-century New Jersey than he did in 19th-century New Mexico? He wondered how Rosita would fit in, leaving behind the dry desert climate and only home she'd ever known? Rosita in New Jersey? It was an unimagined possibility, but suddenly it was a possibility.

"A Jersey girl, huh?" he mumbled mostly to himself. "Bruce would love that."

"Who's Bruce?" asked Billy, overhearing Martin's conversation with himself.

"Oh, Bruce Springsteen. He writes songs," answered Martin, before deciding whether it was a good idea or not.

"Springsteen, huh?" said Billy. "Never heard of him. Is he any good with the iron?"

38.

"Aim at the sky. Maybe you can hit that!" cried Chavez as the rest of Tunstall's ranch hands broke down laughing, some so hard they began to cry.

Now on his ninth shot, Martin had hit exactly one of the 10 bottles that Billy had helpfully lined up for his challenge. Luckily for Martin, he had his only success on his very first shot, so he at least held forth the illusion of a marksman...until the second shot flew high and wide.

"Easy guys," warned Martin, "this isn't my rifle. I'm just getting used to it."

Even the normally stoic Dick Brewer was getting in on the fun. "Go on and put 10 wash basins up there for him to hit, Billy. Maybe he can hit those at five paces!" roared Brewer.

More laughter ensued from the men, who probably didn't get many laughs during these tense pre-War days. Martin aimed carefully at the biggest bottle on the rocky ledge. Somewhere he remembered that he shouldn't so much pull the trigger, but squeeze it as if he didn't know when it would fire. Two out of 10 shots wasn't going to win him any prizes, but at least he could go out on a high note. Sighting down the barrel of Billy's Winchester, Martin suddenly had a vision of Billy Matthew's head pop up in place of the bottle. Martin needed no more prodding. Smoothly squeezing the trigger, he shattered the big bottle with a loud report, which was barely louder than the happily cheering men.

"10 out of 10, you said, Teebsie," challenged Billy. "You was off by just a bit. I'd say now you owe me two boxes of cartridges."

Martin sighed and handed the rifle back to his friend. Surely he must be going to have another opportunity to test his marksmanship? He knew when he inevitably would have to pull the trigger on Mathews, it was as if Martin had shot hundreds of rounds through that rifle. That shot, as gruesome as the outcome was, felt far more natural than his many misses on this day. Being sure that he'd get another chance to practice, he agreed to Billy's terms. "Ok, two boxes it is. But just wait, someday you're not going to be laughing at Martin Teebs."

The men descended into conversation about everything except Martin Teebs while Godfrey Gauss stoked a cooking fire. Martin was ravenously hungry and wondered what qualified for sustenance out here on the range? Before Martin could answer the question, Dick Brewer approached.

"Martin, how's your ass?" asked Brewer as seriously as if he were a physician about to offer a diagnosis.

"Ummmm, it's ok. Maybe a little sore. I've been out of the saddle for awhile," fibbed Martin in return. Truth be told, he'd been out of the saddle his entire life.

"Yeah, awhile," said Brewer questioningly. "Well, tomorrow you can drive the buckboard up to the store. Give your ass a break. Charlie and Chavez will go with ya. This crew's getting bigger, and Gauss is running out of supplies."

Lincoln! A chance to reunite with Rosita! Martin was ecstatic but made sure to offer the dour tone of a man denied another day of his beloved saddle time. "Ok, Dick. Whatever you need."

And with that, Dick Brewer walked off to get himself a drink.

"Gonna get to see Rosita, huh?" asked Billy, as he sat down next to the big man.

"Yes, Sir, it looks like I will, Billy," replied Martin in a voice that he hoped didn't sound too chipper.

"Sir? Who the hell you talkin to, Teebsie? What was you, a cook in the army?"

That Billy assumed that Martin could only be a cook in the army and not a fighting man bothered him. Sure, he wasn't the best shot among the Regulators (truth be told he was the worst, by far), but if Billy only knew how Martin would soon save his life, he would be singing a different tune. He must have looked a little wounded because Billy saw his face and jumped back in. "I'm kidding, Teebsie. That dang Winchester pulls left anyway. Once I fix the sights up, you'll be a bottle-breaking son of a bitch."

Martin accepted Billy's apology without comment, his mind now focused on Rosita and how he'd explain his sudden and prolonged absence. Gauss called supper, and the men assembled along the chow line to refuel from a long day in the saddle. Making their way to the fire with whatever camp plates or bowls they had, they noisily began slurping a fine mutton stew into their bellies. Doc Scurlock came around and wedged himself in between Martin and Billy.

"Howdy, Martin," said the level-headed, soon-to-be captain of the Regulators. "You're from New Jersey, they say?"

"Yes. Up north. A little town called Waldwick," replied Martin, even though he knew Waldwick wouldn't exist for another 40 years or so.

"Always wanted to go see New York City," said Doc, with some measure of awe in his voice. "Who knows, maybe become a schoolteacher or something?"

The reference creeped Martin out. He knew full well that Doc would retreat to Texas and live out a long life farming and ranching. Being a school teacher in New York was the stuff of the *Young Guns* movies. Martin began to seriously wonder if this whole experience wasn't some elaborate computer-generated simulation? Was his mind living in an alternate reality controlled by a man behind a curtain who was frantically pulling levers and spinning dials? Maybe, just maybe, Doc really did want to be a schoolteacher? Perhaps the writers of that movie found some tiny reference to his wish and decided to incorporate it into the film? In any event, Martin wasn't about to explore Doc's career goals while munching on mutton stew, so he simply replied, "Everybody should see New York at least once in his life, Doc," and left it at that.

"You musta fought for the Yankees, then? What unit were you in?" asked Doc.

Caught off guard, Martin's mind immediately went to pinstripes, not union blues. "Huh? What?" he asked quickly.

"War between the States. You look old enough that you fought in it?" clarified Doc.

In this matter Martin was woefully underinformed. His historical knowledge was focused on and limited to Billy and the Lincoln County War. While he knew that there most certainly had been a civil war, he knew next to nothing about it. Just then, Billy leaned in. "Yeah, was you at Gettysburg, Teebsie? What in the hell was that like?"

If Martin had any reference to draw from, he might have been tempted to lie. It's no wonder these men assumed he'd fought in that war. Here he was in 1878, in his early forties. During the Civil War, he'd have been of prime age to take a bullet and join a stack of bodies that other more experienced soldiers would fight from behind. Most of the men here seemed too young to have fought in the War. Maybe Gauss had been a cook, but who else among the Regulators was old enough to doff the union blues or johnnyreb grays? Martin's only Yankee references came from the times they played the Mets in interleague games. Maybe he could have served in the Bronx Bomber's Brigade under the command of Colonel Derek Jeter?

Martin paused for a long moment, thought the better of trying to invent some glorious past for himself, and simply stated, "I didn't fight in the War, guys. I had a medical deferment."

Billy and Doc looked at each other questioningly.

"Medical deferment?" asked Doc. "What was wrong with you?"

Martin thought back to a sweeping documentary he'd seen briefly on the Civil War, all replete with grainy pictures of men with various limbs shot off, missing an eye, or cut in half and perched up in a wheelchair. Those were real men, he told himself. Lose an arm for breakfast and get back in the fight by dinnertime. What could he possibly come up with that would resonate with these hard men of the plains? He drew on the only reference he could capture as the two men intently stared at him.

"I ummm....had bone spurs."

39.

Thirty-nine miles into the forty-mile journey from the ranch to Lincoln, and Martin's ass was on fire again. While the buckboard was easy enough to drive, the unforgiving wooden slat seat punished his bits already tenderized by a long day in the saddle the day prior. He shifted uncomfortably back and forth from cheek to cheek, hoping the ride would soon end. The team, Bobbi and Jake, plodded steadily along, passing Lincoln's only cemetery as they arrived on the cusp of town.

With hard feelings existing between Dolan and anyone who didn't side with him, both Bowdre and Chavez flanked the wagon as they made their way steadily through town. Passing Rosita's house, Martin craned his neck to see if she could be seen. He assumed she might be at work at this late afternoon time but hoped for at least a glance.

Everyone breathed a sigh of relief with the Tunstall store finally in sight. Martin pulled up Bobbi and Jake outside the corral but had no further idea what to do with the team, so he left the task for Charlie. Stepping inside the store, Martin sought out Sam Corbett to drop off the list of supplies that Tunstall had requested. The men wouldn't be making the trip back until tomorrow, so once this was job done, Martin was free to spend the night doing whatever it was he wanted to do.

Martin walked out to the corral as Charlie was attaching a nose bag of grain to each horse's muzzle.

"Hell of a long ride, huh, Teebs?" asked Charlie.

"Yeah. I'm feeling every mile of it right now. How do you guys do this day after day?" asked Martin, hoping for some enlightenment.

"Dunno," replied Charlie, "we just do it. Hell, I been living in the saddle since I was seven years old. Don't bother me none at all anymore. The callouses on my balls have their own callouses."

Martin looked at the slight man with some envy. Charlie, like the rest of the Regulators, could probably live off the land for a month, carrying nothing more than a blanket, a gun, and a knife. These were real men, the type who barely existed in Martin's comfy, internet-fueled future. If Martin got hungry, he didn't butcher a calf, he called for pizza delivery (at least before his gluten intolerance reared its ugly head). If he was tired, he laid on his deluxe memory-foam mattress and Egyptian cotton sheets, not a wool horse blanket under the stars. If he wanted a fire, he would simply flick the switch on his gas log fireplace in his living room, rather than gathering kindling and wood and building one from scratch. If it was possible for him to feel any more out-of-time or out-of-place, he couldn't imagine how that would be.

"How long you gonna keep that woman waiting, Teebs?" yelled Chavez, who had just relieved himself in the trees near the creek.

Indeed, thought Martin. How long am I going to make her wait? How long until I have to lie to her about my absence? How long before I impregnate her and leave my son to be raised a bastard child by my old friend Billy the Kid? All of these questions swirled in Martin's mind as he suddenly realized that he was freezing cold. The sun was dipping quickly behind the mountains, and the jacket that had been more than enough on the ride up now was failing miserably at keeping him warm. Charlie and Chavez were planning to bunk at Juan Patron's place, as instructed by Tunstall. He'd made the same offer to Martin, but the big man remained noncommittal. Not knowing how things would go with Rosita, he felt he should hedge his bets and perhaps bunk at the Wortley instead. He didn't know Juan Patron and didn't feel like explaining who he was and why he was in Lincoln to yet another person.

"I'm gonna get going if you guys don't need me anymore," stated Martin to his two bodyguards. Charlie and Chavez both looked at each other and shrugged their shoulders.

"Let's get on our way by 9 am tomorrow, Martin," said Charlie. "This way we'll get back in time for supper. I'll meet ya back here at 8:30."

"Have a good time tonight, lover boy," laughed Chavez, as Martin meekly waved at the men and walked towards the Wortley.

Martin replayed his story over and over again in his mind. He wanted it to be just perfect when Rosita invariably asked what had happened to him. While he hated lying to the woman he was falling in love with, he knew the truth would never suffice in this situation. Martin's heart began to race, both at the prospect of seeing Rosita again and at the possibility of losing her. Walking up the few steps onto the main portal of the Wortley, he was about to push the front door open when he heard his name being called.

"*Martin?*"

Martin wheeled around to see Rosita looking at him, her face almost in shock at the sight.

"Rosita!" Martin cried as he rushed to wrap his arms around her. As he approached, he sensed a change in her body language. Her hand went up to stop him, and she turned to the side as she backed off.

"What happened to you, *Martin Teebs*?" asked Rosita formally. "One day you are willing to kiss me, and the next you disappear without so much as a goodbye. Is this the way to treat a lady?"

Aside from the obvious chill in the night air, Martin was positively frozen by Rosita's accusation. He knew it might take some work to smooth things over, but he had assumed she'd be happy to see him. He decided he needed to lay it on thick and to do it right now.

"Rosita," he gushed, "I'm so terribly sorry. I meant no harm. I got word that my mother in New Jersey was dying, and I rode out for Santa Fe immediately to catch the next train heading east."

Rosita found it hard to maintain her icy stare when Martin mentioned his mother dying, so she shifted uncomfortably from foot to foot and glanced off to the side. Unsure if his confession was working, Martin decided to play the shut-up game and see what Rosita said next.

"I'm sorry to hear about *tu madre*, *Martin*," was all Rosita could force out.

Martin waited through the uncomfortable silence, unsure of how much more color he should add to the story. Seeing no progress being made, he decided to go big or go home.

"Thank you. I barely made it before she passed. I was able to hold her in my arms as she went. It was sad but quite beautiful too."

Rosita sighed as a small sound escaped from her throat. She desperately wanted to believe Martin's story because she had missed him greatly while he'd been gone. Never before had she given of herself to any man as she did to him, only to have him vanish the next day with nary a word. She remembered asking around town if anyone had seen him, but most people had no idea who she was talking about. She wondered if somehow Jimmy Dolan and his thug Billy Mathews were involved? They could have been looking for payback for when Martin had made them look silly (with Billy's help) earlier in that day. She wondered if those two men were so embarrassed that they might even have murdered Martin? Her sadness had overtaken her so completely that her new man was either dead or had run out on her. Either way, it seemed as if he'd never be back…yet here he was. Her years of waiting came down to the next decision she would make.

Rosita dropped the basket she was carrying and ran into Martin's arms. The moment their bodies touched, it was as if they were two jigsaw puzzle pieces that had finally found their mates. She melted into his chest, tears streaming down her face.

"*Oh, Martin*!" she cried, "I was so worried when you went. No one knows where you go or if you would come back." Rosita's tears soaked at Martin's shirt.

"I'm so sorry. I wasn't thinking," he said quietly as he stroked her hair. "I panicked, thinking that I would never see my mother again. Please, Rosita, forgive me."

Rosita pulled Martin more tightly to her, a month of sadness and worry melting away with each heartbeat. "Forgive me, *Martin*," she said between tears, "I did not want to act badly to you just now."

Martin pushed her slightly away from him so he could look into her eyes. Through the tears, they still shone as brightly as he remembered. "We are together. That's all that matters," he said simply.

Martin reached down to pick up the basket and then put his arm around her shoulder. Unsure of what the next step should be, he asked, "May I walk you home?"

"Yes, yes!" she said, her face brightening. "Where will you stay tonight?"

Martin responded, "I'm working for Mr. Tunstall tomorrow. I figured I would stay at the Wortley tonight. I don't really have another plan, to be honest."

"Come, *Martin*," Rosita replied happily, "let us get out of the cold at my home. We can have dinner and discuss your 'plans' for this evening. *Si?*"

Rosita reached up to free herself from his arm and instead held his hand tightly. Supremely happy to be back with this woman, Martin smiled from ear to ear. They walked gingerly down the main street of Lincoln towards Rosita's tiny hut. Inside Martin imagined a warm fire, hearty food, and his burning desire to once again pull Rosita into him, their bodies coagulating as if into one being.

"What are you thinking, *Martin*?" asked the young lady innocently, seeing her man lost in thought.

Rather than risk telling her all that was on his mind (and other places around his body), he still offered the truth. "I'm thinking this is one of the best days of my life."

Rosita beamed at him, holding his hand even more firmly. She was secretly glad he didn't ask her what she was thinking because the mere thought of it made her blush a deep rosy glow.

40.

The crackling fire warmed the tiny hut, sending off bursts of light that made Rosita shimmer in Martin's eyes. He marveled as she moved from place to place strongly and firmly, always knowing where to go and what to do next. A simple dinner was taking shape before his very eyes, but truth be told Martin would have gladly gone without eating for a week if it meant he could stay here with this woman. Every once in awhile, she would catch him staring at her; and her face would radiate a smile just before she would invariably ask, "What? What are you staring at, *Martin*?" Sometimes Martin would smile and look away, but most times he would answer with a simple, "You. I just can't take my eyes off of you."

With beans cooking over the fire and the smell of freshly baked biscuits emanating from the tiny oven, Rosita finally sat facing Martin. She clasped both of his hands firmly and looked straight into his yes.

"Tell me about your *Madre*. What happened?" she asked, hoping she could ease his pain.

Surprisingly Martin's eyes began to well up as if his mother really had died just a couple of weeks ago. It had been years since he had allowed his mind to revisit that painful event. Sheila Teebs, the faithful wife of Arlo Teebs, was diagnosed with an insidious case of Stage 4 breast cancer when Martin was just a teenager. The diagnosis happened so late because Sheila, always full of life and energy, seemed to will herself past the constant nagging fatigue she had been experiencing. With her husband Arlo bouncing around from job to job (yet always gainfully employed), it was left to Sheila to create a stable environment for Martin and his younger sister Ellen. As the world crept towards the end of the 20th century, cancer treatment options were good, but the prognosis for Stage 4 was not. Sheila fought bravely and put on a good face for Arlo and the kids. Martin watched his mother slowly disappear from a strong, vibrant woman to a mere shell of a human being. Through it all, she never seemed to lose her smile or her faith that somehow she would beat the dreaded monster.

Sheila Teebs lost her fight on September 25, 1991. Martin remembered the lost, scared look on his father's face when the hospice nurse lifted her stethoscope from Sheila's chest and gave a tight little smile to the family. Arlo, he of the peace and love revolution, was not cut out to handle being a widower with two children that would surely need a father to guide them through life. Martin's sister looked on to their mother's body, upper lip quivering but determined not to cry at this, a foregone conclusion. The loss of their mother had shaped Ellen. It was soon after that when she decided to go into medicine. Ellen proudly served as the chief of oncology at a large cancer care campus in Arlington, Texas. For Martin, however, the loss of his mother was something else. Sheila had always been an enthusiastic cheerleader for her children (and for Arlo). Always convinced he could accomplish anything he set his mind to, Martin simply waited until he found something his mind would be set on. With the loss of his mother, his motivation to achieve...well, anything...quickly faded. He had barely escaped college with his degree, and he and Lilly settled into a life of nothing special soon after. The weight of his loss weighed heavily on Martin in the moment as tears began to silently fall from his eyes.

Seeing his pain, Rosita pulled him closer. "I'm so sorry, *querido*. I did not mean for such sadness," whispered Rosita. Martin was embarrassed by his tears, thinking that somehow Rosita might think less of him, but the effect seemed exactly the opposite. Her big brown eyes looked deeply into his and connected with him in a way that no human being ever had before, not even Lilly. If Martin had any hesitations that Rosita might not believe his story, they had been flushed away by his tearful display.

"It's ok. I just hadn't thought about it in awhile," he said, as his woman rubbed his forearms in her hands.

"If ever you want to talk about it, *Martin*, I will be here to listen," replied Rosita with a strong comforting smile. Months of waiting and hoping weighed heavily on Martin's mind, and finally he could wait no longer. He slid closer to Rosita, threading his fingers into her hair and pulling her face towards his. He feared she might protest, but immediately her lips rushed across the space to meet his. They kissed hungrily and deeply, their bodies coming together as if drawn by magnetic attraction. With his eyes closed tight, Martin focused on every bit of the physical pleasure he was feeling. It washed over him like a tsunami bringing him in to shore and then more forcefully pulling him back out. He ran his hands to Rosita's shoulders and then slid them down to her breasts. He wondered if she would stop him, but a soft, breathy moan gave him permission to continue. Not to be outdone, she ran her hands down his chest, sliding them around his back for leverage. With one effortless move, she leveraged herself directly into Martin's lap, her hands plunging further to his crotch. Martin let out a deep and breathless groan as Rosita took him into her hands. Once again Martin's heart was racing. He had assumed that those days were gone for good once he'd married Lilly. He expected never again to feel the rush of lust and passion that comes from physical love with someone new. His breath came in rapid, shallow bursts, and he feared he was hyperventilating. His fingers fumbled at the buttons on the back of Rosita's blouse. Briefly pulling her lips from his, she smiled and laughed as she deftly reached behind and began to unbutton it for him. As the blouse fell to the floor, Martin marveled at her perfect brown skin, now glowing in the firelight. He reached again for her breasts and was stifled by the heat coming off of her. Just as he touched her, she jumped up with a start, yelling, "My biscuits are burning!"

For a brief moment, Martin wondered if "biscuits" was a 19th century term for boobs? If so, he would concur that Rosita's were definitely burning. However, just a split second later, he realized it wasn't the heat coming off of Rosita that was stifling him, it was the tray of now burnt biscuits that the two lovers had ignored for too long in the oven.

"Ohhhh, *Martin*! See what you make me do?" she said with a half smile. "Now I must make more."

"No. Please don't, Rosita. It's fine," replied Martin. "I don't need biscuits when I have you."

Pulling the tray from the fire, Rosita put it loudly on the small table. She stood there in her corset and skirt, looking every bit the most beautiful creature Martin had ever laid eyes on. Noticing him staring, Rosita became shy and quickly picked up and put on her wayward blouse.

"Let us have supper, *Martin*," she said, motioning him to sit at the table. "You must be hungry from the long trip from Mr. Tunstall's ranch." Martin was indeed hungry, but not for a plate of *refritos* and bacon fat. Nevertheless, he sat down across from Rosita and found himself diving into the plate with more gusto than he expected.

"So you don't have a place to stay tonight?" she asked Martin slyly.

"No, not yet," Martin replied, wondering where this conversation might lead.

"*Martin*, I would be honored if you would stay here with me tonight. You must have a good night's rest," said Rosita as she looked calmly into his eyes. Martin tried to ascertain if she actually meant he should get a good night's rest or if that was just the cover story for what they would tell people in Lincoln, who would surely be whispering about it. Either way, staying with Rosita was a far more pleasant offer than walking in the freezing cold back to the Wortley in hopes that they had a vacant room.

"I'd love to. I can sleep in a chair or something," he said, not wanting to be presumptuous.

Rosita let out a joyous giggle. "Chairs are for sitting, *Martin*. Beds are for sleeping. You will sleep right next to me."

Being invited to a sleepover by Rosita Luna...she of the long flowing raven hair, big brown eyes, swaying hips, and voluptuous breasts...was the best invitation Martin had received in a long time, perhaps ever. Even if he had wanted to, his biology would not allow him to beg off. He rose to help clear the dinner plates and heard himself say, "You're the boss" with a smile.

Rosita cocked her head with a questioning smile and replied, "No, *Martin, tu eres el patron*. But tonight we shall just be equals, *si*?"

Martin smiled warmly, glad that his evening plans had finally been sorted. With a full belly, a warm fire, and a long day on the buckboard ahead of him tomorrow, his eyes began to feel heavy. Seeing she was losing him, Rosita guided Martin to the bedroom and slipped off his boots. She helped him scoot up into bed and laid out a bright woven blanket over him. For good measure, she bent down and kissed him deeply on the lips as he faded into that magical twilight zone between waking and sleeping. Giving his eyelids permission to fall, he dozed into a restful deep sleep.

41.

Spying Pajarito Mountain in the distance, Martin bounced and swayed from the seat of the heavily loaded buckboard. The men took the turn off of the main road towards Tunstall's ranch, with the sun high in the early afternoon sky.

Martin reflected on his evening with Rosita. If not for burning biscuits, who knows how much farther they might have gone? He vaguely remembered getting into bed and remembered the warm touch of her lips on his just before he fell asleep. While he wished he had stayed awake long enough to deliver the goods, he also wanted to be fully in the magical moment when he and Rosita Luna finally did make love.

If she was somehow disappointed by Martin's early retirement the night before, Rosita didn't show it. She was happy and cheerful in the morning while fixing coffee and breakfast. Just knowing her man was back and in town, and intended to stay there, was enough for her to wake up smiling. Once fed and dressed, Martin needed to make his way to the Tunstall corral, so he held Rosita closely and told her he would see her in a few days. Truthfully Martin had no idea if he'd see her in a few days or in a few weeks, but he reasoned that if he was able to stay in 1878, then he must make a foray back into town to see his woman before too long.

"Was she good?" yelled Charlie from a few paces ahead.

Caught lost in his own thoughts, Martin could only respond, "Huh?"

"I said, was she good? She looks like she'd be pretty damn good," repeated Charlie, as plainly as if he was commenting on the weather.

"What are you talking about?" said an irritated Martin, although he already knew what Charlie was asking.

"You took a flyer with her, no? Rosita? Bet that felt finer than frog hair," laughed Charlie as he spurred his horse forward.

"Hey!" warned Martin. "That's a lady you're talking about. And no, I didn't 'take a flyer' with her."

"Damn shame. I woulda done it in a heartbeat," said Charlie, mostly to himself.

"Me too. You screwed up, Teebs," parroted Chavez plainly.

"Whatever," Martin growled under his breath. While these men might have had more survival skills than he did, they clearly didn't know how to treat a lady. At very least, they didn't know how to be discreet in the discussion of such. If they knew so much, he thought, why weren't they the ones sleeping in Rosita's bed? Why had she chosen him over all of the rough and tough bravos of Lincoln County? Because in his own way, Martin Teebs was a real man, he thought to himself. The kind of man that could be counted on. The kind of man who wouldn't kiss and tell. The kind of man who could work the same bland, boring job for 17 years without complaint to take care of his family.

As Martin thought about his qualifications as a "real man," he had to admit they looked rather boring. Was Rosita looking for boring? Would the spark they felt fade away over time? It seemed impossible. The physical reaction he had to her was so overwhelming that at times he worried if he might simply die of excitement. Rosita launched herself at Martin with such vigor that he knew she wasn't simply being nice to him. She wanted him…really wanted him. That's something these two clowns would never be able to say or to understand, he finally concluded.

As the sun began to dip in the west, the ranch was finally in sight. Martin did an inventory of his belly and decided that he was hungry, very hungry. Aside from breakfast and a bit of hardtack, he hadn't eaten anything for the balance of the trip.

Charlie dropped behind the wagon to close the gate at the ranch entrance. He shook his head at seeing Martin so lost in his thoughts that he looked like he was watching a private picture show. Slipping a chain over the gate to secure it, Charlie looked up just in time to see Martin and the wagon drift off the road towards the ditch.

"Martin!" screamed Charlie.

Hearing his name shocked Martin out of the dream he was in, just as the heavily loaded wagon lost purchase and slid into the arroyo. He pulled hard on the reins, just as Bobbi and Jake reared back, and Martin went tumbling ass -over-teakettle into the ditch. The impact knocked the wind out of him, and he struggled to breathe.

Again he heard his name being screamed, "Martin! Martin!" He fought to stay conscious.

Unaware of how long he'd slipped into blackness, Martin was surprised to hear Rosita's voice through the fog. "Is he breathing?" Someone must have sent for her to come to the ranch. He felt her lips press heavily onto his, and she began to hyperventilate, forcing her air into his lungs. She pressed heavily onto his chest in rapid pulses. He'd never known a woman so insatiable that, even in his infirmed condition, she just had to have him. Finally, as the blackness subsided, he gave in, grabbing her hair and jamming his tongue firmly into her mouth, searching for hers in return. At first he found nothing, but she finally relented and darted her tongue inside his mouth, pressing her breasts heavily on his chest and moaning in delight.

"Martin! You're ok!" he heard as he opened his eyes...not to his lover Rosita Luna, but to the very modern duo of Darlene Jones and her real estate agent looking at him in a very worried fashion. He'd been laid out on the dirt next to the truck after bashing his head. Darlene hadn't been kissing him, he realized, she'd been performing CPR on the comatose man. Only Martin's brain fog had prompted him to think her as Rosita and kiss back firmly. Confused and a little bit sad, Martin tried to raise himself from the ground, before feeling woozy and lying back down.

Smiling at her sudden good fortune, Darlene leaned in for another kiss before Martin had the good sense to gently push her away.

42.

"So Darlene put the B&B up for sale. Won't be long now, I'll bet," said a beaming Dallas Jones, as if he'd just coached his team to a Super Bowl win.

"Really?" inquired Lilly, with a hint of surprise in her voice, "Did you agree to this?"

"Agree to it? It was my idea, Lil!" said Dallas proudly.

Fighting the urge to tell him once again not to call her Lil for the millionth or so time, Lilly wondered to herself what the sale of the Jones' B&B meant to her? Just as she decided to open that can of worms, Dallas beat her to the punch. "I'll get half of whatever the profit is, and we can get out of this place and head to LA. How's that sound?"

While New Mexico hadn't quite lived up to Lilly's Georgia O'Keefe expectations, it had provided a decent place to live with a reasonable cost of living for her and her two children...Austin and Dallas, who acted like one. It was far too soon for her to feel nostalgic if she left, but there were some things she would miss. Green chile, to name one. The mountains, sunsets, and stark beauty of the desert at sunset were others. With that said, moving to Los Angeles wouldn't be the worst move they could make, especially if Dallas had enough money to help pay the tab. Job opportunities above the meager sales she made of her artwork were sure to be more plentiful in southern California. Lilly could surely do something in the business world with her degree. It had been a long time since she'd had to punch a clock, though, and she wondered if losing her freedom was something she could live with?

"How much do you think you'll wind up making?" she asked cautiously, as if afraid of the answer. Dallas wasn't the brightest bulb in the row, and he'd shown a propensity to waste money and manage it poorly. Lilly decided she'd be equally surprised whether he said he would earn one million dollars or he'd lose that much.

"Not sure, Lil. I think she's listed the place for about seven hundred thousand dollars," replied Dallas.

Job one for Lilly was understanding how much the sale was for. Job two was to figure out how much money they owed on the place.

"Wow, that's pretty high for Lincoln, New Mexico," she said seriously. "How much money do you owe on it?" Lilly braced herself for the answer.

"Well, I don't remember exactly because Darlene always paid the bills, but something like a quarter mil, Lil," said Dallas, smiling at his inadvertent rhyme.

Lilly was silently shocked. Four hundred and fifty thousand dollars of profit, with half going to Dallas? Maybe he wasn't as much of a dunce as she had him pegged for! She did some quick mental math to join his potential assets with her existing ones and decided that, yes, they could live a reasonable life in SoCal, at very least in the Inland Empire. The thought brightened her outlook on life and opinion of Dallas.

"That sounds great. With that money, we should talk about moving to LA. Things just haven't worked out here the way I thought they would," she said, her mind racing with the possibilities. Dallas seemed pleased that he finally had done something that Lilly approved of. He was hoping for a quick sale so that he could uproot his little family and get into the heart of the LA acting scene. When he'd been there a decade ago, he was too young and too inexperienced. With a marriage, a divorce, a baby, and a financial windfall coming his way, he reasoned that he'd be a better actor now that he had more life experiences to draw on. All it would take is a starring role in a big studio feature film or two to allow him to show his talents.

In her own little world, Lilly too hoped the B&B would sell quickly. The sooner it was sold, the sooner she could start the next chapter of her unexpected life after forty.

43.

Martin's car plowed heavily through the salty gray slush of Route 17 in Paramus. It was early February and typically gray and gloomy. With COVID restrictions easing, Martin had taken to going to the office two times per week. Most of the time, it was just to escape the quiet monotony of his home office. He did try to coordinate his office days with Colin, who was also fighting his way through pandemic fatigue.

Before leaving New Mexico just two weeks prior, Martin had a heart-to-heart talk with Darlene about their tongue-to-tongue meeting. He let her know firmly that it had all been a mistake and that he must have been dreaming as she was attempting CPR on him. Seeing the wounded look on her face, he quickly added that she was a beautiful, desirable woman whom any man would be lucky to have, but the constant reminder of her former husband was a boner killer. He definitely did not attempt to explain that he was deeply in love with someone else as that would prompt questions such as…when was she born? What is her name? What century does she live in? Darlene would just have to live with his decision and stay in the dark about his personal life.

Martin had been able to escape back to Rosita one brief time before he left. Knowing he would be gone for awhile, he had explained that Tunstall had a special job for him that would have Martin on the range and at the ranch for at least a few weeks. He promised he would try to visit Lincoln to see her, but he needed to earn some money and couldn't pass up the work. Rosita seemed happy that at least Martin wouldn't just up and leave again, like he did the last time, so she left him with a long and deep kiss and her traditional bright-eyed smile.

Now here he sat in bumper-to-bumper traffic. A race of madmen and madwomen all charged up to go somewhere yet stuck going nowhere. He couldn't help the words escaping his mouth, even though the otherwise empty car held no one to hear them. "How much of my life am I going to waste doing this?" he implored of himself. Stepping back in his mind, he laughed at the absurdity of it all. He spent hours each week going nowhere. Caught in a ridiculous rat race all designed to achieve absolutely nothing. He worked so he could pay his bills. He paid his bills so he could go out and buy more stuff with what was left, which then demanded he go to work to earn more money to start the cycle over again. At that moment Martin Teebs saw himself as a rat on a hamster wheel, thinking he was so slick because he was getting exercise, but never realizing he was going nowhere.

Martin had even wondered why he still lived in New Jersey? Lilly was gone. He had no children...at least not in the 21st century...and his girlfriend lived two thousand miles and 140 years away. His job, when he got to do it these days, was focused on the west coast. What was he doing here? Why hadn't he had this clarity before? Martin told himself he should go into Talbot's office today and let him know that he would like to move to the west coast to be closer to his territory. Of course, he wouldn't live in Albuquerque. The thought of running into Lilly and Dallas at the grocery store was too much for him. But there were other cities. Denver, Phoenix, Tucson, El Paso, Las Vegas, or even Los Angeles? The prospect began to excite Martin. No longer would he have to plan and execute strategies to lay over in New Mexico on his business trips. No longer would he need for the magic wave of Talbot's hand to tell Martin when to stay and when to go. No, now he would be in charge of his time and his location.

Martin felt strong, heady even. For the first time in a long time, he was taking charge of his life, and it felt incredible. Even the dirty remnants of yesterday's snow storm couldn't dampen his enthusiasm. He reached for the radio to flip on some music appropriate to a change in life but froze as a question popped into his mind.

What if Talbot said no?

He wouldn't, would he? How could he? Talbot would have to consider the cost savings of not flying Martin back and forth across the country at the drop of a hat. On the other hand, Talbot had taken firm direction with keeping Martin in line and his sales growing. The man was an encyclopedia of sales and marketing, having studied the Power Shot Training method, and it was largely due to him that Martin was succeeding. Talbot could easily say no just to keep Martin close enough to prevent him from screwing anything up royally.

"What if he does say no?" Martin wondered aloud. Perhaps he would have to find a new job. With his short but successful stint in sales, he figured he could find something to sell. Never one to strike out on his own, Martin wondered about perhaps opening his own business? The idea sounded great, except for his complete and total lack of any business ideas.

"What do I know about?" he asked himself, as his car slipped and slid north towards Mahwah. "Well, I know an awful lot about Billy the Kid," he added. That wasn't the kind of talent that would bring in much money, however. Perhaps Martin could lead tours of Lincoln? He'd seen some people from the museums do it, and they didn't know half of what really went on in Lincoln like he did.

"I wonder how much I could make?" he asked again out loud. As he frequently did, Martin started doing the math in his head. Ten tourists times the not-very-much money they would pay for a walking tour of Lincoln added up to Martin burning through his savings quickly. Besides, if he worked in Lincoln, where would he live? Certainly not in Capitan so he could avoid running into that psycho Steve every day. He thought about some of the towns to the east like Hondo, Tinnie, or even San Patricio, but he reasoned that there wouldn't be anything for sale or rent. Then it struck Martin that Darlene was selling the Patron House. A business. A real, working business that people who liked Billy the Kid would want to stay in. As much as he knew being a hotel proprietor wasn't for him, he asked himself: "or is it?" It was honest work. He could lead tours for his guests and others who would pay the tab, and best of all, he could be right in Lincoln, hopefully with the ability to slip back to see Rosita whenever he wanted to.

Could it be? Martin imagined a world where he lived with his soulmate each day, only heading out the door for work in the mornings. He'd walk through some reliable time portal to the present so that he could take care of his guests. Once five o'clock hit, he'd punch out for the day, dress in his old clothes, and make it back to Rosita's house in time for dinner. Could he somehow pull off the past/present life by living in Lincoln? Could he inherit the best of both worlds and never have to choose between now and then? Could he cheat the space-time continuum to be the luckiest son of a bitch that ever lived?

Of course he'd have to tell Rosita the truth by that point, otherwise she'd be expecting him to come home for lunch at least once in awhile. If he could manage the travel between Rosita's time and his, maybe he could just bring her into the present for a few small moments at a time? He imagined his guests would love her *pastelitos* as much as he did. The incredible thought of it all distracted Martin to the point he almost slammed into a BMW that had slowed to navigate an overly deep puddle of slush at the Paramus Road exit. Pulling himself together, he focused on the road. The plan seemed almost too perfect. As he reviewed it in his mind, he began to get excited. Maybe the answer to all of his problems was the one place that truly felt like home to him!

Now Martin felt emboldened to go in and talk to Talbot. "Tell me no!" he said as if issuing a challenge. He began to hope that Talbot would not approve the change of station so that Martin could dramatically quit his job and find his future (and past) in New Mexico. His gray, cold day was getting sunnier and warmer by the minute. He finally had a plan! He was taking control. His life could resume moving forward.

Visions of vivid red and orange sunsets decorated Martin's brain while the gray mush on Route 17 robbed every other driver stuck in the messy traffic jam of their very will to live.

44.

"Better than expected" was the answer Martin gave himself when he asked the question, "How did his discussion with Mr. Talbot go?"

While Talbot didn't clap Martin on the back and tell him to choose the corner office in LA, he did say he'd consider it, providing Martin would fly back to New Jersey monthly for training and strategy meetings. "Give me a week, Martin" was exactly what he said, and so Martin started the mental clock countdown at that moment.

Arriving home that evening, he put on the lights and stoked up a cozy, natural-gas powered fire over fake ceramic logs. He'd been waiting all day to make an important phone call and didn't want to be disturbed. He tapped out the contact card for Darlene Jones and settled onto his couch.

"Darlene? Hey, it's Martin…Teebs."

"Martin! How are you? So good to hear your voice," answered Darlene sincerely.

"Well, I'm good," he replied, wanting to get right down to business. "You know how you said I should buy the B&B from you?"

"Yeah," came the tentative reply.

"Well, I've been thinking about it. You know, there's no reason for me to stay living in New Jersey anymore. I talked to my boss about moving to the west coast, and he's thinking about it. But I was sitting in traffic this morning and wondering 'what am I doing here,' you know?" Martin was on a roll, as if he somehow had to convince Darlene that this was a good idea.

"So I'm thinking that the thing I know about most is Billy the Kid. I could lead tours, give presentations, and I think I could be a great host. I've been going over my financials all day, and I think I can maybe swing buying the place," he continued enthusiastically, "and you know I would run it like you would. It wouldn't be some stranger coming in and changing a bunch of stuff. God, I have so many ideas and I…"

"Martin," cut in Darlene suddenly.

"Huh? Oh I'm sorry, Darlene. I just got so excited," he stopped.

"I sold the place yesterday. Some investment group from Texas bought it. Full asking price," she said sadly. "I had no idea you would want it. I'm so sorry, Martin. You told me no. If I had any idea you would change your mind, I would have waited."

Martin suddenly had the feeling of a sharp pin puncturing his balloon of hope. His entire day of dreaming and scheming had allowed him to create a perfect post-Lilly life in his mind. His vision was so real on the drive home, he could almost smell the fires he would light nightly for his guests in the fire pit out front of the house. He'd even gone so far as to invite Colin out for an extended vacation to help him with the grand opening, which the young man gladly accepted. Martin had a habit of building things up in his mind only to be disappointed later, and this was no exception. This one was big, though, and the disappointment was real…and it hurt.

"Oh, no. That's ok, Darlene. You didn't know. How could you?" came Martin's reassuring reply.

"Thanks, Martin. I feel terrible. You would have been great for this place," said Darlene. "We're closing next week, then I'm off to Portland for awhile."

"Portland, huh?" asked Martin absentmindedly.

"Yes! It's the tiny-house capital of the world. I'm looking forward to only taking care of myself and not picking up after a bunch of people."

"Well, good luck, Darlene," said Martin with as much enthusiasm as he could muster. "Stay in touch, huh? I really hope you enjoy your new place."

"I will, Martin. You take care of yourself, too. It's crazy how we met, and I wouldn't want our friendship to end just because we're both moving," she said with warm affection in her voice. "Oh, and if you want to visit here, the new owners are putting an online reservation system on the website. Technology, you know."

"Yeah, ok. Thanks," was about all that Martin could mumble as Darlene said goodbye and hung up.

"Damn," said Martin to himself and his empty house. He'd finally made a solid, concrete plan and had it dashed by his obsessive need to plan everything to the nth degree before taking action. There'd be no bed & breakfast in his future. Now his only hopes were tied to Talbot's decision of whether to allow his star junior salesman out of his sight by about three thousand miles.

Martin hung up the phone and dropped it on the couch. The quiet of his house was deafening. If only there were a woman to bring some life to his place, he thought. If only Rosita were here…

45.

Early the next morning, Mr. Talbot summoned Martin to his office for a chat.

"Sit down, Martin," said Talbot, as he graciously swept his hand across an empty chair. "Make yourself comfortable."

As instructed, Martin dropped a bit too heavily on the chair, wondering if he was about to get fired.

"You've done a really good job for us in a short time, Martin. I wanted to put that on the table first," said Talbot. "So I want to give you some leeway with this move you asked about."

Martin gave a funny little smile, at least happy that he still had a job, or so it seemed.

"Now moving across the country is a big deal," continued Talbot. "I've been able to keep an eye on you here and help out with certain accounts."

Unable to deny the fact, Martin simply nodded seriously in agreement.

"Personally, I couldn't care any less where you live as long as you get the job done," Talbot said casually, as if trying to show Martin he was one of the guys. "But there's not much oversight in the LA office for sales yet. You get out there and need help, none of those pretty boys are coming to the rescue. They're too busy with their chai lattes, their kombucha, their gluten-free everything, and their spin yoga strength classes to work like we do here on the east coast. You get what I'm saying?"

Indeed Martin had zero idea what Talbot was saying. He'd worked a number of times with the west coast crew, and they seemed way more relaxed but equally as talented as the people in his current office. Martin wondered if this was just a case of some aging dinosaur trying to carve out another step on the corporate ladder just to keep himself relevant. In any event, Talbot held the key to Martin leaving New Jersey (at least if he still wanted a job), so he nodded in return and managed an "Umm hmmm."

"So let's do this. Let's you and I fly out to LA next week, and we can meet with the team. Run it by them, so to speak," said Talbot, with just a bit of condescension in his voice, "If they can convince me that you'll be supported and we can keep our numbers up, then you'll have my blessing."

Martin couldn't figure out if Talbot really wanted to shore up his west coast support or if the gray, cold, and slushy New Jersey winter was chasing him out west for a few days of warm sunshine. Either way, Martin realized the trip was a formality that he was unlikely to escape. While Talbot had been a good boss, the two men never spoke of anything but work. Martin doubted that the man knew anything about his life and probably would never care to. What would they talk about for six hours on a transcontinental flight? Martin shuddered at the thought. Perhaps Talbot was a heavy sleeper? Maybe he'd pop out his business-class pillow and blanket and sleep the entire flight away? Martin sure hoped so.

"Let's head out Monday. We can get a couple of days in and fly back on Thursday," offered Talbot as a further wrench in Martin's mental works. Now the entire trip would take place during the work week. If Martin had any plans to stop over in New Mexico (as he always did), they would have to wait. He imagined a scenario where he purposely arrived at LAX just as the airplane door was closing, the gate agent forbidding him to get on. He'd desperately text Talbot and tell him he would either catch the next flight or, better yet, spend the next couple of days on account calls and then fly back over the weekend. Of course, the friendly LAX gate agent could give Martin one of those "don't tell anybody I did this" looks and actually let him on the plane. Even in a post 9/11 world, it could happen. That would be a disaster, Martin decided.

Maybe he should just forget New Mexico on this trip and do what he was expected to for a change? After all, he knew that in his past and Rosita's future (March 31, 1878, to be precise) he'd be re-meeting Rosita anyway. His entire effort over the past few months had been focused on meeting Martin Jr. While that hadn't (yet) worked out, the time slips into his meetings with Billy and Rosita were an unanticipated bonus. Selfishly Martin wanted more time with Rosita and Billy. Even though he knew the March 31 meeting would take place, he also knew that it had already happened for him and wouldn't happen again. If he didn't get back to Lincoln, he might never see Rosita or Billy again.

Billy...

Somehow the boy had used Martin's book to cheat death at the hand of Pat Garrett in 1881, but how did he do it? There had been stories about pretenders who claimed to be Billy long after his death. Most of the time, the imposter had either made a secret deal with Garrett or had a wild shootout and barely escaped with his life. Of course now that Martin had certainly altered the course of history, the real Billy the Kid did in fact lead a long life over in Magdalena. Since all the history books still showed Garrett living until 1908, when someone put two slugs in him while he was pissing on the side of the road near Las Cruces, Martin was sure that Billy definitely didn't kill the man. So, he wondered, how did Billy get away?

Martin decided there was too much left unanswered to miss out on a chance to see his friends again, so he swung for the fences.

"Sounds good. I'll book it," said Martin in his most businesslike manner. "Oh, hey, you know what, Mr. Talbot?"

Talbot gave him an inquisitive bob of the head from behind his massive desk.

"My ex-wife lives in Albuquerque," said Martin carefully. "There are still some papers and things to sort through. I think I'll fly out there on Saturday, and I can meet you in LA on Monday. Sound ok?"

Martin noticed that Talbot was studying him carefully. He wondered if the man was some sort of human lie detector. It seemed like Talbot wanted to say something but wasn't sure if Martin was the guy to say it to. Finally Talbot leaned in and motioned Martin forward with a wave of two fingers.

"You've got an ex-wife, Martin?" asked Talbot in a low, secretive voice.

"Yes, Sir. We've been divorced for about a year now," answered Martin truthfully.

"One? Those are rookie numbers! Hell, Martin, I've got four!" roared Talbot more loudly than Martin would have expected. Talbot's body jiggled as if he couldn't contain his laughter and delight that he and his charge were part of the same club. Martin nodded warily and rose to leave, realizing that he never got the ok from his boss.

"Do what you gotta do, Teebs. I'll see you in LaLaLand on Monday," said the now jovial man "Oh, and hey, Martin?"

Martin stopped, wondering what else the man could possibly want to share with him?

"You know why divorce is so expensive?" said Talbot in a way that Martin knew was a set up for a joke. "Because it's worth it!" Martin's boss again roared to himself at the pun and waved Martin off while he dabbed a laugh-induced tear or two from his eyes.

Making his way back to his cubicle, Martin noticed that Colin's desk was empty. With COVID case counts running like a rollercoaster, you never knew from one week till the next what New Jersey's governor would do. Colin was probably working at home in reaction to the latest spike in cases. Glancing out of the window at the sludgy sky, Martin longed for the coming days in April when he and Colin could get together to watch the NFL draft and dream of another Giants Super Bowl. April, he thought, would he even still be here in New Jersey? It seemed likely. He'd have to sell the house and pick out a place to live. He didn't imagine so many changes could happen in just a couple of months. Then Martin remembered his very first visit to Lincoln on the two free tickets he'd won from the company. In literally fifteen minutes, his entire world had changed. He went from bland, boring everyman to Martin Teebs, murderer of lawmen. If that didn't prove life could turn on a dime, then nothing would.

Martin settled into his chair and booked himself a flight to Albuquerque on Friday. He figured by then he'd be working from home anyway and what Talbot didn't know wouldn't hurt him. Besides, an extra day in New Mexico might offer one extra chance to visit his friends in 1878.

As he was about to email Darlene to reserve a room, he remembered that the new owners would have an online reservation system. Figuring he'd check to be sure, he logged onto the B&B's website; and sure enough, right there on the main page, were the calendar and the "Book Now!" button. Martin navigated to the days he wanted to stay and clicked the cheery yellow button. The price tag for his three-night stay shocked him more than a little. It was almost twice what he'd paid in the past. While he realized that Dallas and Darlene offered a bargain when it came to rates, he didn't know some corporate scumbags would come in and try to roll him for almost double. Oh, well, he thought, this would have to be his last stay there. Unsure if he had any other purpose in the past beyond what he'd already done, Martin knew if he did, he'd need to find a cheaper lodging option!

With his trip booked, Martin looked longingly at the clock and wished it somehow would turn enough times so that it could be Friday already.

46.

The unadorned road sign simply said "Capitan" as Martin pushed his foot more firmly on the gas pedal. Not about to stop and invite that weirdo Steve to accost him again, Martin had gassed up the car and laid in some snacks in Carrizozo an hour earlier. All seemed peaceful in the small town on this rather mild February evening. Nearing the margin of town, Martin set his sights on Lincoln and hoped he might see the sunrise from the bed of Rosita Luna. The happy, gauzy thought floated through his brain, distracting him from the twisty road ahead. At the last moment, in the darkness, he saw a vehicle broken down on the side of the road and a man waving his arms for help. Martin slammed on the brakes and jerked the wheel to the left, his heart pounding at the near miss. Just as he reached to lower the passenger side window, he noticed the tall stature and giant white cowboy hat. This was no mere man on the road, this was Steve. Their eyes met as Martin rolled slowly past. Steve's too friendly smile and Martin's icy glare. Satisfied that the man was close enough to town that someone else would help him, Martin pushed down on the gas pedal to make his escape.

"Martin! Wait! We need to talk," yelled Steve, to no avail as he watched the taillights recede into the darkness.

Rather than wait for someone else to come by, Steve started walking towards the lights of his small town. As he did, he mumbled to himself, "Ok, then, if not now, we'll do it later." Steve laughed to himself that if Martin only knew what he wanted to discuss, he'd have turned that car around right now and raced back to Capitan as fast as it would go.

47.

"Martin!" said Darlene warmly. She had been waiting for him on the porch, knowing he was going to arrive late. The closing on the B&B had taken place earlier that day, and Darlene had agreed to mind the store until Sunday, when she'd be taking off for Portland. Thinking this was the last chance she'd have for awhile to see her friend, she grabbed the big man and gave him a bear hug.

"Whoa!" said Martin, surprised by the ferocity that Darlene possessed. "That's some hug!"

Darlene released Martin and stepped back to view him in the porchlight.

"I'm glad you're here, Martin," she said. "I'll be out of here on Sunday, and there's no better guest to spend the last couple of nights with than you."

Normally Martin would be suspicious of the "spend the last couple of nights with" coming from Darlene, but after their post-kiss talk, he knew that she meant it platonically. He had to admit that if this was his final stay at the B&B, there was no one he'd rather have as his hostess than Darlene.

"Agreed, Darlene. Big changes coming for both of us, huh?" he said.

"Tell me about it. The closing was this morning. By Monday my share of the money will be in my bank account, and by Monday night I should be in Portland," said Darlene with a mix of excitement and sadness.

"Yeah. This is probably my last stay here too," said Martin. "I guess you saw the rate increase? I would need a second mortgage to rent a room here anymore."

"I'm sorry about that, Martin. I just can't believe that enough people will come here and pay those rates, but, hey, maybe I'm wrong," Darlene surmised. "If I had raised my rates like that, maybe I wouldn't have had to sell the place."

Darlene looked around wistfully at all she'd be leaving behind. Martin didn't want to interrupt her mental inventory, so he just stood there, waiting for her to speak again.

"Well, onward for both of us then!" she finally said. "New sights, new adventures, and new people."

"Indeed, Darlene," said Martin reassuringly.

"Ok, your casita is ready. You know the drill. I need to pack a few more things, so let me know if you need anything," said a suddenly enthusiastic Darlene. She reached in to give Martin another hug and a very non-sexual kiss on the neck. Releasing the big man, she bounded back into the main house, leaving Martin to find his way on his own.

Entering his casita, he noticed that little had changed. If the new owners were going to raise their rates, it didn't seem like they had any thought of upgrading the scenery. That thought warmed Martin, at least for a few moments. This had always been his home base for his inadvertent travels back and forth in time. He wondered if the place itself, the former home of Lincoln notable Juan Patron, was an irreplaceable component of his forays back to the 1800s? Martin took an inventory of the pieces of his time-travel puzzle. Certainly Bachaca's book had played a part in it. The Patron House could be another. Martin's frequent clumsy mishaps seemed to spark most, but not all, of his journeys. Then he remembered Steve. That day on the steps of the Murphy store, Steve was the last modern-day person he saw before Tunstall showed up to advertise his end-of-the-season clothing sale. Every time Martin had run into Steve, he got creeped out by the feeling that the man was hiding something. What was the endgame? Was Steve a time traveler from the past, coming to lead Martin back? Was he somehow in the know about Martin's exploits in both past and present? Maybe he was some sort of spirit guide, Martin thought. Or a shaman coming to guide Martin irrevocably through the keyhole of time so that he could leave the 21st century behind for good.

Finally Martin had enough mental gymnastics on the subject. He decided that Steve was just a creepy cowboy that enjoyed tormenting Billy the Kid afficionados who came through his town. If it wasn't Martin, it would have been some other suburban nobody with a bookcase full of Lincoln County War tomes and a late night penchant for ice cream.

Reaching to unpack his bag, Martin carefully removed the tiny *Lincoln County Days* book. He'd made no progress in identifying the author on his previous trip, and he intended to close that loop this time. If he could find and talk to the author, maybe he could understand what was written on those final missing pages. Somehow Martin felt that whatever was contained on those pages also foretold his destiny. Pulling out his period-correct kit, he wondered about heading out into town right now. Sure he was tired, but the chance to see Rosita pulled strongly at him. Unlike other times, he hadn't left her with no explanation this go-round. He assumed that there would be no icy stare or long warm-up period and that they could get right back to their burgeoning relationship. He ached to lie by her side in bed and, this time, not fall asleep on her. Martin checked himself and decided that, while he was most certainly tired, the risk was worth the reward. If he was able to get back in time on this evening, he'd dunk his damn head in the icy Bonito to keep himself awake.

As he dressed, Martin began to wonder. When he saw Rosita only a couple of months after they had first made love, her belly was already showing. He had assumed at the time that it was their first experience being intimate, but there was no way for him to know. Would a woman's pregnancy show after only two months? Martin was woefully uninformed about such matters, given that he and Lilly had stopped trying for kids. Was it possible that Martin and Rosita were in the throes of passion sooner...as in, right now? Five or six months after conception seemed like a more likely scenario to Martin for Rosita's pregnancy to be available for the world to see.

"Wow," he muttered aloud. He had just assumed that night by the tree, after the five-day battle, was when Martin Jr. was conceived, but now he was faced with the possibility that he would get the chance to change history much sooner than expected. He remembered how easily Rosita allowed him to make love to her that night. At first he had thought foolishly that it was because they were meant to be. Now he realized that it was most likely because they had already done the deed. They weren't strangers (in the biblical sense), and so there needed to be no formality between them. Having been faced with the prospect of some very blue balls until July, Martin suddenly realized that he was going to sample the delights of Rosita Luna much sooner than anticipated.

He hitched up his suspenders and slipped on his coat as he headed for the door. Remembering the book, he stepped back and gently placed it in his pocket. Having it, he figured, would give him a better chance of confronting whoever wrote it, providing he could find him.

Alive with the possibilities of a night with Rosita, Martin had a bounce in his step as he left the casita. He didn't need any cold water to keep him awake, and he didn't anticipate any need for a cold shower later in the night either.

48.

Martin stepped onto the moonlit street as the evening chill began to take root. He had an easy confidence about him on this night. Usually he fretted as he walked to and fro, waiting for some mishap to dislodge him from his current time. This time, however, he felt the strong pull of 140 years upon him and knew with certainty he'd be heading back there. The street was quiet save for a slight breeze rustling the bare branches of trees. Martin closed his eyes and took an enormous breath of mountain air into his lungs. Releasing it, he opened his eyes, to be greeted by the same modern touches he'd seen only seconds ago. Undeterred, he repeated the process, and this time the smells of old Lincoln permeated his nostrils. Without even opening his eyes, he knew it. He was home.

With his eyes still closed, Martin began the walk towards Rosita's house. As they opened, all of old Lincoln was bestowed upon them. As much bloodshed as this tiny town had seen, and as much as was yet to happen, Martin felt at peace here, unlike anywhere else he'd ever known. If he could dodge a bullet...or twelve...and not make too many enemies, Lincoln seemed like a perfectly fine place to live out the rest of his life.

Martin could barely see the Tunstall store in the distance as he neared Rosita's portal. While the town was mostly quiet, save for some rowdies kicking up dust in the cantina, he did notice a large number of horses tethered outside the store. Rosita's house was completely dark inside, with not even a candle illuminating the interior. While Martin had no idea what time it was, he assumed it would be close to when he left the present behind, about 9 pm. He had a moment of panic: what if Rosita was out on the town? Or maybe she had another boyfriend since Martin couldn't seem to stick around for more than a day or two at a time? He felt a sinking sensation in the pit of his stomach, imagining himself walking into the Wortley, only to find her hand-in-hand, sipping champagne with another man. Worse yet, as he heard the hoots and hollers coming from the cantina, he envisioned her dancing on the bar in some *Coyote Ugly* pose while pouring shots of whiskey into the waiting mouths of whatever cowboys thought they had a chance of getting lucky with her. For a moment, he asked himself if he could handle such a situation. In his mind Rosita had been created only for him. Two perfect matches in an imperfect world. The thoughts of some dirty cowboy roughly yanking his gun belt off to penetrate her and of her actually liking it made him sick. Literally sick. Sick to his stomach.

With half a mind to close his eyes and leave the past, Martin got hold of his emotions. "Stop making things up!" he scolded himself. Deep down he knew that he and Rosita were soulmates. No Dolan-Come-Lately was going to walk in and change that. He stepped up onto the porch and knocked on Rosita's door. Getting no response, he wondered if perhaps he was right about her nightly activities. He knocked again, just a bit firmer this time.

"*Martin*? Is that you?" came the soft voice from the window.

"It's me, Rosita. Can I come in?" he answered, as he secretly sighed with deep relief that she was home.

The door flung open suddenly, missing Martin's nose by inches, and Rosita jumped into his arms. "*Martin*!" was all she could get out before locking her lips to his as they stood swaying in the doorway. Martin decided that her lips tasted like magic. The good kind of magic where everyone smiles at the end, not the black magic that made you feel creepy and dirty. After a few moments, she slid from his arms and pulled him inside the house, shutting and barring the door firmly behind them. Rosita padded to the kitchen and retrieved a candle to light the table as she scurried here and there, picking up things as if the house was somehow not neat enough for guests. Then she leaned over the table to light the candle. Martin slipped up behind her and hugged her tightly as she stood up. The room softly came alive as the flame's light danced upon her hair. Martin pulled her close to him, feeling the form of her body under the cotton nightshirt she wore. If a moment were ever created for total silence, this one was perfectly it. Rosita leaned back into her man, tossing her hair over his shoulders and grasping his hands firmly with her own. The two bodies stood there for what seemed like an hour, swaying to some music they could only hear in their minds, while the candle danced shadows around the room and back.

"It is so good to be here with you again," whispered Martin into her ear.

Rosita breathed deeply before responding. "I am happy, *Martin*. I expected you would come back with the trouble at the store. I'm so happy you came to me."

Martin had no illusions about what he was walking into when visiting old Lincoln during this time. He knew that Brady and Dolan would conspire with the courts to attach Alexander McSween's property to satisfy the proceeds from a ten thousand dollar insurance policy that he had settled for the estate of Emil Fritz. If Dolan and Murphy knew that McSween was not a financial partner in Tunstall's businesses, they didn't let it stop them from acting as if he was. Brady took possession of the store and its contents to the tune of some forty thousand dollars' worth of merchandise. McSween was floored by the audacity of the town's sheriff and his collusion with the enemy. Tunstall was more pragmatic, however. He knew that given his day in court, he would win and probably with damages to boot. He had enough of a supply of family money coming from England that he could withstand the barrage until the spring term of the district court convened. While angered at Dolan's clear overreach and Brady's complicity, he assured McSween that all would be well in the end.

"I heard about Brady taking the store. I'm not sure what Mr. Tunstall will want us to do, but it's better if I'm here and he needs me," replied Martin in a way more confident voice than he should have.

"I keep the lights out at night so no one comes here. So many of those men from Dolan are in town now. No one can even walk the streets and feel safe," reported Rosita.

Martin continued to hold her tightly. In his mind she was safe now, and he wanted her to know it. "I'm here now. We're going to be fine. Everything is going to be fine now," he lied to her. Telling her that Tunstall would be dead soon and Lincoln would become a war zone wasn't likely to make her feel better, nor would it change the last moments of peace the two lovers would feel for months.

Rosita let out a satisfied breath and said, "I know, *Martin*. I always feel safe with you." She leaned back harder into him, practically melting into his arms.

Suddenly wondering what day it was, he asked, "What is today's date, Rosita?"

Rosita snorted a little laugh and replied, "*Si, Martin*, for me, too. When we're together, I lose track of time." Martin appreciated the heartfelt notion, but he really did need to know what the date was. He decided a different approach was in order.

"Is it the 16th or 17th? I've been out working and lost track," he asked again.

Apparently amused by his obsession with the date, Rosita chuckled a bit but answered, "It is 16 *Febrero*. Do you have someplace you must be?" For a moment Martin took her statement as an accusation, but her warm smile let him know she was merely toying with him.

"I do, I do," he said in his most businesslike manner, "I have to meet a beautiful woman tomorrow. She is known as the Belle of Lincoln."

Rosita blushed a little but decided to play along, "Is this so, Senor Teebs? Who is this woman? I may have to have a word with her."

"Well, I don't want to start any trouble, you understand," teased Martin, "it's just that I belong to her, and she to me."

Rosita's eyes stabbed with a tear of joy upon hearing this. She quickly regained her composure to finish the game, wondering what other sentiments Martin would admit to? "So you belong together, *si*? Perhaps I should be the judge of that, *Martin*?"

Martin looked deeply into Rosita's eyes. If they were the ocean, he would gladly plunge in and drown in them, letting his body drift dreamily to the sea floor, he thought. She currently had the tiniest of smirks on her face, which he regarded as the height of cuteness, and all he could think about in that moment was making this woman happy for every day remaining to him on this earth.

"It doesn't matter who judges, we're made for each other," he said softly, wondering if he was even continuing the game, "I love her…I love you, Rosita."

If her eyes could somehow open even wider to draw him in, they would have in that moment. Every day of her adult life, Rosita had dreamed of hearing those words…not from just anyone, but from someone she felt the same way about. There were days when she wondered if it would ever happen…or if she should just give in and settle for one of the very ordinary men who existed within and without Lincoln County? Each time she wavered, she deeply examined a feeling in what she could only consider her soul that told her, "Wait…he'll be here." And now here he was, saying the words that played like a symphony in her ears.

Pretense dropped, Rosita gushed *"Te amo, Martin! Te amo."* Martin's rudimentary Spanish, and his recollection of Maria Elena telling Buddy the same in *The Buddy Holly Story*, gave him enough confidence to know that Rosita felt the same way as he did. Again the two lovers rushed into each other's arms and sought solace from the trouble brewing right outside of their door.

Rosita removed Martin's coat, placing it on a peg near the door, and pulled him by the hand towards the bed. "Come, *Martin*, let us get into bed," she said softly, but with a power that Martin could not ignore. "Our future starts now, my love."

His world spinning, Martin did not resist. You never get a second "first time" with someone in life, yet here he was, about to have another "first time" with Rosita. His breath, once he could breathe again, came in rapid bursts. He slowly unbuttoned his shirt as Rosita lifted her nightshirt revealing her all to him. Try as he might, he could not take his eyes off of her, nor could he swallow the lump in his throat that was preventing him from breathing. If he had commissioned a sculptor to fashion the perfect woman to his specifications, the result could not even compare to the perfection before his eyes. He slowly reached out his hand to touch her, as if to prove to himself that she was real. Before he could reach her, she leaned into him, his hand landing on one of her large and very firm breasts. Not to be outdone, Rosita removed Martin's shirt and then began to release his belt and pants. For the first time, his gluten intolerance proved to be a blessing since he looked far more fit than the Martin Teebs that was going to show up in Lincoln in a couple of months or so.

Both now naked, Rosita helped Martin scoot back on the bed so she could straddle him. Electricity pulsed through his veins at the very thought of the lovemaking to come. Rosita was not shy, smiling directly at Martin while rubbing his chest. She worked her body back and forth against his, feeling his excitement grow with each movement.

"You say nothing, *Martin*?" she asked coyly, "are you not pleased?" Rosita traced her fingers around her breasts and then lightly touched them to Martin's lips.

He swallowed hard before finally being able to answer, "I'm speechless." His eyes wide and his body aching to connect with hers, he pulled her shoulders closer to his and kissed her deeply. Knowing that the moment was about to arrive, Rosita gently kissed his ear and whispered, "for my first time, I could not wish for better than this, my love."

49.

"Teebs! Teebsie! You in there?" The voice came with a sharp rap on the door just as the sun was coming up the next morning. It was Billy.

Martin struggled to open his eyes in the early morning light that flooded Rosita's house. His left arm was currently trapped underneath Rosita, who showed no intention of moving to let him get up. "*Martin*, tell them to go away for now," she said sleepily, "and you join them later."

Knowing that Billy wouldn't come calling unless it was important, he stuffed himself into his pants and shirt and cracked the door open. He was greeted by the buck-toothed familiar smile that would define Billy for the rest of his life. "I heard you was back, Teebsie. G'mornin," declared Billy, as he moved his head back and forth, trying to see if he could get a look at Rosita.

Yawning mightily after a long night, Martin wondered what prompted the early morning visit. "Morning, Billy. It's kind of early. What's up?"

"What's up is we need help at the ranch. This Dolan and Brady shit is spinning out. Pretty soon they'll take the entire county to pay Alex's debt," said Billy, with as much calm as he could manage.

"I heard about the store," replied Martin. "What are they after now?"

"What in the hell ain't they after? Brady's coming for John's cows. They ain't belonging to Alex! This is some bullshit. We're gonna drive em off to a spot that Dick knows so they can't find em. Need ya to help."

Billy stood on his tip toes, trying to see over Martin's shoulder. "Rosita in there? I might could say hello, you know?" said Billy, with a smile and a wink.

"Hey! Enough. She's sleeping," Martin shot back. Billy let out a slightly sinister cackle and responded, "Ok, Teebsie, get dressed and come on. We got a ride in front of us. I got you a roan saddled up."

Not that Martin knew what a roan was, but at least he knew Billy had saddled one for him. He felt guilt tugging at him. He desperately wanted to stay with Rosita but knew he owed Tunstall money that needed to be worked off. He also owed Billy friendship, and when your pards call you, it's time to go. The best he could come up with was a negotiation, "Give me a half hour, ok? I need to wake up and eat something before we get on the road."

"Alright, lover boy. You go ahead and 'eat something,' and I'll be at the Ellis store when you're ready," said Billy through his laughter. Martin turned to go and closed the door. Just before it latched, Billy looked at him in a deadly serious fashion and spoke, "Don't drop out, Teebsie. This is serious stuff today. Life and death stuff. Let's make sure we're on the life side."

Martin nodded seriously as he shut and latched the door. Rosita looked at him with concern in her big brown eyes. Seeing her with a blanket wrapped loosely around her shoulders and her breasts peeking out, Martin was tempted to forget his responsibility to Tunstall and let Billy and the Regulators handle the issue without him. Sighing heavily, he knew he couldn't do that to men that were counting on him. Rosita beckoned him back to the bed, and as Martin slipped in, he noticed blood on the sheets. "Oh, no, are you ok?" he stammered.

She smiled back at him, taking him into her arms before saying, "Si, Martin, this is what happens the first time. Don't you know?" Rosita buried her face in his neck, kissing around the back of his hairline. Martin's eyes were wide. For some reason, he had thought Rosita was kidding when she mentioned her "first time" last night. He figured it was one of those things a woman says to make a man feel special, or to make it more exciting to him. If Martin was honest with himself, had he gotten any more excited about their lovemaking, his head would probably have exploded then and there.

Rosita had been a virgin.

As far as Martin knew, he'd never been with a virgin before. Lilly certainly had been more sexually experienced than he was when they met in college, and the two other girls he slept with later in high school seemed unimpressed with his prowess. Somehow he remembered hearing or reading about the emotional attachment a woman forms with her first lover. It wasn't anything Martin feared, but it seemed like a great responsibility. He didn't speak for fear of saying the wrong thing.

"I told you, *Martin*, I would wait for the perfect man before I gave myself to him…to you," she said softly.

Still mute, Martin was unsure if a thank you was in order. He simply wasn't equipped for the conversation and waited, hoping Rosita would speak again.

"For you, it's not the first time, *si*?" she asked as if she already knew the answer.

"Ummm, no?" said Martin carefully and then lied to her. "But there was only one other, and that was years ago."

Rosita had not expected that this man could have gone his entire adult life without the company of a woman. That there was only one other pleased her, and she vowed to make his lifetime total of women slept with stop at its current number, two. "That was then, and here we are now, *Martin*," she said through a happy smile, "we are only for each other, yes?" Rosita's hopeful eyes implored Martin to voice his commitment to her, which he gladly did.

"I never want to be with another woman as long as I live, Rosita. Only you. I love you."

Rosita's happiness at hearing his words swept over her like a warm bath. She playfully pushed him down on the bed. Martin raised himself up on one arm to get a better look at her, but she firmly put him flat on his back. Quickly climbing on top of him, she made sure he had something to remember her by on his long ride to the Tunstall ranch.

50.

Billy and Martin picked their way along the trail to the Feliz ranch sometime near noon. "You made me wait, Teebsie, I hate to wait," exclaimed Billy. Indeed Martin had made Billy wait an extra 30 minutes, which was the time it took for him to pull himself from Rosita's bed and get dressed.

"Yeah, sorry about that. It's just…you know…forget it," came the insufficient reply from Martin.

Billy got a good laugh from the older man's discomfort. "I know what you mean. Might not know to look, but I shake the sheets a fair amount myself," boasted the young man.

Martin looked over at his complicated friend. Had he not intervened in Billy's future, this boy would be dead in a few years, or at least that's what the consensus of historians agreed upon. As Martin remembered his trip to Magdalena when he saw this boy as an old man, he wondered: did the extra time give Billy any better of a life? Was it better to die a sobbing, bitter old man rather than going out in a blaze of glory? Martin thought back to the dozens (if not hundreds) of books that he had read about Billy. He was portrayed as many ways as there are grains of sand on the beach. Killer, outlaw, punk, avenger, Robin Hood, romantic, comedian, songster, dancer, and more. Who was Billy the Kid though, Martin questioned?

If someone in the present day ever asked him, he figured he'd answer something like this: Billy the Kid was a pretty ordinary outlaw and cowhand. He was a lighthearted, respectful young man…until it was time to not be those things. He killed without a second thought but was not a wanton murderer. Billy had justification (at least in his own mind) for every person he killed. He was living in a time far removed from Martin's, and the prospect of looking at him from a 21st century perspective was ridiculous and foolhardy. No one in 2021 could possibly understand how Billy, Dolan, and the rest lived. They had never faced a land so lawless and remote that you handed out your own justice, and then either made a run for the border or sat in jail hoping the courts would see things your way. Billy was a fine young man, but so then were Charlie and Doc, and the rest of the Regulators. Truth be told, Dolan's boys were no worse than Tunstall's. It just so happened that they were fighting for the enemy on this day.

Teebs wondered what would have become of Billy if he'd been born in Martin's time? There seemed nothing remarkable about the boy that would suggest he'd have been a tech industry leader or a member of Seal Team 6. With Billy's bravery and propensity for fighting, an enlistment in the armed forces would probably have been a good move. Martin imagined that, upon being discharged, Billy would become some sort of tradesman, settling down with a wife and a couple of kids of his own. He assumed Billy would lead a pretty unspectacular life in some suburb of Chicago and bundle up the family to see da Bears play a couple of times a year in Soldier Field.

Martin's daydreaming was cut short when Billy interrupted, "Teebs, where you really from?"

Martin froze in the saddle for a moment, unsure of what the Kid was asking and how he should answer.

"I'm from New Jersey, Billy. You already know that," he answered as nonchalantly as he could.

Billy straightened up in the saddle with his crooked grin. "You know that ain't what I'm asking." The boy stared at Martin with a challenging smile. Martin's heart was beating fast in his chest. Not Rosita fast, but probably faster than it should given the circumstances. He tried to play off Billy's question.

"Ha. I don't know what you're talking about, Billy," which came off much more formally than he wanted it to.

Billy swung his head from his left shoulder to his right so it would be nearer to Martin. He spoke quietly, as if someone might hear them, "You ain't from around here. You don't belong here. I can see it. Hell, everybody can. You ain't just from New Jersey, Teebsie, you're from some other…place."

Martin nervously laughed and shook his head. He guided his horse to the edge of the trail to relieve the crowding that Billy was imposing upon him.

"Listen, I don't care," Billy continued, "I like you. Most of them fellers treat me like a kid. You's the only one who talks with me level, you know?"

Martin glanced over at Billy's face long enough to nod his assent before looking up the trail.

"I'm glad you carved yourself out a little life here, Teebsie," said a smiling Billy. "Got yourself the prettiest girl in Lincoln, got yourself a job with John, and got you a friend in me." Billy's declaration of friendship hit Martin hard, almost as hard as Rosita's declaration of love.

"I really appreciate that, Billy. Truly. I don't have that many friends, and to count you as one of them is pretty special to me." Martin spoke with a sincerity that Billy hadn't heard from the man before. "Now as far as where I'm from," Martin continued, "I'd love to explain it, but I'm not even sure I can make sense of it. Give me some time, and if I can figure it out, then I'll be happy to share with you, ok?"

Billy looked over, his head nodding in acceptance. There was still one more question the boy needed answered. "When you drove that wagon into the ditch, you was there, and then you was gone. Nobody else seen it cause they was chasing the team. By the time they came back, they asked where you was. I just told em you run off, thinking you was gonna get fired. What in the hell happened that day?"

Every bit of energy drained from Martin's body. How could he possibly explain that he was traveling through time from 140 years in the future to this 19th century kid? His shoulders slumped and his head dropped with the weight of Billy's question. He didn't want to lie to the boy, but the truth didn't seem a good option either. Finally he offered, "I'm different, Billy. Always have been. I don't even know what's happening to me, so I sure can't expect you to. I want to stay here. With Rosita, with you. I'm not sure if I can, but I sure as hell want to."

Billy looked at Martin sadly, as if looking at a man with a terminal illness. He hadn't wanted to make his friend sad with his questions. Sensing he might be able to rescue the moment, Billy piped in, "Don't worry bout it none, Teebsie. We all got our problems. For what it's worth, I hope you can stay too. Least then maybe I can teach you how to shoot!" With that, Billy slapped Martin's roan on the rump, causing the horse to run, and the Kid whooped and hollered all the way to the ranch to catch him.

51.

By the time Martin and Billy arrived at the ranch, a full-on parlay was taking place. Tunstall and Dick Brewer were deep in conversation about how to proceed. Brewer favored driving the cattle off the ranch into Tegusa Canyon that very evening. He knew that Brady's posse was coming to attach the cattle and anything else they found at the ranch. With Dolan pulling the strings, Brady had become nothing but a puppet of The House's wishes. Tunstall worried that the men would be chased and if so, that shooting might break out. To this point the conflict, while heated and emotional, had not spilled any blood. Tunstall intended to keep it that way until the district court could convene and hand him a victory.

With the sun setting, someone stoked a large campfire to warm the men. Tunstall counted his chances and decided that a showdown on the Feliz would be disastrous to his men and his interests. Word was sent to Brady's posse that the attachment of Tunstall's cattle would not be contested and that only Godfrey Gauss would be at the ranch. Brewer wasn't happy with the decision. Running his own ranch just outside of Lincoln, he knew that if Dolan were empowered to do as he pleased, he wouldn't stop until he ran everyone but himself out of business. Nevertheless, the decision wasn't his to make, so he and Tunstall decided on the plan for February 18, 1878. The date that would mark John Henry Tunstall's final day on earth.

52.

Martin tossed and turned on the hard bunk for what seemed like an eternity. Knowing full well what would transpire the next day, he wished only to be in the soft, warm bed of Rosita Luna and not the rock-hard bunk in Tunstall's bunkhouse. The night was punctuated by a loud chorus of snores, belches, farts, and someone calling in his dream for a Miss Ruby. If Martin slept ten minutes overnight, that was a lot. As the sun began to color the winter sky, he stirred and swung his legs over the bunk, putting his boots on.

"Now look who's up and at em early?" groaned Billy as he stiffly sat up, trying to stretch his back. The other men slowly came to life to the smell of breakfast being cooked by Gauss. The plan as Tunstall described it, and history confirmed, was to leave the cattle behind and drive the only other stock, nine horses, to be put up in Lincoln until he could regain control of his store. The men wanted to be on the road early to avoid the posse's arrival and to gain Lincoln before dark. Martin was filled with a sense of dread, knowing the ride would be the Englishman's last. Saddling up, the men were on the road just after sunrise. Billy had passed his Winchester to Martin in the event a fight broke out. While he didn't expect much from the big man, if he hit his quota of two out of ten posse members, it would be enough for Billy and company to finish off the rest of them.

The men drove on throughout the day, with Brewer and Rob Widenmann riding point. Tunstall stayed with the horses, and Billy, Martin, and a ferocious specimen named John Middleton were at the rear. Martin tried to divorce his mind from the impending final act of Tunstall life, so he and Billy joked as they picked their way through the trail. Their conversation so irritated Middleton that he growled, "Damn buncha washwomen back here!" and rode up towards Tunstall.

Finally alone, Martin again asked his own morality if he should somehow intervene? Perhaps Billy wouldn't think him insane to proclaim that he knew what would happen, but the others surely would. How could he just sit here and watch his boss be murdered? wondered Martin. Only then did he begin to realize the dilemma that Billy would face in the near future when he found Sergio Bachaca's book. As hard as it was to sit and watch your friends die, you don't risk making things worse by trying to change their destiny. He looked over at Billy, who was whistling his "Wagon Wheel"

PAGE 193

song, with a different understanding. The old man Martin had met in Magdalena wasn't selfish, he was tormented. He had watched Bowdre, McSween, Folliard, and more die, and he could have stopped every single one. Or could he? Just like Martin now, Billy must have known that, as distasteful as these events were, they were necessary to fulfill everyone's destiny.

Martin had another mission to complete on this day. He reached into his coat pocket and removed *Lincoln County Days*. "Hey, Billy. Do you know of a Juan Panchito Baca?"

"Dummy," replied Billy simply.

Martin was a little wounded at the name calling by his friend for asking only a simple question. "Why am I a dummy?" he demanded from the Kid.

"Not you dummy. His name's Dummy. He's a mongoloid or something. Works for Dolan. Don't talk, don't hear," said Billy.

Martin sensed that there must be another Juan Baca. A historian that couldn't hear or speak? How would he even know Martin's name?

"Are you sure? Maybe there's another Juan Baca somewhere in the county?" asked Martin.

"Might be, but there ain't one named Panchito. Dummy was named after Murphy's dog. Little chihuahua that would bark all damn day. It was kind of funny, that the dog never shut up and Dummy never talked. Ya get it?" replied Billy.

Now Martin was completely lost. A "mongoloid" (or in today's terms, a person with Down's Syndrome) that was deaf and mute surely couldn't have written the book, even as badly as this book had been written. If not Baca, then who? Who would go so far as to write a book under the pseudonym of a person who could never have written it? Martin scratched at his chin and shrugged his shoulders. The book had been found in the B&B. It definitely looked authentic. Everything that Martin had been able to decipher had definitely happened to him. Maybe the secret to its author was in those final missing pages. If so, the mystery would have to wait, as Martin had no time to find him and no idea where to start looking.

As the sun began to recede in the western sky, the party topped out at the crest of a mountain and began to slide down the gorge towards the Ruidoso. In the gloaming, Brewer and Widenmann startled a small flock of wild turkeys. The two men lit out after them, guns drawn, imagining a delicious hot supper. Well in the distance, Martin and Billy continued to talk as the killing hour drew near.

With what sounded like an approaching thunderstorm, the posse suddenly rattled over the crest behind the two men. Billy caught Martin's eye, and neither man needed any instruction on what to do. They galloped as hard as they could down the hill towards Tunstall and Middleton. Once within a hundred yards, Billy screamed, "Posse!" causing Tunstall to turn. Martin hung onto his saddle horn for dear life as he followed Billy up a small hill. They quickly dismounted and drew their weapons as the posse closed in on Middleton and Tunstall. With his arms, Middleton gestured wildly at Tunstall to ride quickly off the trail, but to no avail. Tunstall seemed utterly confused and unable to follow even the simplest command. Finally Martin could stand it no more, standing up and screaming down the hill, "Get the hell out there, John!" Martin's orders, although well meaning, served to distract Tunstall from following Middleton, who kept yelling for the Englishman to follow him. Tunstall's horse circled in the road as he shouted, "What, John? What, Martin?" Middleton glared up the hill at Martin as he once again screamed for Tunstall to follow him, until he could wait no more. He dashed up the hill, dismounted, and prepared for battle.

Tunstall was completely turned around and began to ride in the direction of the posse. From the meager cover the rocks provided, Billy, Martin, and Middleton could see Tunstall discussing something and pointing up the hill. Suddenly, three of the posse members rode Tunstall off the trail, and within seconds, a gunshot was heard. Then quickly two more.

"They killed him," said Billy, simply and almost devoid of emotion.

Middleton grunted and flared his nostrils. Martin thought the man might go down and single handedly destroy the posse, but instead he faced Martin directly. "What the hell were you thinking? Screaming like a goddamned school girl! He's dead because of you, shit for brains!"

Martin was incredulous at the indictment. He'd merely been trying to help Tunstall avoid his killers. Sure, his timing was off just as Middleton was trying to guide the Englishman away, but his intentions were good.

"Hack off, Middleton. He's just tryin to help is all," said Billy. Middleton's dark eyes glowered at both of them, but for some reason he thought the better of challenging Billy and began to make his way across the hillside to Brewer.

"I'm sorry, Billy. I only wanted to help," offered Martin apologetically.

"Teebsie, those boys came to kill John, and that's all there is to it. Doesn't matter what you did or didn't do. The only difference if we didn't git up here is they'd be digging a few more graves," said Billy, as casually as if announcing the local sports scores. Martin wondered if somehow the boy was in shock. While it was true that he had never seen Billy and Tunstall in any kind of deep conversation, they surely knew each other. Martin expected a bigger show of emotion, but none was forthcoming. Perhaps this was the side of Billy that many of the books showed to paint him a sociopath?

Night was falling quickly and the five Tunstall men held superior defensive positions, so the posse decided one dead Englishman and nine captured horses represented job done for the evening. They rode off to the ranch on the Feliz, while Martin and the boys made their way down the slippery canyon to break the news that John Henry Tunstall had been murdered and that the fuse that sparked the Lincoln County War had been lit.

53.

While the news of Tunstall's murder made it to Lincoln with his men, the furor over Brady and Dolan's continued harassment of someone the town felt was an upstanding citizen had been brewing all day. Scores of men had gathered at the McSween house, answering Tunstall's calls for soldiers from the day prior. Learning that he had been killed, the house erupted in anger. More than a few men attempted to head to the House of Murphy and burn it to the ground, but intervention by Brewer and McSween stopped them. An all-out war, without planning or leadership, would surely lead to the demise of many of these men swearing vengeance upon their common enemy.

Arrangements were made for someone to retrieve Tunstall's corpse the next day and return it to Lincoln. McSween thought that Tunstall's family in England might want his remains returned, but in any event, the body would be embalmed until his funeral arrangements had been determined.

Watching the scene in Lincoln play out just as he'd read in Sergio Bachaca's book gave Martin the chills. How could an author, or anyone really, know so much about what certain individuals did on a night over 140 years ago? Was it possible that "Serg" was somehow a time traveler too? No, he decided, he couldn't have been. If he were, he would have known about every single historical fact that Martin had now meddled in and changed forever. Still, hearing the words spoken that had heretofore only been written in his history books made him pause. Martin of course realized that much of what people in his time knew came from written testimony collected shortly after the event, but it was eerie to actually see it happening in front of his eyes.

The McSween house was not a welcoming place that evening, and less so for Martin since Middleton had arrived and surely blamed Tunstall's death squarely on him. Once their horses were put up, Martin cautiously walked down the street to Rosita's house. His caution was overkill on this night as the posse, which was nearly all of Brady and Dolan's men, was overnighting at the Tunstall ranch on the Feliz. As Martin approached her house, he saw Rosita standing in the doorway, her eyes filled with tears.

"*Martin*, are you ok, *mi amor*?" she sobbed as he walked up and held her. "I hear that Mr. Tunstall is dead?"

Martin lifted her chin and smiled at her, trying to offer some comfort. He breathed out heavily before speaking. "Tunstall is gone. He was murdered."

Rosita's face took on a look of anger. While no great friend of Tunstall, she had looked upon the man like most of Lincoln did, as someone coming to free its citizens from the financial shackles of the Murphy-Dolan monopoly.

"Those filthy Dolan pricks!" she spat, surprising Martin with her bitterness. He knew Rosita to be strong but had never before seen this level of anger. Martin had no idea what to do or say. He had just taken a front-row view of his employer's murder that he seemed powerless to stop. He was very happy to have Rosita back in his arms but sensed that this night would not be one of romance. He gently guided her inside and shut the door behind them.

"What will happen now?" she asked him, in a voice that portrayed her weariness with the violence in this place that she called home.

Martin knew full well what would happen now. The Regulators would capture and kill Morton, McCloskey, and Baker in the Blackwater Draw. Then, on March 31, an out-of-place, middle-aged man wearing a shirt with fireworks and cats on it would show up in Lincoln on the eve of the murder of Sheriff Brady. Then the town would descend into open warfare, culminating in the five-day battle.

Would any of this mean anything to Rosita? If he told her everything he knew would happen, would she run away with him? Maybe they could go to Texas or Arizona? They could start a life and be far from the killing that was headed their way. Martin considered this for a moment, and then the realization hit him: what if he took Rosita away, and then he disappeared back to the future? How could he abandon her in a place with no friends and no family? How could he be sure he could even get back to any place but Lincoln? He had little if any control over his travels, and the risk was too great. No, he thought, they must stay here. As dangerous as Lincoln was, it was still the safest place for Rosita.

"I don't know. Honestly. I'm sure there will be a trial. I think it was Jesse Evans and Bob Olinger that killed him. Put those guys in jail and move on with life?" was all Martin could offer. While he knew it would never happen, it sounded like a better alternative than the events that would begin in the next few days.

Rosita dabbed at her eyes with a cloth. Martin gently guided her to the foot of the bed and removed her shoes. She looked at him, wondering if he was putting her to bed or preparing for more of what they had done two nights ago. Emotionally exhausted, she decided that either one would be fine. Martin, however, wasn't thinking of sex on this night. He helped her out of her clothes and into her cotton night shirt. While he still silently marveled at her body, it wasn't the time or place to take advantage of it. Propping up two pillows, he helped her lie down and covered her with a warm woolen blanket.

"You take such good care of me," she said with a weary smile.

"It's my pleasure to do that…my honor," replied Martin, "and I want to do it for a long, long time." A flush of happiness spread over Rosita's face at the news.

"Come, *Martin*," she beckoned with her arms, "come lie with me. Let us forget the problems of Lincoln for one night at least."

Martin stripped down to the cleanest thing he had with him, which was his own skin. Rosita had a broad smile on her face watching him strip, and her eyes danced in amusement.

"Will you not get cold tonight?" she asked with a sly grin.

"No, my love. I won't. I have you to keep me warm," he said in return.

Martin cradled her in his arms as their eyes reveled in the heaviness that comes from being perfectly comfortable and secure in the place where you are about to sleep. Her head fell lightly on his chest as his eyes closed and the rest that had eluded him at the ranch showed up just in time. In any other time and any other place, they would just be two supremely happy lovers. They could be in a condo on Maui, at a lake house in Texas, or a hotel in New York City. Martin and Rosita were falling so deeply in love that they could be happy anywhere.

It just so happened that they were falling in love right in the middle of the bloodiest cattle war of the Old West.

54.

Billy pulled silently at the sparse whiskers on his upper lip. The boy would never be able to grow a proper mustache or beard, at least not in the 21 years or so that history had allotted to him. Early that morning, Brady and his posse had clamored into Lincoln triumphantly, as if expecting a parade for ridding the county of one thieving Englishman. No parade nor thanks was there to welcome them, however, as the citizens of Lincoln were horrified and disgusted at the posse's actions. With the large group of gunmen who'd responded to Tunstall's call to raise arms, along with the swollen Brady posse, the number of combatants in town was well over 100. It was like a powder keg, and any false move could light a spark that could destroy the citizenry of the town.

"Nuther dead friend. I wish to hell this would be the last one," said Billy plainly while staring at the dirt. He, Martin, and Fred Waite had been dispatched to Juan Patron's house as sentry to watch the eastern edge of town. While no one expected them to fight off Brady's marauders, they would at least have a show of force in case Dolan ordered any more killing. Similarly, McSween and Brewer had posted small pockets of men strategically around the village to keep Brady and Dolan on their toes.

Fred Waite was a handsome young man who bore an uncanny resemblance to a young Tom Selleck. So much so that Martin began to call him Magnum, much to Waite's chagrin, who was thinking the name was somehow an insult. "We're in it now, Billy. You think the courts are going to convict the sheriff? In this county?" asked Waite logically. "If Brady is going to get justice, it ain't gonna come from anyone with a black robe on."

Billy quickly jumped in. "Unless it's the grim reaper," he said with a wicked smile. That the boy only brightened up when he talked about killing someone was troubling to Martin. For a young boy of 18 or so years old, Billy had seen a lot of death, but was it more than any other of these young men of the plains?

Martin had never seen such a dichotomy in one person. Billy loved the light. He loved people, laughing, singing, and dancing, yet he also loved the darkness. Killing someone was no more an issue for him than deciding what he was going to have for supper. The most troubling part was that it never seemed to linger with the boy. He could kill or see someone killed and file it away in his emotional bank, quick to move on in life.

All of this is what made Billy's behavior on this day all the more puzzling. The Billy that the world knew and loved would be cracking jokes while loading his guns for war.

"It's like when someone gets close to me, they die or disappear. Take note of that, Teebsie, cause you might wanna run for New Jersey or hell or anywhere else you think is safe," said Billy.

"Hey, I'm here, Billy. Magnum's here," said Martin, with a wave of his hand towards Waite, "We don't plan on going anywhere." Waite looked at Martin with exasperation as the now familiar moniker passed his lips.

Billy looked up and cocked his head like when he was about to tell a joke. Instead of a smile, however, his face was plainly serious. "Day ain't over yet, so don't be so sure." The way Billy said it chilled Martin, while Waite had no reaction at all.

"I gotta piss," said Waite simply as he rose and walked off to defile the spot where, 140 years from now, Martin would be luxuriating in hot coffee and freshly made cinnamon buns.

"What's really wrong, Billy? I haven't seen you this down before," asked Martin carefully.

Billy, who had been tracing a circle in the dirt with a stick, kicked his boot to extinguish his art work before answering. "Who ya got, Teebsie?" the boy asked.

"What? I'm not sure what you mean?" answered Martin truthfully.

"Who ya got? In your life? You got family? Who are your friends…besides me, of course," the boy clarified.

Billy seemed so incredibly small, young, and lonely at that moment that it nearly broke Martin's heart. What was the point of the discussion? To prove Martin had a life and Billy didn't? If Martin were honest with himself, he didn't have much of a life left either. He worked all day in his New Jersey home and walked downstairs at the end of the day to complete silence. He had been locked down variously for the better part of two years with no ability to see anyone, and no one to really see if he could. His only life at the moment consisted of making his way to Lincoln, when his schedule would permit, and living a fool's dream in the past with a woman who was so far out of his league he shouldn't have even earned a tryout. In any event, the boy had asked a question so Martin felt compelled to answer.

"Well, you know my Mom passed," began Martin.

"What was her name?" Billy cut in.

"Sheila. Sheila Teebs," replied Martin.

"I'll bet she was a nice lady. Had to be if she had you for a son," said Billy fondly.

The compliment disarmed Martin. For the most part, he always felt that Billy tolerated him. Well, that and that he was amused by him as well. Never had the boy been so honest and forthright with him, except when he talked about killing. Martin didn't know if he blushed when he answered seriously, "Wow. Thanks, Billy. That's a really nice thing for you to say."

Billy grinned a little, and it wound up he was the one turning red at the discussion.

Martin continued, "My dad's name is Arlo. He's still alive. Lives in New Hampshire, where he was born."

"Good guy? Or is he a bastard like that good-for-nothing stepdaddy of mine?" said Billy, with some bitterness in his voice.

"He's good. Maybe not the best role model, but he was a heck of a good dad," said Martin, wistfully remembering the good old days. "And I've got a sister. Ellen. She lives in Texas now. She's about four years younger than me," added Martin.

Billy laughed at the geography of the Teebs family. "Mostly damned Yankees. Shoulda known, Teebsie."

Martin laughed, knowing that Billy meant no harm, then added, "That's about it. I've got a friend named Colin. I work with…well used to work with him," corrected Martin to account for the 140-year gap in his resume.

"Your friend Colin ever killed a man?" said Billy, with his steely blue eyes locked on Martin. Martin felt uncomfortable with the question. A moment ago Billy was joking, and now he'd flipped the switch into killing without so much as a warning. It was unnerving how quickly the boy could change.

"Colin? Noooo. I don't think Colin could hurt a fly," said Martin carefully, wondering what Billy was driving at.

Billy swallowed hard, his eyes avoiding Martin's. He looked down into the dirt where a few minutes ago he was drawing pictures.

"What you want with me, Teebsie? I mean, what's a guy with a nice family and friends and the prettiest girl in Lincoln doing slumming with me?" asked Billy. "You should go on and live this great life you have and leave this place behind. Leave me behind."

No credible response formed on Martin's lips, so he let the moment linger before Billy continued. "I expect if you spend too much time around me, you'll either be in trouble with the law or you'll be the filling of a pine box. Either way your family and your girl ain't gonna be able to help you. You really wanna give all that up for…this?" Billy waved his hand around the surrounding environs to make his point.

"Hey, Billy," Martin cut in, "we're friends. I don't know how, but I know that I like you. I think you're a great young man. If you get the chance, you'll develop into a really great older man."

Billy tilted his head up to see if maybe Martin was joking, but he saw no signs that he was. "This is a hard life that you live," Martin continued, "and it's not for everyone. I admire you. How brave you are, how loyal you are. You're one of the toughest guys I know."

Billy gave an "aw shucks" shake of his head, as if he didn't want to hear more, even though he was definitely hoping he would. Martin didn't disappoint. "When I met you, for some reason I felt like I'd known everything about you. Almost like I read a book or something. Then I get to know you and find out you're way more than what I expected. Billy, I'm proud to call you my friend."

Billy sat staring over Martin's shoulder into space. While he had friends and business associates (if that's what you can call rustlers and outlaws), he'd never had a real friend that was so far removed from his lifestyle as he had in Teebs. Billy wondered to himself if he truly thought of Teebs as a friend, or was he some replacement for his father and stepfather? After pondering the question for a few moments, he decided that Martin was a friend. A true friend. Billy had not ever known his real father and wished like hell he could forget William Antrim, the stepfather that went off and left his mother to die under Billy's care. If the Kid had needed a father figure, by now that need was long gone. At only 18 years old, he'd already been formed into the man he would become. It would be a waste of energy to try to correct his path at this late date, he decided.

Billy was careful to let the bitterness of the memory of Antrim wash away before responding, "I'm proud to call you my friend too, Teebsie. Thanks for tellin me that."

After what must have been the world's longest piss, Fred Waite walked back to where the men were sitting. "Keep eyes out. They'll be bringing in John's body right quick. Gonna put him over in Alex's place. I'm heading there now," he said, and without asking anyone's permission, he walked up the street and out of sight. As he went, Martin imagined him sliding into the front seat of a Ferrari 308 with a Hawaiian shirt on, on his way to bed some local honey before solving the week's new murder mystery.

It occurred to Martin that all of these men would be something different if they existed in his time. Nobody rustled cattle in 2022, did they? There'd be no merchant war, other than perhaps Dolan and Tunstall taking out competing Facebook ads to sell their wares online. Billy Mathews would bore his friends to tears during every summer Sunday barbeque by recounting how he made the big catch during the homecoming game that allowed his team to win the state championship for Polk High. What of Dick Brewer? Martin thought. As solemn and serious as he was, Brewer would probably open a chain of car dealerships. He'd work tirelessly behind the scenes to grow his empire, while offering fair, no negotiation pricing, and use the catch phrase "Come in for an honest Dick" in his commercials. McSween would probably be a "let-us-sue-someone-real-good" lawyer with a slick marketing campaign and a great phone number like 1-800-MAC SUES U.

And what of Tunstall? What would the earnest, ambitious young man be like in modern day? While the man had much potential and drive, Martin imagined he'd stay away from the Americas and become a YouTube influencer in jolly old England. He'd date Taylor Swift, and with the attached gravitas, he'd probably jet off to Lake Como to spend weekends with George and Amal Clooney. At some point, he'd become hooked on smack and have a spectacular crash and burn. From the ashes of rehab, Tunstall would rise up with his motivational message to host his own midday talk show on ABC, sandwiched somewhere between Dr. Oz and Ellen. That only left Billy…

"You ever seen a dead body?" asked Billy.

Billy's voice jolted Martin out of his repainting of history. He immediately thought of Brady, Mathews, McSween, and Morris, among others. Although they wouldn't die in Billy's timeline for a few months, Martin had indeed seen them all die. In fact, he thought, he'd even sent one of them to the great beyond.

"I have, Billy. Lots of them, to be honest. More than I should have," answered Martin.

"It don't look right for some reason. You look small when you're dead. I don't like it," said Billy. Martin could not be sure what point the boy was driving at. "If you're around when I die, don't let them show me off, ok?" asked Billy as he looked directly at Martin. "I don't want no ladies seeing me even smaller than I am."

Martin nodded but it was too quick for Billy, and he took it as being dismissed. "I'm serious here, Teebsie!" the boy said with a raised voice, "let the damn buzzards pick me clean. I don't want no grave and no cross and no place for people to go thinking they're going to talk to me…that is, if anybody even cares I'm dead."

The irony of Billy's wish wasn't lost on Martin. Here was a youth who would become the most notorious outlaw in the west (if not by deed, then at least via the press he received) and who would be buried in Fort Sumner after being killed by Pat Garrett. Billy's grave…if he was even in there…was one of the most visited sites in New Mexico. People came from all over the world to pay their respects to the young outlaw who would lie in eternity next to his pals, Charlie Bowdre and Tom Folliard. This Billy didn't even want a grave for people to fawn over, yet the historical Billy got exactly that. It was one of those rare times that Martin wished to explain to Billy exactly where he came from and everything he knew about the Kid. He could imagine Billy oohing and aahing over the ridiculously minute facts of his life that 21st century people were obsessed with. He'd have to tell Billy that he wasn't picked clean by buzzards (at least not that anyone knew about), but he was behind a steel cage in the old post cemetery at Fort Sumner, and the object of films, books, photos, and stories. Despite Billy's protestations to the contrary, Martin had a feeling that upon learning that news, the young man would most likely be pleased.

"Listen, Billy. I'm going to be gone from this world a long time before you," said Martin, tapping his finger in the dirt to emphasize he meant this physical world in 1878. "So whatever happens to you when I'm gone is going to be up to somebody else. I wouldn't worry too much about it. We'll be gone, and people can do what they like."

"I guess so," replied Billy simply, as he returned to drawing circles in the dirt.

Martin spied Rosita walking to her house. She must have finished working early. "Hey, Billy, can I meet you at Alex's later? I have to...umm...do something," said Martin, trying to avoid a long discussion.

"Sure, I got this," said Billy helpfully, "and, Teebs, give Rosita one for me!" Billy howled and slapped his knee so hard he actually hurt it. Martin could only shake his head and roll his eyes as he trotted up the road to spend whatever time he had with the love of his life.

55.

Martin gently held Rosita's hand and guided her to the front door of her home. Although the young woman worked hard and surely put her hands through the ringer each day with the demands of life on the frontier, to Martin they felt as soft as milk. While happy to see each other, the somberness of the day was not lost on the two lovers. Word around Lincoln was that Tunstall's body would soon arrive so that the townspeople could pay their last respects. While Martin already knew the outcome of the event and that it wouldn't bring any gunplay or death (at least not at the moment), the feelings were sure to run high on both sides. If his experience in the past was any indication, he knew that things could most certainly change without impacting the future, so he remained on guard.

"This is sad, *Martin*," said Rosita seriously. "That young man lost his life and that pinche Dolan brings his men to the Wortley all day to celebrate. I wanted to be sick."

It didn't take much for Martin to envision Dolan and his crew raising glass after glass at the demise of Tunstall. While he always portrayed himself as one of Lincoln's most upstanding citizens and business owners, Dolan's thirst for money and power even outshone that of his mentor L.G. Murphy. Small in stature, he nevertheless cut a large figure in the history of New Mexico. If someone had gone back to Lincoln ten years after Dolan had died, he'd have been hard-pressed to find anyone who would say something nice about the man.

For a moment Martin had a burst of an idea. What if he marched right up the street to The House and shot Dolan dead right now? What would happen next? Martin certainly knew that he played some part in the upcoming events of the War. If he killed Dolan, would the Dolan men then be able to kill him, being as Martin had already seen his future (and that he was most definitely in it)? With Dolan gone and Murphy on his deathbed, perhaps the War wouldn't come off at all? The domino effect would be substantial. Brady wouldn't be murdered, Brewer would live on to be an old man, Billy wouldn't be indicted for the crime, and McSween's law practice would probably flourish until young Harvey Morris would take over years from now.

If Billy were never indicted for the murder of Brady, what course would the boy's life take? Fine upstanding citizen, or would the Kid continue to be a petty cattle rustler?

While the Billy that Martin currently knew didn't seem to crave the attention that he would in coming years, would he be able to stay out of the limelight and live an ordinary (yet long) life without the help of Sergio Bachaca's book?

It was then that Martin remembered that this Billy would in fact live a long ordinary life due to Martin's carelessness. Billy would be a sick old man sitting on an old porch in Magdalena, NM, waiting for death to come and claim him, albeit 60 years too late. The stark difference between this developing Billy and the sad old man was almost too much for Martin to bear. No one likes their heroes to fade away. Like the paunchy George Reeves playing Superman for a season too long on TV, it seemed far better to flame out spectacularly than to go sadly and quietly into that long night. While it seemed like history would always regard the boy bandit as a legend, the truth that Martin had helped create was much less impressive. Billy the Kid would be an ordinary old man whom few would remember and fewer would care when he was gone. Aside from all else that Martin had ruined, he'd destroyed the legend that would fuel a million social media group arguments.

"What is wrong, *Martin*?" asked Rosita, seeing a single tear course down Martin's cheek.

Martin was embarrassed at crying in front of his woman, so he quickly wiped the tear away and lied, "Oh nothing. Nothing. Just got some dust in my eyes is all."

Much like Lilly, Rosita was always a step ahead of Martin and could see the pain in her lover's eyes. She didn't want to pry further, so she gently stood in front of him and wiped the corners of his eyes with her soft fingers. "Yes, when the wind blows like this, this happens to me too," she said, while smiling reassuringly at him.

Martin ran his hands down the length of her shining black hair. Once during his business travels to California, he had slept in a hotel with Egyptian cotton sheets. He remembered them feeling like the softest, most supple things he'd ever felt…until now. Rosita's hair felt like fine spun silk as it danced with his fingers. In Martin's time, he'd see commercial after commercial for expensive hair products that women would use to thicken, lengthen, soften, and straighten their hair; yet here was a simple woman of the southwest who had all of that and more, and probably used a rough bar of soap to wash up with. While he couldn't make sense of it, he supposed it was the fog of love that amplified every facet of Rosita to perfection in his mind. Or maybe it wasn't? Maybe Rosita was as absolutely perfect as she seemed to Martin, just because that's who she was. Maybe she was one of the rare perfect beings that existed in past and present who didn't need makeup, stylists, or fashion designers to create an illusion for her. If Rosita existed in Martin's time, he thought, she'd be a supermodel. So stunningly perfect that she'd never have an interest in the likes of him. In Lincoln County, Martin was the best available option. In the future, Rosita would have options, options that didn't exist in 1878. She'd jet around the globe and post half-naked pictures on her Instagram account for her twenty-three million followers. She'd use hashtags like #blessed #livingmybestlife #happy and #thankful to let people know she was both one of them, and nothing at all like them.

Martin began to have a sinking feeling in his stomach that the only reason this woman loved him was because he sucked the least out of all of the men in Lincoln. It was like visiting the donut store and having only a choice of yesterday's stale leftovers, so you pick the one that looks bad, but not as bad as the rest.

Could it be? Could Rosita really have settled for Martin? The more he thought about it, the more he could not believe it. She had waited for him. She told him so. The electricity when they touched wasn't something she was settling for, was it? It was something she craved. Sure, in his own time, Martin was an average husband in a lackluster marriage, but something in Rosita had changed him. It had made him better. This wasn't the Martin Teebs of 2022. This was Teebs 2.0. Everything this woman was helped him be a better man. Would that dynamic change if they were both magically transported to Martin's time? No, he decided. He'd still be the better version of Martin Teebs because Rosita's love made him so. If she was jetting off to Monaco for a beachside photo shoot, it would be with Martin sitting right beside her on their Learjet. This woman belonged to him just as surely as he belonged to her, and the difference of a century or two wasn't going to change that.

"Can we sit and talk?" asked Martin, while still unwilling to let her hair go. If this was the last time he saw her, he wanted to feel every sensation she could produce upon him so that it might last a lifetime.

Rosita sat in the chair that Martin pulled out for her as he sat down heavily just across from her. He didn't know exactly where to start. He was about to tell his love that he was going away again and it might be some weeks until he returned. While Rosita would eventually be happy to see him again, their next meetings had already happened on Martin's timeline. He wouldn't be there to relive them again. If he could, he'd certainly leave out the part about having a wife...and probably not go with the cat and fireworks shirt again.

The whole point of his return to New Mexico had been a vain attempt to connect with his son Martin Jr. This trip back earlier in time to the start of his relationships with Billy and Rosita was a bittersweet bonus. If Martin had indeed never met his son, then this could very well be the last time he would be in the presence of Rosita Luna. He couldn't fathom the fact and truth be told, he didn't want to. He knew that between now and March 31, many people in Lincoln would tell her that he was gone and would not return. The Dolan boys would probably paint him as a coward, running to save his life; while the Regulators (other than Billy of course) would probably barely remember he even existed, caught as they were in the fog of war.

"What is it, *mi amor*? What's wrong?" asked Rosita softly but seriously.

Martin cleared his throat and began, "I have a good idea that things are about to get bad here, Rosita. I was there when they killed Tunstall. Brady is going to want to get rid of the witnesses." He paused to see if what he was saying would register on her face. Rosita only nodded slowly, waiting for him to continue.

"I can't be here with you when that happens. If anything happened to you, I...I couldn't go on living," he said with sadness, a tear again threatening to escape his eye. Thanks to Billy's unannounced visit to Martin's home in New Jersey, he already knew that something would happen to Rosita. At this moment Martin couldn't focus on that thought, however.

"We will be fine, *Martin*. With *Billito* and the others, we will be safe, no?" asked Rosita, with her eyes imploring Martin to agree with her.

"I don't think so. Not here anyway," he said to Rosita's clear dissatisfaction. "I need to get away from here to protect you. Do you understand? I love you, Rosita. I have to protect you."

Now it was Rosita's turn to cry. Big swollen tears dripped silently down her face and dropped heavily on the table. How could she explain to this man that she had waited her entire life to find him and wasn't ready to lose him, no matter the cost? "I won't lose you, *Martin*," she said in a strong and rising voice, "I have waited too long to find you. Whatever our fate, we will meet it together, *entiendes, Martin*?"

Martin simply shook his head slowly, unsure of how to respond. When Lilly had made her mind up and laid down the law with Martin, he knew to go along with it to save the fight. Rosita was cut from the same strong cloth as Lilly, but going along with her could mean death this time. Martin knew it was time to be strong. Perhaps stronger than he'd ever been in his past.

"No, my love. I can't let that happen. You will stay here. You'll be fine. I will be back as soon as I can. I promise," said Martin seriously.

Rosita looked helplessly at her man, knowing his mind was made up and she would not be able to change it. Her frustration spilled out. "How long this time, *Martin*? How long must I wait for you again!" It broke Martin's heart to see her this way, and he reached across the table to hold her hands. At first she pulled them back in anger, but he reached again more firmly until she relented. He rose from his chair and lifted her into his arms. Her defenses down, Rosita sobbed heavily into his chest. "If you are killed, I don't want to live, *Martin*. They should put us in the same hole in the ground!"

Martin fought to keep his composure as the thought of him and Rosita being lowered into the earth played out in his mind. He knew that their fate was not to end that way and wanted her to know it.

"I will be back. I promise," he repeated, as he wrapped his arms more tightly around her.

Rosita cried for another few minutes that felt like hours to Martin. Eventually her tears faded, and she decided to make the most of the time she had with him. He felt her body relax in his arms, while she wiped away what remained of her tears.

"Kiss me, *Martin*," she said simply as she pulled his face to hers. Their lips met with the same electricity of that first time. Her movements became more insistent, and she pushed Martin firmly to the bed. Her eyes had come alight, and a slight smile had returned to her face. Stepping back, she pushed him hard until he fell backwards onto the bed. Her laughter filled the small hut. Martin smiled back, pleased that she was finally seemingly happy. Rosita slowly peeled off her clothes as Martin looked on, marveling at the delicate yet strong creature in front of him. In his time women would pay many thousands of dollars to nip, tuck, and implant things in a vain attempt to look anywhere near as perfect as Rosita did. There wasn't a hint of shyness in her actions as she kept her eyes locked to his to make sure he was pleased. Martin slid back on the bed to make room for her. Just as she was about to climb on top of him, a cacophony of sound rose from the east. Wagon wheels clattered along the dirt road, and people began to cry out. The sound got louder and louder as it approached Rosita's house. The voices, some soft, some at the peak of anger, formed a chorus of noise that woke the sleepy town from its twilight daze. Even Rosita, standing there almost completely naked, was caught off guard by the swell of emotion coming from just outside her door. She quickly covered up as Martin rose from the bed and peeked out of the window. In the distance a gunshot or two was heard. In a moment the whole of Lincoln seemed to be yelling, crying, or threatening retribution, while the death wagon slowly rolled along the town's only street.

John Henry Tunstall had come home.

56.

Martin threw on his clothes and boots quickly and pecked Rosita on the cheek as he made his way out onto the street, warning her to stay inside until he returned. The din of furor that night would only be matched by the coming five-day battle some five months in the future. If Brady and Dolan's crew had designs on celebrating any further that day, they were quickly cancelled as the partisan Tunstall crowd took to the streets en masse.

The wagon containing Tunstall's body creaked and groaned along the pitches of the road as it approached the dead man's store. That store was currently still being held by Brady and his men, a fact that infuriated McSween, Brewer, the boys from the ranch, and many of the townspeople. Martin followed at a safe distance, and the wagon finally wagged to a stop in front of McSween's house. In his shirtsleeves, Alex walked out of the front door, hands on hips, to take in the sight. At his appearance, a great swell of sound and fury was heard from the crowd as they demanded he take retribution on those responsible for Tunstall's death.

McSween held up his hands to the crowd in an attempt to calm them. He stepped to the back of the wagon and gently pulled back the tarp that had been laid over the Englishman's body. At the sight of his dead friend, McSween swooned and tears tormented his eyes. Tunstall had taken a bullet to the back of the head...a difficult bit of business since the posse said they had shot him in self defense when he fired at them...with an exit wound just over his right eye. The other shot to his chest was hidden by his cloak, and the young man appeared, if nothing else, to be in a deep and restful sleep. Brewer immediately dispatched two men to carry the body into the house.

From the margins of the crowd, Martin looked on as if seeing again a movie already watched once or twice. The scene was exactly as the history books described. There must have been 100 people milling about as Tunstall made his final visit to his friend's home. Martin imagined the shadowy figures of Dolan's men hiding in the dark, arms at the ready in the event Brewer decided to start and finish the War off in only one night.

Billy stepped out of the darkness from the side of the house, taking in the crowd. He spotted Martin and waved him over.

"Hey. C'mon in. Let's pay our respects," he said somberly.

In the lead, the diminutive Billy pushed his way through the crowd, with the much bigger Martin in his wake.

Entering the McSween house, they saw John's body laid out on a table in the parlor. Susan McSween came in briefly, clutched her hand to her mouth, and ran out in tears. The rest of Tunstall's men looked seriously at their boss's body and shouted threats of retribution through gritted teeth. Conversations began about which of Brady's men would be killed first and if Dolan should be dispatched to hell on that very evening. Although not one for confrontation, McSween stepped up and shouted the men to order.

"Quiet! All that talk can wait for tomorrow. Respect the dead in our presence tonight, will you?" he shouted above the men. While McSween was never a wartime leader, the men surprisingly quieted down to a soft murmur, and some jostled forward to take a last look at John Henry Tunstall. History told Martin that Billy alone would make a proclamation over the body that he would "get some of them before he died." If reading one of the many books Martin had poured his discretionary income into buying, a person could come away with the idea that Billy's missive would be a dramatic pause for all to see. That's the way reporting works. When someone reports only what one person did, everyone might believe that was the only person to do something. On this night, however, that could not be further from the truth. Each man in the house took a step up to Tunstall and pledged some kind of thanks, revenge, or profanity, while the other men continued their conversations. Martin had a front seat to history in the making as Billy jostled through the crowd and stared at the body for a few long moments. The men continued to talk and argue about what should happen next, but surely one or two of them heard the boy say, "'ll get some of them before I die," in far less dramatic fashion than history would allow. Had any of the rest of these men achieved the level of legend that the Kid would, Martin was sure that someone would have remembered and reported that speech over the body of Tunstall.

Billy's eyes met Martin's in an invitation for the big man to make his own vengeful statement over the body. Martin hesitated. He barely knew Tunstall. He'd worked for him for all of about three days, not even long enough to earn the money needed to pay the man back what was owed. Besides, Martin had no idea what he'd say. He knew this day was coming and the outcome was no surprise, so what could he possibly add that would make a difference to these men? Martin held up his palm to Billy as if to say "not now," and the young man went swearing to the others in the room.

A man entered, carrying a bag and a bucket of some sort with liquid sloshing around in it. McSween waved the man to his side of the room, as Martin realized this was the embalmer. Unsure if Tunstall's parents would want the remains shipped back to England, Alex had made arrangements to have Tunstall preserved just in case. The sharp smell of formaldehyde filled the room as the man stepped carefully between the warriors still embroiled in conversation.

Never one to take no as an answer, Billy worked his way over to Martin and grabbed him by the sleeve. "C'mon, Teebsie. Say your last goodbyes."

Reluctantly Martin stepped up to the corpse and looked upon him in the lighted room. He was struck by how right Billy had been. Tunstall did look smaller than he did in life. It was as if the soul left the body and took something more with it. While Martin could have made a grand speech about Tunstall and the coming War based upon his knowledge of history, none of that felt right. He felt guilty he hadn't been able to help the man when help was needed most, so he simply looked down and said a heartfelt, "I'm sorry, John,"

"Sorry nothing!" came a roar from across the room as John Middleton's black eyes sliced through the crowd. "If you would have shut your Goddamn mouth, he'd still be alive, you moron!"

The men in the room gasped. While most everyone was up for a fight on this night, none expected it would be amongst their own men.

"No!" said Martin defensively, "I was just trying to help. That's all."

"You helped him into the grave, you fucking imbecile!" roared Middleton.

Martin was caught somewhere between anger at the accusation and fear that the obviously very drunk Middleton might beat the crap out of him right here and now. While silence would be the best option, he was being dressed down here among men who would surely brand him a coward if he didn't respond.

Before he could stop himself, the words sprang from his lips. "Maybe if you didn't run and leave him alone in the middle of the road to die, he'd still be alive!"

There was a huge gasp from the room and then dead quiet. It took Middleton's alcohol-addled brain just a second to register Martin's accusation before a guttural scream filled the air. The hulking man launched himself at Martin, pushing him hard into the table holding Tunstall's body. The weight of the Englishman's body and the two combatants was too much for the table's spindly legs, and it collapsed underneath them, with Martin falling on Tunstall and Middleton falling on Martin. There was a great cry throughout the room as Middleton gained his knees and punched down hard at Martin's head. With surprising dexterity, Teebs rolled out of the way at the last moment, and Middleton's punch landed squarely on the jaw of Tunstall, creating a look of surprise... or maybe shock...on the dead man's face. Another cry was heard as Martin jumped up, right into the embalmer, who let loose with the entire contents of his bucket onto Martin, Middleton, and Tunstall. The fumes coming from his soaked clothes overwhelmed Martin, and he collapsed heavily to the floor, slipping from consciousness. The last thing he remembered was being nose-to-nose with a very surprised looking and very dead John Henry Tunstall.

57.

Martin blinked his eyes back to consciousness as he lay on the cold ground. The faint smell of formaldehyde lingered in his nostrils, but in checking, he found his clothes were as dry as a bone. As he pushed himself from the ground, he immediately noticed he was outside, on the empty lot that used to contain the McSween house. After the house was burned to the ground during the five-day battle, it had never been rebuilt, and its location was now marked only by a sign near the road. Doing a quick mental inventory, Martin realized that he had come to in exactly the same spot he'd been knocked out. He twisted his head from side to side to work out the kinks and rose to his feet.

It was cold and dark, and Martin didn't have any idea what day it was. If this trip back in time had followed others, he might be only a few minutes from the time he left his casita on Friday night. Brushing his pants off, he slowly walked the half mile back to the B&B, to make some sense of what had happened and to get some rest. There wasn't another car or person on the street as he shuffled along. He approached the area that he well knew used to contain Rosita's hut. Now it was home to the Lincoln National Monument museum and administrative office. While the building was a definite step up in value for the neighborhood, it made Martin sad to know that Rosita's small house didn't survive the intervening years. He longed to touch the rough-hewn wooden door or the adobe walls. He wished that there was some reminder, some remembrance of Rosita Luna in this town, other than the sad picture at the B&B that haunted his waking moments. With a woman so incredibly beautiful as Rosita, was it possible that no one remembered her? No one cared about her? Had she simply vanished from history at some point after giving birth to Martin Jr.? Martin could not believe it. Rosita was so incredibly special that there must be something of her left in this town. How could a woman who was pursued by every non-married male (and some married ones) in the whole of the county simply be forgotten? No memorial, no plaque, no official sign to mark her existence? It was unfathomable to Martin.

A thought that had never occurred to him entered his mind as he walked. Where was Rosita buried? Martin had been so involved in changing the past that he never thought about seeking out her grave to pay his proper respects. Was she buried in the old Lincoln cemetery? If so, it would be easy enough for Martin to walk the hallowed grounds and find her tombstone...or would it? Many of the old graves had been marked with wooden crosses or in some cases, nothing at all. Would Rosita's have survived the last 140 years? What about Junior? Was he also buried in Lincoln? Did the two members of his family lie side by side in eternity? Mother and bastard child? While Martin thought about the possibility, his heart sank. Would he find them in some lonely corner of the cemetery under the shade of a *pinon* tree? Would he make pilgrimages there to lay flowers on the ground, maybe taking a blanket to sit and talk with the family he so suddenly abandoned? Would their spirits rise up from the dirt, turning their ghostly backs on him, telling him to leave and never return? Just the thought of it made him retch. Combined with the lingering scent of formaldehyde, Martin was afraid he'd pass out again. Pushing the questions from his mind, he decided that focusing on the alive version of his love would be much more productive. A smile visited his face as he saw hers dancing in the glow of the firelight. His mind replayed their time together as he walked past the spot where the hut had been and approached the B&B.

Martin's car was in the driveway, just where he'd left it. The main house looked dark, and he assumed that Darlene must have turned in after a long day of packing. Trudging to the front door of his casita, he saw a tray with breakfast on it, two newspapers, and a note. Picking up the entire lot, he opened the door and pushed his way in.

Martin snapped on a light switch and placed the tray on the table. As his eyes adjusted to the light, he looked at the two newspapers and realized that one was the Saturday edition and the other was the larger Sunday paper. The realization that he'd been gone two full days was reinforced by the now sour milk that graced a tray, which Darlene had obviously left many hours ago for his breakfast. Martin wasn't prepared for this. He usually had a day or more to decompress after his travels back in time. This time he'd need to be up at the crack of dawn to drive to Albuquerque and catch his flight to LA. He groaned wearily at the knowledge.

Finally he picked up the note, which bore the familiar handwriting he knew to be Darlene's.

Martin,

Are you ok? I know you like to go on these adventures, but you're usually back the same day. I'm a bit worried but know you can take care of yourself. When you get this, please text me to let me know you arrived back safe and sound?

I soooo wanted to see you before I left, but I have many miles to go to reach Portland and needed to get on the road! The new owners should be here sometime today. I expect you'll see them when you check out. It's been wonderful getting to know you. Please know you have a friend in me and if I can do anything to help you, just reach out and ask!

Well, I'm on my way. If you're ever around Portland way, let me know. It might be a little cozy in my tiny house for two of us, but I'll fit you in somehow!

Love,
Darlene
XOXOXOXOXO

Martin smiled at Darlene's final parting sexual innuendo as he dropped the note on the table. He was ravenously hungry but also dead tired. If he was to meet Mr. Talbot in LA tomorrow, he didn't want to look like he just lived through the Lincoln County War, so he decided sleep was more important than food and slowly shuffled up the steps to the loft.

58.

The chirping coming from Martin's iPhone became more and more insistent. He cracked open his dry, crusty eyes, knowing he didn't have time to lounge around before making the long drive to the Albuquerque Sunport. He had wisely packed a carry-on bag with his business clothes that had been left in the trunk of his rental car. He pulled his travel clothes out of the suitcase and let them relax on the bed while he quickly showered and shaved. As the hot water washed any remnants of sleep from him, he thought back on the last few days. His bond with Rosita seemed stronger than ever. He felt he'd set her up properly so that when he didn't arrive back at her home last night, she would patiently wait for him to wage war with the rest of the Regulators. While not seeing her for six weeks wasn't ideal, he was certain the two-years-younger version of himself would pick up where he left off, save for mentioning that he had a wife in town at the time.

Martin poured a half cup of hot coffee as he began throwing items into his suitcase. His old clothes, lacking in modern-day synthetic fabrics, were bulky and took up more room than three of his regular outfits. As he pushed his coat into the case, he felt a firm object that wouldn't yield. The book. He reached into his pocket and removed Dummy's book. Still unsure about who wrote it and certain it couldn't have been a deaf mute with Down's Syndrome in 1881, Martin simply sighed as if he'd just used up his final chance to solve an issue of importance to the entire world. He slipped the tiny book into a pocket in his suitcase and slugged down the last bit of coffee, anxious to get on the road.

"Hello, Martin," said Lilly plainly, standing outside his door as he rushed out. Little Austin was standing hand-in-hand beside her.

Martin's eyes went wide. He'd become used to all sorts of unexpected arrivals and departures in his life, but he was in no way ready to see this.

"What the hell are you doing here?" he asked incredulously. If he had intended to use more forceful language, the presence of the young boy prevented it.

"I own this place. I bought it from Darlene and Dallas," replied Lilly, staring nervously into her ex-husband's eyes.

"What?" cried Martin more to himself than to Lilly. "Some investment group from Texas bought it. Darlene told me!"

Lilly smiled a rueful little smile and tilted her head towards little Austin, "Austin Enterprises, you know?"

Martin closed his eyes heavily and buried his face in his hands. This was his former wife Lilly, who hated everything about Lincoln (except apparently for Dallas). She had taken every opportunity to denigrate the historical little town and Martin's interest in it. While her move to Albuquerque had shocked Martin, he at least could make sense of it, with the lower cost of living and all. This, he could make no sense of.

"You hate this place!" he said loudly. Austin had a worried look on his face, so Martin throttled back his tone. "You've never liked it here. Why this? Why here? Why now?"

Tears began to well up in Lilly's eyes as she pondered the question in her own mind. "Dallas is gone. He's in LA. I didn't go with him. I couldn't stand him, Martin. Sure, the sex was incredible. I mean, it was unlike anything that I've ever…."

"I get it!" shouted Martin, wanting her to get to the point at hand.

"But he was dumber than a drawer full of screwdrivers. I never loved him, Martin. Never," she said as her tears began dropping on the wooden porch. "I always loved you. I just made a huge, horrendous mistake and couldn't find my way out of it."

Martin stared at her, trying to find some thread of his former self that used to love this woman. He turned his head to Austin, who seemed unfazed by the early morning confessional going on in front of him.

"That doesn't answer my question. Why did you have to buy *this* place?" Martin demanded.

Lilly dropped her head and slowly said, "Because you love it, Martin, and because I still love you."

Martin was shaking both with anger and disbelief at what he was hearing. At this moment he wished that Lilly would simply up and disappear and that this might be the end of a very strange and unhappy dream.

"You cheated on me. You got pregnant. You had a baby, and you ran off with your lover. None of that adds up to you still loving me," he said firmly. Only after he said it did Martin realize that he had done the exact same thing...and probably before Lilly had.

"I know, Martin. There are no words. I did do all that, and those are things you would never have done to me," she said sadly. That Lilly had stood in their guest room and heard Farber and Billy accuse him of adultery and fathering an illegitimate child wasn't lost on him. At the time, at least to Lilly, the story seemed so far-fetched that she wrote it off as ridiculous indictments made in the heat of the moment between two men she barely knew. Martin had never cheated on her, she thought. He had no opportunity. When he wasn't with her, he was at work. How in the world could he have a girlfriend and a child in New Mexico when he'd only been there one or two times? The logistics of the whole thing didn't work out, and so, in the end, Lilly simply dismissed it.

"You're such a good man, Martin. Faithful. Reliable. Honest. Loving. Caring..."

"Stop!" he shouted, unable to bear the weight of his own guilt. He was in love with another woman in another time. He'd fathered a child that existed somewhere out there in a time that Martin could not reach. If Martin could have found a way to stay with Rosita, he would have done so in a heartbeat. He thought about his first days with Lilly and admitted they had never held the same weight in his heart as Rosita did. It was as if he had discovered that what he thought was love, actually was something else, and that Rosita had taught him the true depth and soul of the emotion. If Martin had ever loved Lilly, he certainly did no longer. He felt only pity as he looked at her standing there, vulnerable, after making the second biggest mistake of her life by purchasing the B&B.

"Stop," he said more softly. "Whatever your idea was, it's not going to work. I'm not in love with you." After a long pause in which Lilly could find no words, Martin said simply, "And now I have to go."

He turned and began walking to his car amidst the sounds of Lilly gasping through her cries. "Don't turn around," he told himself, as he placed his suitcase in the trunk. Martin opened the door and slid into the driver's seat as Lilly cried out one more time, "Martin, please! Martin!"

Martin slipped the car into reverse, backed out onto the road, and drove to the west without ever looking back at the devastation he had left in his wake.

59.

His heart racing and his body shaking, Martin accelerated past the western edge of Lincoln town bound for Albuquerque. He couldn't believe the ridiculous lengths Lilly went to in order to win him back. What did she think he was going to do? Wrap his arms around her and put little Austin on his shoulders as they walked into the main house to resume their life as one happy family?

"Bullshit!" he yelled to no one, as the broken yellow stripes on the road rushed past.

Truth be told, most of his anger was at himself. Hearing Lilly profess what a great guy he was revealed the truth to Martin. He was a creep. He'd cheated on his wife well before she ever cheated on him (or so he thought), and his obsession with Billy the Kid had given him a welcoming respite from his stale marriage. Lilly was no saint, but Martin couldn't assume the title either. This mess was of both of their making, and he for one wasn't interested in going backwards to try to figure it out.

Lilly's audacity at confronting him without warning did make his blood boil. Here he was, trying to get to the airport so he could earn the money that paid her alimony, and she just stood there on his doorstep like some demented episode of *Candid Camera*. How could she possibly imagine he was going to raise little Austin, the child of another man, while the boy's father was out starring in toothpaste commercials in LA? Ok, Martin thought, why don't I bring Rosita and Martin Jr. to the present too? Maybe we can all live at the B&B like some big happy polygamous, time-traveling family? Lilly and Rosita could be sister wives, and the kids would at least have each other to play with. How would Lilly respond to that? he wondered. Not well, he thought. It would be insane for her to accept Martin Jr. to the same degree that she expected him to accept Austin.

Martin neared Capitan, and his head began to buzz with the beginnings of a seriously bad tension headache. His usual dose of 4-5 cups of caffeinated coffee had been severely cut back in his haste to leave Lincoln. As he neared the gas station, he decided to pull in before his pain got away from him and he missed his flight. Pulling off to the side of the parking lot, Martin reached to open the door and suddenly saw the hulking figure of Steve blocking him in the car. The man had a smile on, but it was pasted over a look that let Martin know he wasn't there to ask about the weather.

"What do you want with me?!" came Martin's muffled scream through the window.

Steve reached down one of his giant hands and opened the driver's door, inviting Martin to exit the car. As he stepped out, Martin snapped, "I don't have time for this today!"

In a calm and patient voice, Steve said, "I think you want to hear what I have to say, Martin." He put a heavy hand on Martin's shoulder, beckoning him to walk and talk. The weight of Steve guided him, and Martin looked around to see if there was any escape. This reckoning, whatever it was about, had been coming for a long time, and there was no sense further avoiding it.

In a weary voice, Martin asked, "What do you want with me, Steve? What have I ever done to you?"

Steve laughed gently before speaking. "You haven't done anything to me. Nothing at all. I've been trying to talk to you about your past."

The mention of "his past" froze Martin for a second. "What about my past?" Martin questioned carefully.

"Did you find Dummy?" asked Steve, with a light dancing in his eyes.

Martin's head snapped around as if on swivel. "How did you know about that?"

As they walked around back of the station, Steve reached his free hand into the pocket of his jacket. He rustled around for a second and pulled out a small stack of papers… the missing pages from Juan Baca's book!

Martin's eyes opened wide as if he'd seen a ghost. "Where did you get those?"

Steve ignored the question and asked one of his own. "You know Dummy didn't write this book, right, Martin?" Martin turned his head just a little and nodded.

"When I got it, I couldn't believe the shit in this thing," said Steve with a hearty laugh.

"Somebody's either got one hell of an imagination or this shit really happened." Again Martin turned his head slightly but fell short of looking Steve in the eyes.

"So, *amigo*, which is it?" asked Steve, as he stopped walking and stared straight into Martin's eyes. Martin suddenly felt as if he were naked in front of a room of supermodels. Totally exposed and totally inadequate. If he wanted to put this all behind him, now was the time to tell the truth...or to lie through his teeth. Martin felt small, alone, and afraid. He let loose a giant sigh containing all of the lies he'd been telling to everyone to conceal his sordid past.

"It happened. All of it," he began, "at least as much as I read in the book. I don't know what the hell happened. I have no idea how the hell I got picked for this, but it happened. Every damn thing!" Martin's voice rose with the anger of all he had gained… and then lost.

"So you got the book? You read it? Everything on those pages...that was you?" asked Steve in disbelief

No longer afraid of the truth, Martin looked him in the eyes and nodded.

"Holy shit!" exclaimed Steve. "What a trip, Martin."

Martin thought about it and silently agreed it was indeed a trip. His only remaining question was to find out what was written on the pages that now resided in Steve's rather large hand. From what he could read of the book, Martin had been documented all the way through Billy's escape from The House. Everything upcoming that he knew about was written on the pages of the book that Martin had in his car. What Steve had in his hand contained something else. As if he were a psychic reading Martin's mind, the large man held the pages up and asked slowly, "You haven't read these yet, have you?"

Never taking his eyes from the pages, Martin replied "No, I haven't."

Steve's lighthearted mood was gone. He seemed deep in thought as the smile left his face.

"But I'd like to. I need to," Martin continued. "I've left people behind, and I need to know what happened to them."

Steve winced at the notion as if it pained him. He didn't know what to say, although he had certainly already decided what he would do. He imagined the pain these pages would cause Martin. The anguish. The finality of what was written on them.

"Please, Steve," Martin implored, "I have to know."

"No. Can't do it, Martin. Can't. No man should know his future so he don't try to change it," said Steve reluctantly, as he held the pages more firmly in his hand.

Martin stood shaking in the cold, tears beginning to well up in his eyes. Across from him, Steve stood firmly, but with a look of compassion for what he was about to do for...not to...the man. He slowly reached into his vest pocket and removed a lighter. To Martin's horror, Steve raised the lighter to the pages and lit them on fire. Martin tried to scream "No!" but no words would come. Steve stared directly at him, very slightly shaking his head as if to let Teens know he shouldn't try to stop the fire from consuming Martin's past...and perhaps future. When the fire licked at his fingertips, Steve let the ashes blow from his hand to be scattered to the four corners of the wind.

Martin stood, numb. He wasn't mad or sad anymore, he was just empty. Finally when he could speak, he mouthed a solitary word, "Why?"

Tilting his head to recollect, Steve answered, "The guy that wrote it gave me those. Said to hold em while he went to Lincoln to drop the rest of the book off. Said I should only give them back to him if he ever needed em. I swear to God I thought it was all a bullshit game, Martin." If Steve had ever thought this was fun, it certainly wasn't now. Caught as a pawn in a horrific game of life and death, Steve wished he'd never agreed to take part.

Martin stood, confused. Guy? The book wasn't written in 1881? What guy would have the knowledge to write such a book?

"Guy? What guy wrote it?" Martin demanded.

Steve looked thoughtfully as he tried to remember. "Name was, umm….Farber. Carl Farber."

Martin's shaking amplified by a factor of ten upon hearing the name. Farber must have written this and planted it at least a year and a half ago. The son of a bitch had planted a parting shot at Martin before his demise at Billy's hands. That conniving, wretched piece of shit Farber. Martin wished only to reach back through time and pull Farber's eyes from the sockets, leaving them dangling, and him screaming and writhing in pain. Martin's anger was as fresh as if they were all still standing in his guest room.

"Two years? You've been holding onto those for two years?" demanded Martin.

"Two years? Shit, Martin, he just came through here back in December..."

December?

The news struck Martin like the steel of a ball peen hammer to the back of his skull. Farber was alive? His body twitched and convulsed at the news, finally going limp. Martin blacked out and fell heavily at Steve's feet, as the large man looked down and wondered just what in the hell kind of game he'd been talked into.

The End.

ABOUT THE AUTHOR

Michael Anthony Giudicissi is an author, screenwriter, and speaker from Albuquerque, NM. Michael hosts the internationally popular YouTube channel, "All Things Billy the Kid". In addition to the Back to Billy series, Michael has written a number of other books focused on personal growth, business, and sales.

Disclaimer: Due to the shifting nature of fiction versus reality, we're unsure exactly who is currently writing these books. Clearly a fictional character named Martin Teebs is not writing them, but who is Martin Teebs, really? Recent reports point to the fact that a Martin Teebs might just exist after all. We're not clear on whether Michael Anthony Giudicissi is a real person, or perhaps Michael Roberts might be the driving force behind the manuscript. It's possible, as disagreeable as it may seem, that even Carl Farber could be at the helm of current and future Back to Billy stories. Anyone with any information on this vexing puzzle is encouraged to contact the "author" at the links below.

To Contact the Author: billythekidridesagain@gmail.com

Books in the "Back to Billy" saga:
Back to Billy – 2nd Edition (Mankind Media, 2023)
1877 (Mankind Media 2021)
Sunset in Sumner (Mankind Media 2021)
Bonney and Teebs (Mankind Media 2021)
One Week in Lincoln (Mankind Media 2021)
4 Empty Graves (Mankind Media 2022)
Pieces of Us (Mankind Media 2023)

COMING SOON:
1950, Book 8 in the Back to Billy Saga (Mankind Media 2023)